The Firefly Jar

The Firefly Jar

A Crickley Creek Romance

Laurie Beach

TULE
PUBLISHING

Dedication

For Bryan Reese

and

in loving memory of Bari Lokken

Chapter One

CHARLOTTE WAS LATE. Few things bothered her more than arriving late, even if it was just a party. *Oh, please, let Mrs. Buchanan be understanding.* She'd never met the hostess, an unfamiliarity that added to the headache behind her eyes.

How would she explain that she'd been so engrossed in creating a new recipe for goat cheese quiche that she'd lost track of the time? She'd sound like an irresponsible idiot. Or worse, the kind of person who was so much the center of her own universe that she didn't care about appointments or expectations or invitations trustingly extended by good friends. Sweat beaded along her hairline, and the sound of her tires rolling on the gravel road echoed her thoughts exactly. *Crap, crap, crap, crap.*

Hush with all that now. Her mother's voice filled her head. Charlotte was ten years old again, her mother's gentle hand stroking back the bangs from her forehead. *Everything's gonna be just fine.* It took leaving California and moving across the country to South Carolina to find her mother's voice again. Charlotte held on tight to every word and relaxed her foot from the gas. *Everything's gonna be just fine.*

She neared a circular drive topped by an enormous white-columned mansion. Her mother had spoken so often about her life in the South while she was alive, Charlotte thought she would be prepared for a party in a gigantic antebellum home with the sounds of live classical music coming from the window. But, no. Despite her mother's thick Southern drawl, her love of Southern foods, country music, and sweet-smelling flowers, Charlotte had no clue what to expect. And no matter how often Charlotte begged, going back to the South, even for a visit, had always been out of the question.

A white-gloved man opened her door and surveyed her torn jeans and Beyoncé concert T-shirt. If she could have moved from that spot, she would have jumped back into her car and sped away. Instead, the valet spoke quietly, "Ma'am, we can both pretend like you were never here."

Charlotte must've looked like a horned owl with her eyes so wide. "I can't leave. I promised Birdie I'd be here, and I'm already late." She surveyed the area again, her stomach clenching. "You know, what? It's all good. I will just text Birdie if you can hold on a minute."

Another car kicked up gravel as it drove up the driveway. "I'll just pull your car to the side," said the valet, climbing in.

"Birdalee Mudge, you are a dead woman," Charlotte hissed under her breath as she moved off the driveway to text her. In return, she got a phone call.

"Charlotte, seriously, how bad can it be?"

Charlotte began to speak, but Birdie interrupted. "I can't hear a darned thing. Just get your bony little behind in here." And she hung up.

Her mother had always impressed upon Charlotte that, no matter how big your heart, what people are going to judge first is what's on the outside, so you've got to make sure you dress appropriately. Which is probably why Charlotte panicked before every date, school dance, and party she'd ever been to, despite having called at least two of her closest friends to find out what they were wearing. The only friend she had in Crickley Creek was Birdie, and she was really Charlotte's mother's friend, a Southern woman, drawl and all, with a heart as big as her bosom and a mouth even bigger. But Charlotte didn't have time to listen to her go on and on about the private lives of other people, so she never made that phone call.

The perfectly symmetrical home loomed in front of her, and people in long dresses and tuxedos milled past a window in a room on the right. It was going to be like walking into a wedding wearing a bikini. Forcing herself to move forward, she muttered, "Damn it, Birdie. This was supposed to be a crab cook. In California, crab cooks are beer-drinking, jean-wiping parties." She stomped up the front steps. "How could she forget to tell me this was formal? For God's sake, Birdie can't keep any detail to herself. Why would she start now?"

The door opened as she raised her hand to knock. A stiff

man in a tuxedo answered, "Good evening, ma'am. May I take your items to the coatroom?" His pity was apparent in his expression.

"Oh, thank you," Charlotte said, handing him her purse and keeping the brightly colored gift bag stuffed with tissue paper. At least she knew enough about Southern customs to bring a hostess gift. She held on to it like it was a sack of money as she made her way across the grand foyer toward the hallway, her old sneakers making squeaking noises on the polished heart-pine floors. To her left was a staircase almost like Scarlett O'Hara's, and to her right was the parlor full of formally dressed people, all with their heads turned toward her. She smiled at them and, in return, most of them smiled back, but they lacked something. It was the feeling she got when the mean girls in high school smiled at her. She'd inevitably find out later that they'd stolen her lunch or covered her locker in maxi pads.

She renewed her vow to kill Birdie upon sight.

Charlotte looked up to see a tall, imposing older woman in a form-fitting pale blue gown and white chignon walking toward her. What, for a barely discernible second, looked like a stunned expression on the woman's face turned quickly into a vague, somewhat annoyed smile. "Hello, dear. How may I help you?"

"Hi," Charlotte sputtered. "Oh, I don't need any help. I was just—Well, I think I'm supposed to be a guest."

"Oh, my." She paused. "I see. Well, then, I am Mrs. Virginia Buchanan, the lady of the house." Her blue eyes were hazy, almost purple. She looked too old to be one of Charlotte's mother's friends. Maybe it was the hair. Or the condescension. "I don't believe I've had the pleasure of meeting you."

Charlotte reached for a handshake. "I'm Anna Grace's daughter, Charlotte Sinclair." Virginia's cold hand hesitated before reluctantly meeting hers in the middle. "I'm told you were my mother's friend in high school." The woman squinted but said nothing. "It's nice to meet you." Charlotte squeezed confidently.

Mrs. Buchanan pulled her hand away and held it a few inches from her side as if making a mental note to wash it immediately.

Judging from the woman's expression, maybe the friendship wasn't quite as close as Birdie made it sound. She could hear her mother saying, *Kill her with kindness, honey.* So she pulled her shoulders back and smiled sweetly. "You have a beautiful home." Down the hall and through a screened-in porch, she could see a green slope ending at the Atlantic. It truly was beautiful.

"Well, aren't you just a sweet little thing." Her singsongy South Carolina twang was not nearly as convincing as her tight, closed-lip sneer. "So, dear, how is it that you have an invitation?"

"Birdalee Mudge invited me." *And I'm gonna break every stinkin' bone in her body when I see her.* Charlotte forced another smile and looked around. A few of the partygoers stopped talking in order to watch. "She thought it'd be a great way for me to meet new people, maybe some of my mom's old friends."

Mrs. Buchanan remained silent.

"Birdie told me it was a crab cook." Charlotte tugged at her T-shirt and smiled apologetically.

Virginia gestured grandly toward a round table piled high with crushed ice, pieces of blue and red cooked crab, and slices of lemon. "Why, bless your heart, this *is* a crab cook, honey." A few of the crabs were left whole, one of which was still alive. Charlotte watched as his pinchers moved slowly, half-anesthetized by the cold. Was she expected to eat it while it was still alive? Her heart broke for the poor, cold crab.

"May I help you with your bag?" Mrs. Buchanan drawled.

Charlotte clutched the brightly colored gift bag. "Oh, this is nothing really. Just a little hostess gift," she said, regretting it immediately.

Virginia extended her arm, palm up. "Oh, how lovely." It was a bad idea, but Charlotte didn't have a choice. She handed her the bag. Using only her forefinger and thumb, Virginia pulled out the contents. "Well, now, aren't you just precious." The guests were openly watching. "Red plastic crab forks and...what do we have here?" She held up a long, white cotton bib. "Are these...bibs? Why, yes. Yes, I believe they are." Her voice was raised for the rest of the guests to enjoy the scene. "And what do these bibs say? Let's see now..." She moved toward the sitting room of people, turning the bib around to show them. "FEELING CRABBY. How sweet. They will certainly add to the décor." A few of the guests giggled. Virginia turned to Charlotte and waved her hand toward the back of the house. "I believe Ms. Mudge may be found in the sunroom." And with that, thank God, Charlotte was dismissed.

Charlotte found a window-filled sunroom next to the screened-in porch in the back of the house. Scanning the people for Birdie, her eyes landed on a puffy, brown hairdo in the corner. Birdie's large, pasty-white body was stuffed into a wicker chair, stationed next to a plate of crackers and a half-empty bowl of pimiento cheese.

Charlotte whispered, "Birdalee Mudge, you are in so much trouble. I swear if I had a gun, I'd kill you."

Birdie's eyes popped open like two hot pieces of corn. "Gracious, child! What have you done?"

"What have *I* done? *You* did it, Birdie!" She looked at the people in the room apologetically. Every last one of them pretended not to notice. "You never said this thing was formal." Charlotte gestured at her outfit and lifted her foot to show Birdie her grungy old sneakers. "Thanks a lot. I'm feeling good. Feeling *real* good right now."

"Sarcasm ain't necessary, darlin'. Something appropriate to wear is." Birdie wrestled with the chair to free herself.

"Did Ginny let you walk through the house like that?" She appraised Charlotte as if she hadn't caught the full effect of the outfit the first time. "Durn it all." Grabbing Charlotte by the elbow, she stuck her neck out the door, checking to see if the coast was clear. "Now, we've got ourselves a situation here. I'm gonna have to hide you upstairs."

Charlotte was hustled up the creaky old stairs in the kitchen typically used for staff, and hidden in none other than Virginia's own bedroom. A thick, four-poster mahogany bed, with monogrammed pillowcases peeking out from behind shiny apricot-and-beige paisley shams and a mass of at least six coordinated throw pillows, stood in the middle of the wall. People only had beds like that if they had someone else to make them. There was a sitting area next to a pair of French doors leading to a balcony. The chairs positioned around the bookshelf were done in the same shiny fabric as the bed and they looked so delicate, she feared they might rip. So, she stood next to the brick fireplace and studied the oil painting hanging above it. In it was a much younger version of Virginia, a serious man, and a boy who looked to be around twelve years old. None of them were smiling, yet they were an uncommonly good-looking group.

A whiff of lavender made Charlotte turn her head. Standing in the doorway, still as the Doric columns out front, was Virginia, glaring at Charlotte as if her perfectly orchestrated evening had been ruined by the arrival of a petite, brown-haired girl from California.

Birdie walked up from behind, chirping, "Alright, Ginny, let's find this girl a dress." She practically shoved Virginia forward and gave Charlotte a wink.

Charlotte didn't know whether to follow them or stay put, so she held still while the two women walked into a closet nearly the same size as the bedroom. It was easy to hear them whispering.

"Oh, come on. You haven't worn that since I told you it looked like your meemaw's couch," said Birdie. Hangers scraped across metal closet bars, and Birdie's voice rang out again, "Good Lord, Ginny Buchanan, I can't believe you still have the dress."

Virginia answered Birdie in a low murmur. She sounded angry.

"And with the tags still on it, almost thirty years later!" Birdie squawked. "If Anna Grace were alive, she'd tear you to pieces."

"Give me that," said Virginia. "Where do you think you're going with that dress?"

"She's wearing it," said Birdie. "This is the dress."

"Absolutely not."

"You know darn well you only bought this dress so Anna Grace couldn't wear it. It doesn't even fit you. I remember."

There was silence.

Finally, Virginia spoke. "She's in my house. I'll give her the dress."

Birdie walked out first, grinning so widely her bright

pink lipstick nearly smeared against her ear. Virginia came out next, holding a gold dress. Charlotte knew from her college fascination with vintage clothing that it was a silk Christian Dior slip dress. It looked like something Jackie Kennedy or Audrey Hepburn would have worn. Without a glance at Charlotte, Virginia threw the dress on the bed.

"Are you sure?" Charlotte asked Virginia's retreating back. She wanted to give her a way out, an opportunity to say no to lending such an exquisite dress, and in turn, give herself an excuse to slip out the back door and drive home.

Virginia swung around, her squinty eyes belying her fake smile. "Of course, I insist. It wouldn't do to have you running around here like *that*, now would it?" She marched from the room.

Birdie picked up the dress and held it in front of Charlotte. "At least she lets us know what she's made of right up front. Been that way her whole life. Now ignore that old biddy," said Birdie. "Put this on."

Charlotte took it from her carefully. "Why'd she keep this from my mother?"

"Those two were a couple of queen bees competing over who had the better stinger. They'd fight over who could roast their friggin' marshmallow better. 'Course Ginny was more willing to play dirty, which is why she bought this dress after she found out your mama was saving up for it. Now, go ahead and put it on, honey. It's time."

Charlotte changed into the dress slowly, stunned by the

perfection of it and awed by the fact that the dress was so suited to her own taste.

"Oh my," Birdie cooed. "Now if you just straighten yourself up, you'll look like a princess."

Charlotte turned toward the mirror above the dresser. The dress tapered in at her waist, cut in a way to maximize a woman's body. The neckline was high and wide, showing no cleavage, only a lovely silhouette. Not bad for an accountant from Santa Monica. The dress might just equal redemption.

Shoes were a problem. Virginia wore a size nine, and Charlotte wore a six. Birdie flopped herself onto one of the silk chairs in mock exasperation, and Charlotte sucked in her breath, anticipating the sound of fabric tearing. Nothing happened.

"No one wants to wear them old heels all night anyway. Painful is what they are." Birdie removed her own wide, magenta-dyed square-heeled shoes. "If any of those hoity-toities down there has a problem with our goll-danged feet, I dare them to say something. We're in this together, darlin'."

Charlotte wiggled her bare toes. Unless she wanted to wear sneakers, there was no other choice.

Birdie looked Charlotte up and down, obviously pleased. "Your mama would have loved you in that dress, except, of course, for the fact that it belongs to Virginia. Anyway, I must say, it makes you look older."

"Older than twenty-six? What kind of compliment is that?"

"Naw, sugar. It's just that your face is all lit up, like you're wise to something, or like you're just plain comfortable with who you are. I haven't seen you look this way since you moved here."

Charlotte smirked. "You're just digging the hole, Birdie. Making it deeper."

"Honey, what I mean is that you look like you finally got your feet under you."

"Yeah, bare feet." Charlotte giggled as she pulled her dark hair loose from the ponytail and shook it upside down, fluffing it. She checked herself in the mirror again. "If we're going to do this, let's do it."

They walked down the grand curved staircase in the front of the house, Birdie looking like an oversized powder puff stuffed into a sequined purple tent dress and Charlotte feeling like she'd just been transported to Civil War Tara. Conversations ended abruptly as the first few guests noticed their arrival. In the window above the front door, Charlotte saw a reflection. It was an angel in soft focus, floating down the stairs, the glow from the chandelier lighting the natural gold strands in the long waves of her dark hair, her creamy skin translucent. She paused for a moment to squint at the image. Lifting her hand, she touched the blazing hair. The angel followed suit.

Birdie leaned over and whispered, "I'd say I'm forgiven for forgetting to tell you to wear a dress."

Trying to stay near the edge of the sweeping staircase, she

held tight to the handrail, the pine floor cold on her feet, Charlotte whispered back, "Keep dreaming."

When they got to the landing, Birdie said, "I don't know about you, but I'm in desperate need of a toddy. You stand here and look pretty. I'll go get us a drink and be right back." She practically hopped her way toward a tuxedoed man tending the bar.

Charlotte was just beginning to feel awkward again when an elegantly dressed young man approached her. He was dark and attractive, in a grown-up frat-boy sort of way.

"You must be Charlotte Sinclair," he said, extending his hand. "I'm Jack Buchanan." At the mention of his last name, she recognized him as the boy in the picture upstairs. "I heard you're here all the way from California."

"Yes," she squeaked. Not much else was going to come out of her mouth. There was something powerfully alluring, and disquieting, about this boy who'd clearly been discussing her earlier. Plus, he looked way too much like Virginia for comfort.

"Welcome to the South. I see you survived your first test." He chuckled.

Test? She may still be standing, but she didn't feel like she'd passed anything yet.

"Don't let my mother make you think badly of the rest of us, I think you'll find we have a lot to offer." His lilt was masculine, welcoming. His eyes crinkled at the corners.

Charlotte breathed in hope. "Thank you." She smoothed

her hair so that it was behind her shoulders.

Leaning in, he whispered, "Look, I saw her messin' with you, and the fact is, she can be a bit ornery sometimes, but she's really not a bad person." He chuckled again, and Charlotte sensed a glitch in his smile. She tried desperately to think of something to say, outside of how horrible his mother was. Nervously, she fiddled with the fabric on her thigh. "Word has it you just opened a coffeehouse," he said, expertly filling in the silence like he was accustomed to girls acting nervous and fluttery around him.

"Yes, Tea and Tennyson. It's downtown. Actually, it's a tea shop and bookstore, but we sell coffee too." She was torn about inviting him to visit the store. He might be incredibly attractive, but he was also the son of the witch whose dress she was wearing. Unsure of what to say, she did what she hated most and began babbling. "See, I went to Paris for a semester in high school, and there was a store there and they had brownies and peanut butter, and there was this really nice cat that wandered around, and they had books in English, and I just always thought I'd have a store like that someday."

She needed to shut up.

An extremely tall man with a long nose, narrow face, and short, ill-fitting suit shuffled over and placed his hand on Charlotte's arm. "You must be Charlotte," he, thankfully, interrupted. "I'm Pastor Ashby Crane. I knew your mama when she was a girl. I mean, uh, I was a few years older, but I always knew who she was." He blushed furiously, and Charlotte wondered where he just came from. "So sorry to hear of her passing. She was a fine lady." Concern made his face look even longer, and he pulled gently on Charlotte's arm, as if to lead her somewhere. Somewhere away from Jack. "Didn't you come here with Birdalee? Let's go find her. Excuse us, please, Jackson."

Jackson didn't put up a fight.

"The girl's with me, Ashby." The pastor nearly fell down at the sound of Birdie's voice. She handed Charlotte a drink and glared at him. He blushed a deep red, released his hold on Charlotte's arm, mumbled something about trying to find her, and walked away.

Charlotte had never been so happy to see Birdie as in that second. She tried to smile her appreciation, but Birdie was distracted by a beautiful blonde staring at Jack. Jack turned to look too, then sighed deeply. "Well, Jackson," said Birdie, "if you don't mind, Miss Charlotte has had herself locked in that store of hers so long, she's got to catch up on her socializing." Jack said a quick goodbye and trotted after the thin blonde moving quickly toward the powder room.

Dragging Charlotte around the entire first floor, Birdie introduced her to the who's who of Crickley Creek. Big-haired women and big-bellied men greeted her kindly. There were no short skirts, no spilling cleavage, and very few stretched faces—the opposite of what she'd find at a party in Los Angeles. Mayor Sonny Compton shook Charlotte's hand

and welcomed her to the great state of South Carolina, even though she'd lived there three months already. John Franklin and Suzanne Egan-Franklin invited her no fewer than four times to join them at church on Sunday which, according to Birdie, was a gutsy move, considering they were the only Catholics in a room full of Baptists.

Jesse Bixler couldn't take his eyes off her and kept saying over and over that she reminded him of someone. It wasn't her mother, Anna Grace, but for the life of him, he just couldn't "figger out" who it was. In her presence, each guest was sweet and welcoming, but Charlotte sensed that once she was out of earshot, plenty was being said about the girl from California who had the audacity to show up to Virginia Buchanan's party with no shoes. She could see the questions in their faces. What was she doing there? Who were her people?

Chapter Two

THE HOUSE WAS silent, no singing of old hymns from the kitchen, no easy listening from the stereo, no dogs barking or cats knocking knickknacks from their shelves. It wasn't her earliest memory, but for Charlotte, it was her most vivid. Her mother sitting at the old round kitchen table, illuminated by a stream of sunlight, a peaceful set to her rosebud mouth, strands of blonde hair catching the light like dust motes near a lamp. Time stopped in the silence as she watched her mother meticulously paint bugs onto an old Mason jar. Charlotte must have been eight, maybe nine, and to her, everything in the room that day was yellow: her mother's hair, the kitchen table, the sunshine, and the tails of the bugs on that jar.

Like coming home to warm cookies in the oven, the memory was transcendent and comfortable. Her mother was beautiful, and her stepdad was invincible. On the kitchen table next to the jar were the pictures that usually sat on the fireplace mantel. Most of them were various combinations of Charlotte's stepdad. He was fishing with his dad, posing at the beach with his older sister, sitting by the Christmas tree surrounded by all of them, the one common theme his enthusiastic smile. Anna Grace had only two framed pictures of herself. There was the one and only picture Charlotte ever saw of Anna Grace with her parents, taken when she looked to be about three. She was standing in between her mother and father, holding their hands, wearing a knit dress, a matching hat, and a carefree smile.

But the most familiar picture was the one set closest to the edge of the table. It had always been Charlotte's favorite: Charlotte as a newborn, with a little pink bow pasted to her head, looking into the eyes of her mother. Her mother gazed back at her, appearing both completely in love and thoroughly exhausted.

David Sinclair, holding his briefcase, had walked into the room and stopped at the sight, sucked into the same universe Charlotte had just discovered. His presence and their shared vision sent joy surging through her little body like a solar flare. She didn't need anything but these two people for her whole life.

Daddy broke the silence. "What are you making?" he asked. Or maybe it was, "Whatcha doing?" Charlotte couldn't remember. But what was as clear as the glass of the jar being painted was her mother's tearful reaction. The mood in the room shifted, the air became heavy, and Anna Grace Sinclair wept fiercely. Why was Mommy crying? Had something hurt her? Maybe she was crying because she missed her parents. Just the thought of losing her own was too much to bear. She looked to her father for help. She needed him to make it better, to use his gentle strength to coax Mommy's mind back home like he always did when she got upset. She needed him to tell them both that everything was going to be okay. She wiped at her tears, determined not to let her mother see her upset. She didn't want Mommy to feel worse.

Daddy set his briefcase by her chair and cupped his hand on his wife's shoulder. In his deep, steady voice, he said, "Those are some nice-looking fireflies."

"Back home, we call 'em lightning bugs," came her mother's broken reply.

Lightning bugs. From that day on, those tiny bugs had a home in Charlotte's soul.

That Mason jar was now Charlotte's greatest treasure, more than her mother's wedding ring or favorite coffee mug. Now that her parents were gone, most of their household possessions were in a storage unit back in Santa Monica, but the Mason jar came with Charlotte to Crickley Creek. It held her mother's soul, her essence.

It was late, and Charlotte was home from the most disastrous party of her life, grumpy and exhausted, sitting on her couch, holding the jar in her lap, making sure not to nick one of the painted-on fireflies and trying to stop her brain from reliving the viciousness that was Virginia Buchanan.

Never forget who you are, came the echo from somewhere in the middle of her brain. It was something her mother once cross-stitched onto a kitchen towel. She felt like she'd read it every day for most of her life. Yet somehow, she'd forgotten it the moment Virginia Buchanan shook her hand. For heaven's sake, Charlotte was a professional woman, a certified public accountant, and now an entrepreneur. She'd quit a good job and left every friend she ever had to move alone to a small town in South Carolina and set up a business she'd never run before. That took bravery and gumption. Plus, it made good business sense as long as Starbucks stayed out of town. She was nothing if not realistic.

Here she was, smart and ambitious, and yet all evening she'd allowed some backward lady named after a state to make her feel like a stupid little girl. She squeezed the jar against her chest, unscrewed the lid, and inhaled the vague, sweet odor of the dried honeysuckles her mother once kept inside. "Mom." She sighed. "What is it about this place that you could never let go?" Anna Grace told stories about fishing with friends, sinking up to her knees in pluff mud, finding shark teeth on the beach, and a million other perfect-sounding stories. But so far, the South hadn't been the fairy tale Charlotte had imagined.

"Seriously, Mom, these were your friends?"

There were no feelings of warmth, no visions, no motherly voice in her head, just the usual emptiness in her heart that her mother once filled. She placed the jar back on the bookshelf and shuffled to the bedroom, the dress whispering against her calf as she lifted a foot and frowned at the blackness of its sole. *Mrs. Buchanan may think she's got it all together, but her floors are filthy.*

A bath then sleep. That's what she needed. If she couldn't force out the visions of Virginia, maybe she could wash them out. Her mother used to say that a good soaking could drown a world of worry.

Chapter Three

F IRST THING MONDAY morning, Charlotte took Virginia's silk dress to the dry cleaner and paid extra for rushed service. She passed the time at her little tea and bookstore, decorated in black and white with clear acrylic chairs, crystal chandeliers, and a twisty pathway made of white tile heading toward the secret garden out back. It was the most modern interior in all of Crickley. Charlotte happily rang up customers and helped her two employees, Krista and Scruggs, handle the morning crowd. As usual, Krista, contrary to her blonde beauty-queen looks, worked without a smile, quickly and with determination, while Scruggs stomped his cranky, college-boy self around the store, making rude jokes and occasionally wiping a table.

When the crowds died down, Charlotte took a moment to google "plantations of South Carolina" and there, listed by city, next to the words Crickley Creek, was Buchanan Manor.

Founded in 1772 by Lord Thacker and Lady Belle Buchanan, Buchanan Manor sits upon a rich and diverse island in the Atlantic near Charleston. Done in the

Greek Revival Style, Buchanan Manor is today much as it was over three hundred years ago. The manor sits on Katu Island, a private island originally known as Caretta Caretta, *the scientific term for loggerhead sea turtle. The name Katu, as it became known in more recent years, came about as a nod to local Gullah culture and is the casual, common term for the island. At more than 12.8 square miles, Katu is home to saltwater marshes, beaches, cypress swamps, and even a small freshwater estuary. Many endangered animals find shelter on Katu, including the brown pelican and the loggerhead sea turtle. For many years, it was a working plantation, growing rice and indigo, and is one of the few plantations that has been successfully passed from father to son through the generations. It still remains in the Buchanan family today.*

Charlotte had just enough time to appreciate the idea of endangered animals finding safety on Virginia's island before the clock struck ten. She drove to the dry cleaners and picked up the dress. Holding it above her head, she tried to keep it from touching the asphalt parking lot, determined to return the dress in the same condition in which it was given. She would bring it, along with a basket of teas and pastries, as a thank-you to Mrs. Virginia Buchanan. The whole encounter was mapped out in her head. She'd sit with Virginia in the sunroom and laugh comfortably about the silly dress code mix-up. Virginia would laugh with her, having been completely won over by Charlotte's wit and charm. Over tall glasses of sweet tea, Virginia would share stories of life on Katu Island and tell Charlotte to feel free to call her Ginny. Any woman who cared about endangered animals must have some goodness to her.

A gust of wind picked up the dress and nearly blew it off its hanger.

Charlotte began the ten-minute drive east to Katu, humming along in her silver Jetta, feeling centered for the first time since the party. The sun was shining, the air was clear. She rolled down the window and stepped on the gas. She was ready for this. This would go well.

The fresh air was cool and smelled like grass and pine, much different from the eucalyptus and smog smell of Los Angeles. A chill ran through her body, and she rolled up the window. What if Virginia had treated Anna Grace like she'd treated Charlotte, like someone with no "name," no rich Southern history with which to claim a place in society, someone who wasn't worth her time? The only thing Charlotte knew about her mother's family tree was that her grandfather had been born in New Jersey. Like Birdie had told her, *Virginia thought she was above Anna Grace's raising.* Surely, Virginia never let her forget it.

Charlotte turned on the radio to distract herself and listened to "No Shirt, No Shoes, No Problem" for about twenty seconds before turning it right back off. The bridge to the island was ahead. For heaven's sake, they even had their own bridge. Everything about the Buchanans was ostentatious: the old, imposing mansion, the oil-painted family portraits, the waitstaff, the private island. It all screamed wealth and historical significance. Even the front door was off-putting. She gritted her teeth and squeezed the steering wheel, trying to focus on the green and brown blur that was the road ahead.

I'm just returning a dress.

Pulling into the circular driveway, she parked by the front steps. *Everything in life is an attitude.* She walked between the pillars to the front door. *That woman can't make me feel inferior if I don't let her.* The door was ajar, as if she were expected. *I am in charge of my state of mind.* She knocked. No response. Not even the sound of footsteps. *She is not better than me.* She knocked a second time. Still nothing. For a minute, she was relieved.

Sticking her head through the crack in the door, she said, "Hello?" There was no answer, but a slight sound caught her attention: a sad, crying sort of sound. Someone was here—at least a maid, cook, or gardener. She stepped back out and reached for the doorbell, balancing the dress and the basket of goodies on one arm. A pleasant chime rang loudly. Charlotte waited.

She thought she heard a voice call faintly, "Come in." Pushing open the door, she stepped inside. Someone was talking near the back of the house; this time, it sounded less like crying and more like someone speaking softly, yet urgently.

"Hello? Is anyone home?" She squeezed her toes downward in an effort to quiet the clicking of her backless kitten heels as she walked into the foyer. She considered taking the shoes off, but imagined what Virginia would think if she showed up barefoot again. "I'm coming in." The mood of the house was eerie, like the ghost of Scarlett herself would walk down the stairs, beckon her in, will her to uncover long-hidden secrets.

Charlotte scooted down the hall, passing two watercolor portraits of shorebirds before stopping to listen again. Gone was Virginia's lilt, replaced by a steady, worried hum. "Hello?" Charlotte called out as she tiptoed forward, past a third bird portrait and the doorway leading to the dining room. The house itself seemed to pull her in. The feel was more male, now, maybe the handsome man in the portrait upstairs, Virginia's dead husband, the former master of Katu Plantation.

"Will not allow it…" Whatever Virginia was saying, it was serious.

Stretching her neck to the right, she watched as the breeze moved a strand of white hair from the woman's perfectly coiffed twist. Ready to say a cheery *hello*, Charlotte stepped forward into Virginia's line of sight. At the same time, a small round springer spaniel puppy ran at her, barking, causing Charlotte to wobble in her short heels and fling her arms outward for balance. She dropped the basket with a thud, and a cranberry walnut scone flipped out onto the floor, which the dog quickly ate.

Virginia's head swung toward her. "What on earth are you doing in my house?" She slammed down the phone.

Charlotte had never seen anyone so unstrung. For a moment, she was struck silent. Then bending to pick up the basket, she babbled, "I'm sorry. Really. I just..." She clutched the basket and the dress to her chest. "The door was open, and I thought you said to come in. I rang..."

Virginia was standing, heading her way, shouting, "Middie? Middie! Where are you? How'd this girl get in here?"

Charlotte took a breath. "I'm so sorry. I just came to return your dress." She held out the basket, accidentally dropping the dress to the floor.

A short slip of a blonde woman in black pants and a white shirt swooped in and picked it up. "Yes, ma'am," she said. "I'll see her out." She was already hustling toward the front door.

Virginia gave Charlotte a look that said, *follow her, you bumbling, idiotic fool.* "Leave whatever it is you brought and go."

"Yes, ma'am. I'm sorry, ma'am." Charlotte bowed awkwardly to place the basket on the floor, then bent again, like a geisha upon leaving a room. Hurriedly, she turned around and caught up with Middie, who held both the dress and the front door and, with a grave smile, gestured for her to exit.

"I'll make sure Ginny gets this," she whispered. Charlotte

was still too stunned to move. Middie looked at her strange-ly. "Ma'am, if you're smart, you'll hightail it on out of here."

Charlotte practically ran out the front door. She wanted nothing more than to get out of that house, away from that awful woman, and drive directly back to Santa Monica. Climbing into the driver's seat, she turned the key, put the car in gear, and stepped hard on the gas. Her tires spun on the driveway, but the car didn't move. She pressed harder on the gas pedal. Just when it registered in her mind that the tires were spinning because the driveway was wet, the wheels caught and her Jetta lurched, sending Charlotte's head backward and her car forward through the white picket fence on the side of the driveway and into Virginia's creek with a loud smack and a shock of white.

Chapter Four

THE BOTTOM HALF of Charlotte's black cotton dress was soaked, hanging like a wet sheet to her knees. She stood in the cold water, balancing on the rocks in the creek, moving carefully toward the edge. One kitten heel slipped from her foot and floated with the current. She reached for it, and when she did, her purse fell from her arm and plunged into the water. Grabbing the shoe with one hand and her purse with the other, she straightened and looked around. Considering the front third of her car was underwater, it was clear she wouldn't be driving herself home. How did these things happen to her? Ever since she moved to Crickley Creek, she'd been cursed.

She made it, muddied, up the steep slope leading to Virginia's front lawn. The same springer spaniel puppy who ate the scone waited for her at the top, barking loudly. "Go!" Charlotte yelled, sweeping her hand toward the mansion. "Go home!" The last thing she needed was Virginia's dog announcing her mistake. Marching off the driveway toward the pea gravel and crushed oyster shell road, she tried to outpace the puppy, but he ran along beside her.

Bruises showed up immediately on her right arm from the impact of the air bag. Her lips felt fat. But the more pressing issue was how in the heck she was going to get her car towed out of there without having to deal with Virginia. That prospect was more painful than her injuries. She glanced back toward the house, and a flash of silverish-white hair caught her eye. It had to be Virginia, peeking out the window, watching her, and probably reveling in her humiliation. Charlotte turned away and touched her upper lip, angry that Virginia Buchanan had won again. When she pulled away her hand, blood covered her fingertips. She didn't care. A cut lip was the least of her worries.

Rummaging through her soaked purse as she walked, Charlotte was going to first call a tow truck and then Tea and Tennyson. Hopefully, the store wasn't busy and Krista or Scruggs could leave long enough to come get her. There was no way she would call Birdie for a ride. Birdie'd probably march her back to the mansion and make Virginia give her some ice and a Band-Aid.

Charlotte pulled out her cell phone. It was cracked and soaked, useless. She threw it back into her purse. What had she done to deserve to be stranded with a ruined car and a ruined cell phone, alone on an island with a devil woman? Here, where instead of California's day-long sunshine and light ocean breezes, the air turned suddenly heavy and thick. Where gray clouds covered the sky like a dirty old sweater and Spanish moss stuck to ancient oaks like spider webs blowing sideways in the wind. Where drops of rain the size of elephant tears pounded relentlessly on her head. Her mother had made Crickley Creek sound like heaven, but it was turning out to be more like a Hitchcock movie.

Civilization was roughly five miles away. She could walk it. Bending her soaked head into the wind, she trudged down the road, trying to distract herself from the pain and anger by thinking of all the things she missed in California: jogging near the Santa Monica Pier, shopping at the Third Street Promenade, sorority sisters, palm trees, sushi, four-lane highways, Mom.

Mom. She'd found parts of her mother in Crickley Creek, mostly in the memory of Birdie, who told her about Anna Grace Byrne, homecoming queen, "Fairest of the Fair," the girl all the boys wanted to date. Birdie told of the time they sat in front of the sun lamp over a rainy spring break. Their arms were pale as White Lily flour, but their faces ended up as red as a cooked crab shell. When they returned to school, the two girls told everyone they'd gone to Hawaii on vacation. Birdie was a wealth of knowledge, an endless source of overblown embellished stories of Anna Grace as a young girl. Charlotte hoped to discover the girl Birdie knew. She needed to replace the guilt and trauma the memories of her dying mother had left. She needed to live out the life her mother had deserved. But at the moment, Anna Grace seemed further away than ever. Charlotte kicked the gravel from her shoe and dabbed at her bloody lip with the back of her shaking hand. She didn't know how, but she would not let Virginia bully her anymore. She would uphold her mother's honor, and her own. Even if that meant taking on the queen of the South.

Thunder resonated through the clouds like a rumbling earthquake in the sky and, for a moment, Charlotte was grateful the dog was still following her. "Wag your tail if that scared you too." The puppy's stubby tail moved furiously side to side. With every step, sharp pieces of oyster shell from the road caught in her shoes, slicing and poking Charlotte's feet. She unsuccessfully tried to shake them out, then gave up. Crossing her arms and ducking her chin to her chest, she shivered in the cool summer wind, imagining she was walking home to her mother's tender buttermilk biscuits and sweetened condensed milk pies.

The puppy nudged Charlotte on her calf. "Little doggie, you have to go home now." She bent to pet his wet fur. "Go home, puppy." *Please, go home.* On top of everything else, she couldn't be responsible for taking one of Virginia's dogs. The dog continued to waddle along beside her, wet brown-and-white fur plastered to his back, his stunted tail trying to move in circles.

The wind whipped her hair into her eyes and mouth. Blood oozed from the cuts on her toes and heels. She was biting back tears again when the sound of tires crunching along the road caught her attention. First, she felt a warm relief then a powerful urge to hide behind a tree. Pushing away thoughts of serial killers, she pulled her clingy wet skirt from her legs and stepped into the roadway, praying that whoever it was had a good heater and a towel.

In the distance, a large, white pickup truck appeared around a corner, moving fast. She waved her arms, expecting the vehicle to slow. It moved quickly, kicking up dust despite the rain. She hopped, jumping-jack style, as well as she could in heels, while the puppy barked next to her. The truck hurtled forward, showing no sign of slowing. Was it going to stop? The crunch of tires on the road grew loud.

"Stop!" she yelled, waving frantically. "Stop!" She could see rust on the front bumper and a wide-eyed man look up from behind the wheel. He slammed on the brakes and the truck slid sideways, spraying gravel and mud directly onto her. Charlotte fell backward, landing on her rear, stunned, somewhat blinded.

The puppy barked furiously. A hand pressed onto her shoulder. "You okay?"

Grayish-black mud caked her hair and dripped from her nose. "I think so." She couldn't focus her stinging eyes on the man standing before her.

"Your lip's bleeding," he said.

She watched as his blurry body ran toward his truck, returning seconds later with, thank God, a towel. He gently dabbed the mud from her face and lip, whispering, "There now, you'll be okay." The condescension in his voice made her want to punch him. She struggled for composure as he placed his arm around her waist, pulling her up and into the side of his warm body. He was tall, at least a foot taller than Charlotte. And muscular. Her eyes focused on the outline of his bicep through his wet shirt as he tenderly guided her toward his truck.

She could see him now—white teeth, smiling eyes, and a brown cowboy hat. "Sorry about that, hon. I get to daydreaming on this road sometimes. Sure didn't mean to nearly turn you into roadkill."

"You're a cowboy," she blurted.

A slight dimple indented his left cheek when he smiled. "Did something hit you on the head?" He stopped and used the towel to wipe mud from her forehead, chuckling. "Name's Will. Will Rushton."

She'd had enough of people laughing at her to last a lifetime. Embarrassment fueled her fury. She grabbed the towel and used it to wipe her face. "My head's fine. I'm fine."

He chuckled again. "You look like you need a shot of whiskey."

"Stop laughing at me. This isn't funny."

"Aw, come on, maybe it's just a little funny? I don't come across muddy girls wandering around in the middle of nowhere every day."

She wanted to push this self-righteous cowboy into a puddle. "I wouldn't be covered in mud if it weren't for you."

"Yeah, but you'd still be lost."

"Who says I'm lost?" She stood with her hands on her

hips, slightly wobbly, her mud-caked hair slicked back.

He laughed again. "From the looks of things, you need me."

She needed his patronizing attitude about as much as she needed a mud bath. "I said I'm fine."

"Fine, is it? Alrighty. Guess I'll be on my way then." He walked toward his truck, leaving her standing there like a dirty, soaked, orphan girl. *Damn him.* Charlotte tugged at her skirt and, wincing at the pain, walked a few steps down the road. There was no way she was going to let some obnoxious redneck have the upper hand. Even if he was good-looking.

"Look out for funnel clouds on your walk," he yelled after her. "They start with a little point hanging down, kinda like that one over there."

Charlotte turned her head toward the sky, searching the clouds. "You mean a tornado?"

"That's right. The twisters around here are deadly."

She stopped cold. Earthquakes didn't scare her, but tornadoes were a whole different monster.

"I'm just messin' with you." He walked back toward her. "There won't be any tornadoes today. Come on now, I'm sorry."

"That was rude," she said. "And mean."

"I know. I really am sorry. Let me help you." At least he wasn't chuckling. And he was right about the fact that she needed him. She allowed him to put his hand on her lower back and lead her to the passenger side door. The puppy followed. "Are we taking the dog?" he asked.

"Can't. He's not mine." She climbed into the seat, refusing to look down at the waiting puppy.

"Too bad. He's mighty cute."

"It's not that I want to leave him, okay? He doesn't belong to me, and on top of everything else, I am not going to steal a dog today."

Saying nothing, he scooped up the dog with one arm, placed him in Charlotte's lap, and closed her door.

The truck bounced as he climbed inside. He was sitting beside her now, his white shirt and faded blue jeans as wet as her clinging dress.

"You're stealing this dog, not me," she clarified. "I won't have anything to do with this." She breathed in the puppy smell and held him tighter, his little body warm and wet.

Placing his Stetson on the dash, Will wiped his face with the same towel he'd used on her. His hair was short, thick, and the color of a burnt sugar cookie. "Don't you worry about it. Only one person he can belong to on this island. I'll take him home." He reached over, turned the air vent to point directly at her, and twisted the heater on full blast.

For a second, Charlotte almost liked him. "Thank you."

"Guess since I darn near killed you, I ought to take you someplace dry. Where to, hon? Hospital or home?"

"You can take me downtown, please, to Tea and Tennyson." She moved the puppy to the middle of the bench seat in between them, where he made himself comfortable with his head on her lap.

"You want a cup of tea that bad?"

"No, I live there. I own it."

"Really? You're telling me you own that little frou-frou place out by the courthouse?"

"Yes. And it's not frou-frou, it's gourmet."

"Right. Because there's a big ole difference between those two things." He turned the old truck around and drove away from Virginia's mansion. Charlotte breathed a sigh of relief. "So, I'm guessing you're not from these parts," he began.

"No. California."

"Swimming pools, movie stars…" He chuckled.

"That is so 1970. You sound like an old man."

"Hey, I have always wanted to ask about why all y'all Californians eat that sushi out there. I like fish and all, I just don't see what the heck is wrong with cooking it."

"You should be having this conversation with Virginia Buchanan. She's the one who had live crabs walking around on a table with the dead ones."

He chuckled again. Why did he seem to think that everything she said was amusing? "Bet she thinks that's fancy or something. Probably read in some magazine that they do that in France."

"Yes, and, apparently, you have to wear a formal gown to attend a crab cook around here."

"Not the way I do 'em." She caught him looking at her,

so she turned toward the window. He kept talking like he didn't notice. "We wear jeans to catch 'em and jeans to eat 'em. Nothing's better than fresh-caught crab cooked up with a bunch of crab boil. Except maybe a bloody ole steak."

"That's gross."

"What? A steak? Nothin' gross about it. I mean, it's not like I eat it raw. I put it on the grill for a couple seconds first."

"You know what, Cowboy Will?" She turned toward him. "I don't eat beef, I've had a really bad day, and I don't want to be having this conversation."

"Did you just call me cowboy again?"

"If you're going to degrade me by calling me honey, then I can call you cowboy."

He turned the entire top half of his body toward her, taking her on. "Good. I like it. I'll rustle you some cows any day, honey."

"Watch the road, please." They were nearing the narrow bridge leading to the mainland.

He went back to steering with his wrist, looking more like he was lounging than driving. "You know, us cowboys, we get to wondering when pretty ladies decide to take walks in the wilderness during a thunderstorm."

Charlotte ignored him.

"Doesn't look like you meant to be out walking. You know, judging from the kind of shoes you got on. Your feet are all tore up."

She sighed. "Let's just leave it that my car isn't working."

"Car trouble, huh? Okay, honey. I won't ask you any more questions."

"Good. And stop calling me honey."

"Well, if you tell me your name, I'll give it a shot."

His attitude was infuriating. She almost gave him a fake name. "It's Charlotte."

"Just Charlotte, huh? Well, then I guess your last name has to be Honey."

"Sinclair." She turned toward the window and practiced her yoga deep breathing. Out with the negative, in with the positive. What she really wanted was to smack the guy.

The drive to downtown from the coast was a quick one. You couldn't see the ocean from that far inland, but you could sure smell it. When they came to the row of shops that included Charlotte's store, Will parked in the handicapped spot near the front door. "Figure we got a reason to park here today, Charlotte Sinclair."

She looked out the window at her portion of her old red brick building. Before she could unbuckle, Will came around and opened the passenger-side door.

"Thank you," she said, uncomfortable with the help. She gently moved the puppy's head off her lap and expected the cowboy to step aside as she climbed out. Turning her knees toward the open door, she felt a hand slip under her thigh and jumped. Will's tanned face was only a few inches away. Jerking, she fell back into the truck.

"Don't get upset now," he ordered. "I'm just carrying you in."

"I can walk, thank you." She tried to use her knees to push past him.

"There's no way I'm letting you walk on those bleedin' feet of yours." He pulled her closer, and the puppy began to wag vigorously. "Now, scooch on over here and let me carry you." She didn't move, yet somehow he still managed to cradle her in his arms.

"My feet are fine!" She looked down at her swollen, bloody feet. They were as mangled as if she'd walked a mile on broken glass and then stuffed them into heels.

"Charlotte Sinclair, if you don't loosen up, I'm gonna switch this to a fireman's carry."

He was maddening, but she really did need the help. She took a deep breath, gave the dog a quick rub goodbye, grabbed her purse, and relaxed her body enough to bend. Will carried her through the front doors of Tea and Tennyson where, thankfully, Krista and Scruggs were the only ones present. Krista nearly knocked over the display of teas from India when she saw her mud-covered, bloody-lipped boss arrive in the arms of a man. Scruggs stood with his hands on his hips.

"Ummm, Charlotte? You okay?"

"Fine." Charlotte waved a finger at him. "Don't judge me, Scruggs. My feet hurt." Will carried her to the back of the store toward the locked door leading to her upstairs loft.

"Put me down, put me down." She squirmed, pointing frantically toward a nearby chair. Will placed her down gently. By now, both Scruggs and Krista watched them openly, soaking in every moment of this new development.

Charlotte turned to thank Will, who was smiling at her, rugged and confident in his worn jeans and boots. She stared at him, annoyed with her stomach for fluttering. Cowboys were not her thing. Especially not rude, annoying, condescending cowboys. Scruggs chuckled loudly. She shot him a look and turned back to Will. "Thank you for the ride. Can I pay you for gas?" She opened her sopping wet purse.

"Of course not. I'm just glad I came along when I did." He half grinned at all of them, as if to show off his dimple. Then, to Charlotte, he said, "I'll stop by tomorrow and see how those feet of yours are doing."

All three of them watched him walk away, his wet shirt plastered to his muscular back, his backside, well, perfect.

"Lordy, lordy, lordy, Miss Charlotte," Scruggs said as soon as the coast was clear. His eyes were as wide as a dinner plate. "Can I get you something? An ambulance, maybe? You're nothing short of one hot mess."

"I'm fine." Charlotte waved him off, but he sat at the table with her anyway.

"I'd like to know what you did to get Will Rushton himself to carry you in here." Charlotte frowned at him. She had no intention of sharing with anyone the depth of her idiocy. He tapped his pointer finger on the table. "And here you are lookin' like you fell into an alligator pond."

Charlotte dropped her head into her hands. "This was not done on purpose. This whole day has been a *Titanic*-sized disaster, and I'd rather not talk about it." She looked up. "What I have to do now is get my car back." Digging around, she pulled her ruined cell phone from her purse. She'd have to call a tow truck from the store phone but didn't want to stand on her aching feet yet. "So, how do you know that guy?"

"Everyone knows him." Scruggs whistled. "If I had girls flocking to me like they do to him, I wouldn't need to be working here. I'd have me a sugar mama."

Krista, who had clearly been listening, snickered. "Maybe a sugar mama would teach you how to wear matching socks." Scruggs shot her a *what does that have to do with anything?* look, and Krista kept going. "I believe color blindness is an inherited trait. Just like assholery."

Scruggs held up a hand. "Whatever online classes you are taking at the junior college do not make you an expert. We are talking about our beat-up and sopping-wet boss right now." He huffed.

Charlotte limped around the store in her slippers the rest of the day, feeling anxious, her mind consumed with thoughts of broken fences and puppies, wet shirts and pickup trucks. She hated herself for hoping Will Rushton would keep his word and see her again.

Chapter Five

JACK BUCHANAN CAME into the store twice on that horrible Monday when Charlotte crashed her car—once for breakfast before she left for her fateful visit to his mother, and again for an afternoon snack, at which point Charlotte was moving slowly and sporting a swollen lip and bruised arm. Jack didn't seem to notice. Both times, he ordered a cup of black coffee and a lemon poppy seed muffin and sat at the same small table by the front window next to the reference section.

Nothing in his face or demeanor suggested he knew about the fact that she'd just crashed into his mother's creek, probably because it was gentlemanly to spare her the embarrassment of discussing it. But all three tow companies she'd called told her that the property owner said it was an "inconvenient" time for her. She couldn't let her car wallow in the water, even if the last thing she wanted to do was ask Jack for help.

Charlotte sighed. She'd try the tow companies again in the morning, and if Virginia still wouldn't let them get the car, she'd call Birdie for help.

Jack showed up again early Tuesday morning, only this time, he brought with him something large, flat, and square, wrapped in packaging paper. "This is from my mother," he said, handing the gift to her.

"Really?" Charlotte asked, stunned. It was heavy, so she put it on the floor and leaned it against her leg. "Can I open it?"

"Please."

Inside was a watercolor painting of dogwood flowers in what appeared to be a weathered, vintage-style frame. It was stunning, a perfect Southern souvenir. "This is beautiful! It's from Virginia?" She didn't know the woman had it in her. Was it possible she wasn't evil after all? Had Charlotte misread her?

"It's one of her flower prints," said Jack. "Before she got into her shore bird stage. See?" Jack pointed to the bottom right corner of the picture.

Sure enough, next to the print number, the signature read V. BUCHANAN.

The truth was, Charlotte didn't want anything from Virginia. "Are you sure she wants me to have this?"

He nodded. "The frame is made out of wood from our old horse stables. When Mother had them torn down, she commissioned frames to be made for her paintings and prints. It's more than one hundred years old."

"Really?"

"Yes," he said. "And it's for you with sincere apologies

from the Buchanan family."

It was hard to believe that Virginia had it in her to be so nice. "Wow. Thank you so much. Please tell your mother thank you. I'll write her a note." Maybe Charlotte needed to rethink her budding hatred of that bitter, haughty woman. She was, after all, quite a talented artist.

"Don't bother with the note," he said. "I'll tell her you liked it." He walked toward the table in the corner, pulled out his laptop, and left Charlotte wondering if she should send a note anyway. The coffee rush was in full swing, so she ran the painting up to her loft and came back down. She brought Jack his muffin and was delivering a scone to a nearby table when Birdie flew in.

"Mornin', Jackson!" she yelled from the front door. "How's my favorite lawyer?" Charlotte watched as Birdie forcibly hugged him. "You gonna put some more criminals away today?"

"How ya doing, Ms. Birdie?" Despite his good manners, when Birdie was around, his face took on a look of strain. Plus, he was a defense attorney, not a prosecutor.

Birdie sat herself in the chair across from him. "Oh, I'm fine, fine. This bum knee's been barkin' at me, but I'm trying to quit complaining about it."

Scruggs, carrying a hot apple blossom with fresh whipped cream, passed Charlotte and shot her a look. She knew exactly what it meant. Birdie was the bane of Scruggs's existence, the splinter in his toe, the blister on his backside.

Birdie knew it and loved it. She'd known Scruggs Willingham III since he was four years old, sitting at her kitchen table, drinking her sweet tea, back-talking and sass-mouthing her because he lived next door and didn't take kindly to the word *no*.

She had admitted that she might have gotten some enjoyment from watching that boy devour her homemade cookies with gusto, and she might have been amused when he bounded into her house, singing something loudly and off-key, but that certainly didn't mean she loved him. That boy never did know his place. Now that Scruggs was an adult, annoying each other had become their favorite sport. Those two couldn't be in the same room together without one of them stirring up trouble.

Charlotte watched as he delivered the pastry to a woman at the table next to Jack and Birdie. He made quite the show of ignoring Birdie before jogging toward the back door. Without a doubt, he was going to get Waffles, his old Yorkshire terrier and partner in crime. On cue, Waffles came running inside, barking her high-pitched yip, and went straight to Birdie's bright red loafers.

"Scrooge!" Birdie yelled. "Get your rat-dog out of here. She's supposed to be outside."

Scruggs walked to Birdie's table and picked up Waffles, repeating his mantra along the way. "Be peaceful, Ms. Birdie. Just be peaceful, and the dog will stop barking at you."

"Peaceful, my foot. You trained that dog to bark at me

and you know it. You are a mean-spirited man, Scrupid. Just plain mean." Waffles barked again. Birdie made a show of reaching over and pinching Jack's cheek, cooing, "But *you* are just perfection on a plate, young man. So much better than any short, dog-totin', know-it-all college boy."

"Or a fat old ninnyhammer," Scruggs added.

Birdie rolled her eyes as Jack packed his computer and stood to leave. "You're lucky I know I'm gorgeous," she said.

"Don't let that hateful woman run you off, Jack," said Scruggs. "I'll put the poor little puppy outside."

"Oh, quit your boo-hooing, Scruggly," Birdie said before turning toward Jack. "Jackson, you go on to work now and do something real good and purposeful for the folks in this town, alright?" She pulled a face at Scruggs.

Charlotte watched Jack leave, the perfect creases in his suit folded behind his knees as he walked, his back straight and head held high, green eyes scanning the room for something. They landed on her, and he waved goodbye. She waved back, more intrigued than ever. *No*, she told herself. Virginia's son was not the man to set her heart on. Then again, the woman had given her artwork.

She picked up a plate of hot ham buns and moved forward to deliver them to Mayor Compton, who was boisterously visiting her store for the first time since Virginia's crab cook. Scooting toward his entourage, she was self-conscious about wearing slippers but grateful to have footwear that didn't hurt the cuts on her feet. She looked down to see how badly they stood out, and by the time she saw the gray suede oxfords, it was too late. She'd walked directly into Jack, the hot ham buns sliding from the plate and landing squarely on one of his obviously expensive and very stainable suede shoes. Jack jumped backward.

"Oh! I am so sorry." Charlotte looked back and forth from his face to his shoe. "I ruined your shoe." Reaching down, she picked up the gooey bun, which had now made its way to the floor, leaving behind a cheesy, mustardy trail.

"It's okay. No harm done." Jack waved her off. "It's my fault, anyway. I came back to ask you something."

"No. No, it's not okay," Charlotte said from her position on the floor. "I'll get a napkin. I'll fix this. I'll pay for a new shoe."

"A new shoe?" Jack laughed. "Where are you going to find one shoe?"

The store full of customers was staring. "Two shoes, of course. I'll buy you two shoes." Grabbing a handful of napkins, she stooped again to clean his shoe, but the butter and mustard had seeped into the fabric, making a yellowish oil stain on either side.

"Give me those," he said, reaching down and taking the napkins from her. "I'll get this. You go ahead and get back to work."

Charlotte refused to give him the napkins and continued wiping the mess, managing only to make the stain bigger. At least he had the decency to keep his foot still.

In the confusion, she forgot about Mayor Compton, who was looking rather irked at the fact that his breakfast had been dumped and he had not received the attention he was due. Apologizing and running behind the counter, Charlotte went to work preparing two more buns. The mayor used the opportunity to loudly proclaim how happy he was to show her mercy in this instance and how it was a good thing he was a patient man. It would be no problem for him to wait for his meal *again*. Then he added in a hushed voice, "Although I wouldn't turn down a little something free for my trouble."

He beamed sweetly, cheeks shining, as Charlotte added two iced oatmeal cookies to his order, on the house. She was hyper-aware of Jack walking out the front door. Her hands shook as she handed the bag to the mayor.

Jack Buchanan had something to ask her.

Chapter Six

THE TUESDAY MORNING coffee rush was tapering off when Will came back to check on Charlotte. Mud had obviously, and unsuccessfully, been brushed from his jeans and stomped off his old worn boots, but his hair appeared wet and freshly combed. She led him to a table by the stairs, the one where he'd set her down just the day before. He pulled out a chair for her to sit. He smelled of strength, like fresh air and dirt.

"How're those feet of yours?" he asked, sitting across from her.

"Fine. A little sore but good." There was an awkward pause. "I can't sit here long. I have to work."

"Alright." He looked directly at her face, which made her nervous and a little mad. "Your lip looks better."

Her tongue automatically went to it. "Yep, getting better." She looked around the store. Anywhere but at him.

There was an uncomfortable pause. "So, tell me, Charlotte, where'd your name come from? Did your folks name you after the capital of North Carolina?"

Charlotte felt like she was back in sixth grade and the

popular boy had just chosen her to flirt with. "My mother named me after a dessert."

"Well, you're sweet, alright."

There went the dimple again. Clearly, he was a sweet talker. "Cute," she said.

"Yeah. You're that, too." His eyes never left her face.

The guy was too much. Too bold. She reached for a book from the shelf beside them and pretended to flip through the pages. He couldn't possibly be interested in her. Boys like Will didn't choose girls who owned tea shops, wore vintage clothing, and refused to eat red meat. They just didn't. Plus, he was obnoxious.

"So, what's in this 'Charlotte' dessert?" He leaned closer and she noticed that one of his lower teeth was slightly crooked.

She put down the book. "Pretty much just ladyfingers, custard, and chocolate. It's made in a special pan called a Charlotte mold." Will's eyes moved to the book, and he bit his lips together like he was fighting a smile.

For the first time, she noticed the title: *Fifty Shades of Grey.*

Charlotte snatched the book and stuck it face down on top of the neatly aligned books on the bookshelf. Her face felt as red as her work apron. "Um, the cake is—you know, um, Mom would make it for my birthday. The Charlotte. Instead of a cake. My mom would make me a Charlotte instead of a cake." She took a steadying breath. "It's tradition."

Will's eyes twinkled, and she looked away as her face burned.

"So, I've been asking about you," he said. "I heard about your mama. She's from Crickley, right? Ran off after high school?"

Asking about her? "I don't know who you've been talking to, but my mother did no such thing." Charlotte's emotions shot high. Too many customers had asked about her mother with a glint in their eye and gossip in their questions. "Why does everyone around here care so much that my mother left? She wasn't running, she didn't go to California to try to become famous, it was just time to get out of Crickley. I don't blame her, either. This whole town needs to stop with their ridiculous assumptions. She's not even here to defend herself." She had to stick up for her mother, only she wasn't sure of the truth herself.

He reached out to touch her hand. "Don't get all riled up. I'm just saying what I heard."

"What isn't true should not be repeated." She pulled her hand away. "She loved this place. Talked about it my whole life."

"So she left a place that she loved for no reason." He leaned in, appearing unbothered by her annoyance. "And you decided to up and move, too."

"There doesn't have to be a reason. She moved. I moved. People move. Why can't—?" Will's face flushed red and his eyes fixed on the front door. She turned. An overweight man with camouflage shorts, a filthy T-shirt, and orange baseball cap looked smugly in their direction. He sauntered to the counter to order. Something about him made Charlotte shiver. She looked back at Will, who was now calmly looking at his cell phone.

"Is everything okay?" she asked.

"Yeah, good. It's all good." He seemed to have run out of conversation.

They watched Krista smile sweetly as she served the man a large mocha milkshake. Charlotte was proud of her employee. When a customer stared at you with a tight-lipped snarl and squinty bloodshot eyes, it was practically impossible to smile back.

"Is he a friend of yours?" she asked Will.

"Nope."

Something was definitely up. "Is there a problem with him?"

"Always." He leaned back and stretched his legs lazily. "So, we were talking about you."

"Let's not, okay?" There ought to be a less touchy subject. "How about you tell me what you do." As an afterthought, she added, "And what you were you doing on Katu Island yesterday."

His eyes switched back and forth between her face and the man at the counter. "I work in the construction industry. We build homes." Running his fingers through his hair, he sighed and refocused his attention fully on Charlotte. "I was on the island yesterday taking measurements. We're building some guest homes on Katu." He paused, and Charlotte knew what was coming. "What were *you* doing on Katu?"

She couldn't blame him. She'd brought it on herself. "Walking."

"No kiddin'." Leaning in again, he covered his phone with both hands. "And what were you doing before you were walking?"

Charlotte would rather walk on crushed oyster shells again than think about it. "Driving into a ditch." She leaned over to pet Waffles, who'd just snuck back inside, successfully avoiding his gaze.

"Is that right." It was more a statement than a question. Will reached down to scratch Waffles's head, and his hand briefly touched hers. Her breath caught.

I do not like this man. I do not like—the memory of the feel of his arms and chest when he'd carried her inside flared—*cowboys.*

"I'm gonna guess your accident had something to do with Virginia Buchanan," he said.

"You'd be correct." She forced herself to look at him again.

"She has that effect on people," he said. "You wanna talk about it?"

"No. But thanks."

The man in camouflage caught her eye. He was making

his way to the front door, his snake-like eyes boring a hole through Will, his fleshy mouth a threatening smirk. He switched the look to Charlotte, and his expression changed to a mix of lechery and excitement, like she was a doe caught in his crosshairs. She'd never been more repulsed by a person in her life. Thank God he was leaving.

Now that the morning rush was over, she needed to call the tow company again. Will pretended to stretch and yawn. "Do you want to sit outside and get some sun? It's a nice day, and things look like they're under control in here." He nodded toward Krista, who was diligently refilling the pastry display, her long, blonde hair pulled back into a ponytail.

"Maybe just for a second. I have a phone call to make."

Will stood and reached for her hand. "Let's go."

She ignored his hand and walked in front of him toward the door. "Krista, I'll be right back," she called out.

Once outside, Charlotte squinted in the sunlight. It was a warm, blue-skied April day. She inhaled deeply and was about to ask Will which of the sidewalk benches he preferred, but he turned his head to the left, indicating the spot where his old white truck was parked parallel to the curb. She narrowed her eyes against the glare.

"My car!" She gasped. Attached to the tow hitch on the back of his truck was a trailer holding her little silver Jetta. First, she ran toward the car, then turned back to Will, jumping toward him and throwing both arms around his neck. She squeezed him tight, and he lifted her off the ground. "Thank you! Thank you! Thank you!" she gushed.

After a minute, he set her down, beaming. "I fixed the fence, too."

"Oh my God," she whispered. "You did?"

The front of the car resembled crumpled tin foil, but Charlotte didn't care. It was out of the water, back in her possession. She couldn't believe it. Will's hair was barely moving in the breeze, his face flushed, offering her this gift, saving her from further embarrassment, from the anguish of dealing with Virginia. "This is the nicest thing anyone has ever done for me."

"You're welcome." He touched her upper arm before putting his hands in his front jeans pockets and sauntering toward his truck. "I'll drop it at Jimmy's for you. He's the best one for fixing things around here."

Charlotte never wanted to kiss anyone so badly in her life.

Chapter Seven

THE NEXT DAY, Charlotte alternately rode high and low each time she thought of Will. It had been a long time since anyone treated her so kindly. Since the death of her stepdad six years ago and her mom's passing just last year, Charlotte had no soft place to fall, no one to count on. If anything was to be done for her, she was the one who had to do it. By going through the trouble to rescue her car, Will made her feel significant. And while that felt good, it also felt too good to be true. After all, what the heck kind of a weak girl would fall for his "I'm a big man, you're a little woman" act? She totally could have handled getting her own car from that creek. And she could handle Virginia Buchanan and cuts on her feet and thunderstorms and stolen puppies, too.

But she didn't have to. And that was nice.

Charlotte set to work unpacking boxes of the newest bestsellers to place in the front window display. Caught up in her thoughts and humming, she felt genuinely content for the first time in recent memory.

Midmorning, Birdie marched in for her usual snack of a chocolate chip flaxseed cookie and large mango iced tea with six Splendas. Birdie might have a personality that could annoy Mother Teresa, but Charlotte saw through the façade. Birdalee Mudge was a lonely, aging woman who only got into other people's business because she had none of her own: a long-dead husband, no children, and no life outside of Crickley Creek. Maybe it was sentiment for her old friend Anna Grace that led Birdie to stay in Charlotte's life. Or perhaps it was because Charlotte brought with her a certain element of life outside of that small town. Either way, Charlotte knew for certain they had one big thing in common: They were both alone.

"Hey, Birdie! How's your day going?" she asked.

"Aw, honey, it's just giggles and grins." Birdie frowned and stomped to her table, scanning the room for Scruggs. "Where's my nemesis? Messin' with him always makes me feel better."

"I don't know why he puts up with you," said Charlotte.

"It's how I show my love."

"He's late," Krista said, pouring the sweeteners into Birdie's tea. "Probably stayed up all night studying or something."

Charlotte took note of the time. Should she be worried? Scruggs was on the schedule for fifteen minutes ago. He was rarely late. She pulled out the new phone she'd paid extra to have mailed overnight and dialed his number. "You've reached Scruggs Willingham the third. Do not leave me a message. I will not listen to it. If you want to reach me, text me. Have a good day."

Charlotte texted.

Birdie seated herself where Charlotte was setting up the display, and Krista brought her tea and cookie to her. The three girls were alone in the store, an excellent time for sharing secrets.

"Charlotte," Birdie began. "I do believe it is time for you to spill the beans about Will Rushton. I want all of it, honey. Every shameful detail."

Charlotte moved away from Birdie's prodding foot. "No, *I* want the details," she countered. "And I know you have them. Who is Will Rushton?"

"Only the best catch in the whole county. Bless his bones, that boy's got it all: looks, job, family, smarts. I'd take him if he'd have me." She seemed completely serious. "But, since he seems to prefer skinny little teahouse girls to mature women with a little meat on their bones, whyn't you go ahead and start tellin' me what happened?"

"There's nothing to tell." It wasn't anyone's business but hers. Charlotte kept her eyes focused on her piles of books; her inattention would drive Birdie crazy.

"Scruggs and I saw him carrying her in like she was Cinderella herself," Krista chimed in. "You know that boy suffers big with wanting to be the hero all the time. I believe they call that a savior complex. Miss Charlotte, I just hope you are smarter than to believe he is a prince."

Charlotte was stunned. Will may have rescued her, but

she was no sad little victim.

"Go ahead, now, Charlotte," said Birdie. "Open your mouth and speak it. I'm gonna get the goods one way or another."

Charlotte knew she had to give Birdie something or she'd be hounded to death. "He gave me a ride when my car broke down. That's it. End of story."

"Mmmm. Hmmm. Keep going."

Charlotte shrugged innocently.

"Well," Krista said. "He did come back to check on her." Obviously, Krista was unaware that Will actually towed Charlotte's car and surprised her with it. *That* would certainly have given her cause for speculation.

"Okay, how can I make this clear?" Charlotte said, shifting her eyes to make eye contact with both of them. "Nothing happened. There's nothing to tell."

"Alright, darlin'," Birdie said. "Then why don't we go ahead and talk about *how* your car broke down."

She knew. Of course she did. "Go ask Virginia."

Krista threw a questioning glance at Birdie, who, to her credit, revealed nothing. Unbelievably, no one spoke for about ten seconds, an uncommon occurrence when Birdie was involved. Charlotte figured she was waiting her out.

Krista broke the silence with a drawn-out sigh. "Look, y'all, I don't know what's going on here with Virginia and your car and all, but before we give up on this Will thing, I just feel strongly that I need to say something."

Both Birdie and Charlotte faced her.

"I'm just gonna come right out with it, alright? Will Rushton is no kind of superhero or prince out of some fairy tale."

"Oh, and just the other day, I saw him in a cape," smirked Birdie.

"Hush, Birdie," Charlotte scolded.

Krista's voice was sugary sweet. "You have to see past the whole smart, good-looking business-owner image. The word for him is disingenuous. He acts one way to your face and another way behind your back. You know?"

"No, Krista, we don't know," Birdie said.

"Birdie, let the girl talk," Charlotte said.

"What I'm trying to say is, you can't trust him." Krista cut her eyes to Birdie, who sat with her cookie on her lap, tight-lipped. "Don't get me wrong now. I have nothing against the man. It's just that I've spent a lot of time reading things and learning about people. Will Rushton is a straight-forward narcissist." She nervously rubbed the corner of her apron with her right hand. "Look, Charlotte, I would feel horrible if you got hurt 'cause I didn't say something. Okay?"

Charlotte wasn't sure how to respond. She was dying to know details about why Krista had a problem with him, but she was Krista's boss. It might not be appropriate to dig.

"Well, thank you, Krista, for enlightening us," Birdie said. "It has all become clear now. Just about as clear as this here cookie I'm holding."

"I appreciate your concern, and I'm happy to tell you that I have no interest in Will Rushton," Charlotte said. It wasn't exactly the truth but close enough.

"Soooo," Birdie stated too loudly, "The Junior League is having a bake sale, and I told 'em, I said, 'Don't you go competing with my precious Charlotte's pastries now.'" She pulled her chair close to Charlotte, effectively cutting Krista out of the circle. "They're the best in town, I said. I swear on my dead husband's grave." Krista took the hint and walked away. Birdie waited a second, then whispered, "Some people think they know an awful lot about other folks when truth is, they've probably never said two words to them in their entire life."

"If you know something, Birdie, you'd better tell me."

"I have nothing to share on the subject. Except this: Will Rushton never did anything wrong outside of drinking beer in high school." She shook her head as if no one should ever be judged for that. "Whatever the hell a narcissist is, he's not one of them. I'm telling you, Will Rushton and Jackson Buchanan were shoo-ins for the Citadel. Both of them went in the same year, too. That's something, you know. Did us all proud."

She dropped her chin to her chest and looked at Charlotte through her stubby top lashes. "That school won't take just anyone." A faraway look shrouded her eyes, her flair for melodrama building to a crescendo. "Both those boys went off to serve in Afghanistan. Same unit. Came under mortar attack and some serious gunfire, too. This whole town was holdin' its breath, waiting for our special soldiers to come home."

She grabbed for Charlotte's hands. "Screw Krista. This is serious. Hold my hands." Her soft, warm fingers squeezed gently. "Jackson's daddy had his heart attack and died while Jackson was off at law school. Ginny was so beside herself, it was all I could do to get that woman out of her house for some fresh air." She squeezed again, as if the memory were physically painful.

"Will's family suffered, too. Good heavens, they had some real hard times while he was gone. His mama had a bout with breast cancer, and his daddy wouldn't leave her side, sat in the waiting room holding her purse on his lap at every doctor's appointment. He stopped working. Nearly lost everything." Birdie took Charlotte's hands up near her own chin. They were almost nose-to-nose. "Honey, Will gave up his army career to come home and tend to his family. So don't you let that Krista go bad-mouthin' him to you. He's good people."

Charlotte was wondering if she'd been too hard on Will, when Scruggs burst through the front doors, wearing black spandex biking shorts, a skintight red sports shirt, and a neon blue biker's helmet. He had a very unhappy Waffles strapped into a baby carrier on his chest.

"Oh dear Lord." Birdie sighed.

He sauntered toward the front counter while extricating the dog from her straitjacket. "I wasn't trying to be late," he stated. As soon as she was free, Waffles jumped into Charlotte's lap and curled up, shaking and too traumatized to bark at Birdie. Scruggs fumbled around, simultaneously taking off his helmet and logging on to his cash register.

When the cyclone became still, he looked into the faces of the women staring at him, and shrugged innocently. Charlotte laughed.

"Boy, what on earth have you got on?" Birdie snarled. "That"—she pointed a red nail up and down—"is not appropriate attire for a fancy tea shop."

He tied an apron around his waist. "Unlike a certain person named after a small winged creature, I believe in exercise."

Birdie stood, huffy and bothered. "The shorts are stupid, and you're late." She stuffed her napkin into her tall glass and placed them both on top of the trash can. "See you later, Charlotte, honey." She headed for the front door. "Why you ever hired that pile of horse crap, I'll never know."

"Go take a pill!" Scruggs yelled to her retreating back.

She waved him off, and the door slammed shut behind her.

"Sorry about being late," he said. "But, Gawd, it was worth it to set fire to that old biddy."

Charlotte was still comforting Scruggs's trembling dog. "I'm not sure Waffles agrees, but I'm glad you're okay."

Chapter Eight

C HARLOTTE AWOKE AT ten o'clock Saturday morning, her favorite day of the week. Warm sunshine streamed in through the front windows of her loft like a hazy yellow cashmere wrap, soft jazz played on the radio, coaxing her, like the voice of an old friend, into feeling hopeful. Sunday was preparation day, which left Saturday as the one day all week that held no responsibilities.

The beauty of her downtown historic district location was that her business was limited strictly to weekdays. In the center of the block stood the courthouse, surrounded by law firms and other businesses with bankers' hours. Despite the fact that a few boutiques stayed open, the area was mostly quiet on the weekends. Crickley Creek was not a tourist destination, as the nearest island was private and the beaches were more marsh and pluff mud than sand. Some might see this as a drawback, but Charlotte didn't. Her desires were simple: do a good job, earn enough to live comfortably, and sleep in at least once a week. So far, her dream was coming true.

Sitting on the couch in her fluffy robe, she allowed the

peace of the moment to possess her. It could take years for a small business to become profitable and she was prepared for it. Even if her venture failed, she'd never regret the time spent running the store. She was single-handedly bringing high quality, organic foods and drinks to a small town that, for the time being, didn't even have a Starbucks. That had to count as community service.

Charlotte took a sip of her hot green tea. The truth was, there was no way she could compete in Los Angeles where coffee shops sat on every corner. Already, Crickley Creek had given her the opportunity to create what she'd dreamed of all her adult life. And the town gave her pieces of her mother, a remembered voice, an insight into Anna Grace as a spunky, determined child and a studious teenager whom adults loved and her peers envied. No matter how small the bit of information, each piece made Charlotte feel more in touch with her mother, and by extension, herself. Crickley was where she needed to be, where fate or destiny or God himself determined she should be. It was where her mother should have been.

The one thing she absolutely had to do today was buy Jack Buchanan a new pair of shoes. There was no way any of the tiny stores in Crickley carried what she suspected were suede Ferragamo wingtips, so she hoped to order them online. She missed the freedom her car afforded, but she hadn't been too put out by its absence yet. She read and piddled around the loft until late afternoon, procrastinating on calling Birdie for Jack's number. Now, if she could just find her cell phone.

She hunted for the phone in the covers of her four-poster pine bed, her mother's slipcovered sofa, and her father's old leather chair. She searched under antique white side tables, in the black-and-white bathroom, and all through her built-in bookshelves, stopping for a second to hold her mother's firefly jar. She carefully inspected the chipping brown and gold paint before placing it back on the bookshelf by her 1884 edition of *The Poetical Works of Alfred Tennyson* and her leather William Faulkner anthology. The phone was nowhere to be found. She would have to go downstairs and use the store phone.

Her big leather Birkin-style bag hung on a hook near the front door. Oh, what the heck, it probably wasn't in there, but she was out of options.

Naturally, the phone was there all along.

When Charlotte finally called Birdie, she patiently answered what felt like a hundred and fifty questions but eventually won out and got the phone number. She called Jack and left a message requesting his shoe size and the color and designer of the shoes she ruined.

It was after dinner, almost six thirty. She dressed for the first time all day and sat on the sofa, turning on the television. After catching some news, she planned to slip on her running shoes and leave for a walk before it turned dark. Her feet had finally healed enough to function normally.

The news was bleak. She labored through stories of arrests and political antics, waiting for the weather report, but perked up at the mention of the Loggerhead Festival committee making plans for its annual bash. They'd hired a well-known band, so the turnout was expected to be good. Maybe she could convince Krista or Scruggs to go. She really needed to get out and have some fun.

Charlotte's doorbell rang, and the buzz sent her three inches off the couch. She rarely hosted visitors, especially in the evening. Looking out her front window to the street below, she saw the top of the head of a man who looked like Jack Buchanan. It couldn't be. Didn't the man believe in calling back?

Pulling on her sneakers, she ran down the stairs and through the store, hitting her knee on a chair along the way. She limped to the front door, turned the lock, and opened it.

Jack stood in the doorframe, casual in an ARMY T-shirt tucked into his jeans. It was the first time Charlotte saw him in something other than a suit. She forgot all about her sore knee.

"Are you here about your shoes?" she asked.

He raised his eyebrows. "No." He paused. "I'm coming back to ask you what I meant to ask earlier. But, since you mention it, maybe we could make a trade."

"A trade? Like, I ruin your shoes, you get coffee?" She chuckled nervously.

"Not quite." His confidence was disarming. "How about

I forgive the shoes if you give me a little piece of your time?"

A list of possibilities raced through her mind. "What do you want me to do?"

"Come with me." He stood tall, his brown hair brushed up in the front, his eyes glinting like a schoolboy daring a girl to meet him behind the bleachers.

"Where?"

"It's a surprise."

Her heart lurched. "You want me to leave with you when you won't even tell me where you're taking me?" No self-respecting girl would agree to something like that.

"Yes."

"That's not fair. You need to tell—"

Jack smiled, and she completely melted. "Trust me. It'll be fun," he said.

Charlotte hadn't had much in the way of fun since moving to Crickley Creek, and even though his mother was a force to be reckoned with, there was something about him that made her feel safe. "Okay, but I can't stay long." After all, she had a date with her couch and a movie.

She expected a BMW, Mercedes, or other lawyerly, Buchanan-y type car. What she ended up climbing into was an old green Jeep. The plastic side windows couldn't keep the air out, causing strands of her hair to swirl around her head as they drove toward the sea, passing pockets of mobile homes inland and bigger homes as they neared the coast. Vast green lawns surrounded two-hundred-year-old plantation homes flanked by giant oaks as they neared the bridge leading to Katu Island. She remembered Birdie mentioning how, back when Bill Buchanan was alive, he was able to coerce a local state senator into sneaking funding into a bill to build that bridge. Before taxpayers had unknowingly paid for a bridge that would only be used by the Buchanans, the island had only been accessible by boat. The small, two-car-carrying barge sat now docked near the bridge like a rusty symbol of political corruption.

Jack's expression was serious. Did he notice the barge? Did he care?

"You're not taking me to your mother's house, are you?" Inside, she shuddered, but her rational mind thought it might be good to see Virginia in person—an opportunity to thank her for the gift and apologize for the car accident.

"No, this place is much better. It's always been my favorite place to play, or think, or—anything." He tapped his hands on the steering wheel, beating his own tune, while Charlotte slumped into the seat with relief.

They drove the now-familiar dusty road beneath Spanish-moss-covered live oaks and longleaf pines, but after the rookery, Jack turned right instead of continuing straight toward the mansion hidden on the far north side of the island. They'd gone half a mile before she realized the forest was behind them and marshland lay on either side.

"If you look closely, you might see an alligator," Jack said, clearly in his element.

"We're not going to be anywhere near alligators, are we?"

"No." This time, he caught her eye, and she relaxed a little. "Although that's fun, too. When I was a kid, I'd feed them marshmallows. They love 'em."

"Good to know." Charlotte took in all the colors and life outside the car window, wondering how growing up on Katu compared to her childhood.

"Pretty much every time we'd go crabbing, I'd bring some marshmallows for Ernie. He'd hang out a few yards down the creek and watch us." Jack looked directly at her, like a little boy anticipating a reaction.

"Watch the road!" She pulled up her knees when the Jeep veered near the shoulder.

He righted the car and kept talking. "That gator'd sit still as a statue until I threw a marshmallow at him, then jump halfway out of the water like one of those sharks on the Discovery Channel. It was the coolest thing ever." He steered with his knee, grinning broadly. "After a while, every time I'd come around, Ernie would open his mouth as soon as he saw me, waiting for me to toss the marshmallows in."

"It's a miracle you're still connected to your limbs." What the heck kind of mother would allow her son to feed marshmallows to alligators?

Several minutes passed in silence. Charlotte soaked in every detail of the landscape, every sinewy cypress, every clump of marsh grass, every tall bird on the shore. The occasional deer would catch her eye with a flick of a tail and a bounding departure. California had beautiful spots of its own, but she'd never seen such a richness and variety of life as on Katu Island.

"See that black bird flying over the water?" Jack pointed excitedly. "That's a black skimmer. He uses his red bill to attract fish, then he scoops them up and eats them." He turned toward Charlotte as if to gauge her reaction. "You'll only see him out on days like today when the water is smooth and calm."

"It's beautiful." Her eyes scanned the swampy bird-filled estuary. "I love this place."

"I haven't shown you the best part yet." The intensity of the tune he'd resumed beating on the steering wheel increased. He was much more little-boyish than she expected.

A few minutes later, they parked against a patch of sea grass behind a tall sand dune and hopped out. Standing in front of the Jeep, he yelled, "Come on! You'll love this."

Charlotte climbed out and walked toward him. He took her hand and pulled her up the dune, their feet sinking and slipping in the sand as they climbed. "We like to protect our dunes," he said, "but this one is so big, we've always used it for a little something else."

She gasped when she reached the top. Spread before her was a small, secluded beach. Clean and untouched. The tropical fruit colors of the sunset reflected for miles across the water, each wave bringing with it a smattering of diamonds glistening on the crest. It was the most splendidly spectacular beach she'd ever seen. A miniature paradise. "Oh," she breathed.

"Red sky at night, sailor's delight." Jack smiled, still holding her hand. "That means we'll have nice weather tomorrow." Charlotte turned her face toward the sky, absorbing the fading heat. A squadron of eight pelicans flew overhead.

She was living a scene pulled straight from an epic movie: the secluded sandy beach, the Technicolor sunset, and two people getting to know each other with no one around for miles. Tall and proud, he stood atop his hill. "Your surprise isn't over yet!" he yelled as he surfed down the sandy backside to the beach.

Charlotte watched him balance his way to the bottom, excited to join him, but worried she'd wipe out.

"Come on down!" he called from the bottom of the dune.

She laughed out loud. "Coming!" Digging her feet into the sand, she angled her body right, then left, and skied down the hill after Jack.

Chapter Nine

THE BRILLIANCE OF the sunset provided plenty of light on the beach, yet Charlotte noticed Jack brought along a flashlight. He must have been planning to stay awhile.

"Come sit with me," he said. They walked to a flat spot ten yards from the water's edge. Sitting, he patted the sand to his right. Charlotte flopped down beside him. The khaki-colored sand was surprisingly cool, much different from the hot yellow sand of her California beaches. Her body soaked in the heat of the fading sun and the warmth of Jack's arm touching hers.

"Not too far from here is Drunken Jack's Island." He pointed proudly toward the sea. "It's been said there was once a pirate named Jack who got marooned out there. They found his old bleached-out bones months later next to cases and cases of empty rum bottles."

"Are you named for him?"

"For Drunken Jack?" He chuckled. "Not as far as I know. My full name's Jackson Parker Buchanan. Jackson is a nod to ole Andrew, and Parker is my mother's maiden name."

Buchanan, Charlotte thought. She couldn't figure that family out.

"They say Blackbeard's treasure is buried there."

Charlotte stared straight ahead, her head swimming with thoughts of pirates and Buchanans, drunks and greed, secluded beaches and developing situations.

"My friend Will and I went out there once, back in high school," he said. "But like everyone else, we didn't find a darn thing."

"Are you talking about Will Rushton?"

Jack nodded.

"Birdie told me you guys were friends. Seems like everyone around here knows each other."

"You know him?" Jack asked.

"Yeah." She almost mentioned the accident, and flushed. "I guess you can say he sort of rescued me." Surely, he knew already; she didn't need to go into it.

"That was good of him." Jack appeared to be deep in thought.

"Yeah, he's a real gentleman cowboy. Sort of." She laughed to herself.

"Ruth, uh…" Jack flinched, and his demeanor turned down like a light. "A friend of mine always said Will should have been born in the 1950s." His eyes stayed stuck on Drunken Jack's Island.

Who might Ruth be? "I don't think Will is innocent enough for the 1950s."

"Yeah." For several minutes, they said nothing as the sunset faded and the cadence of waves slipping on and off the beach began to quiet. What just happened?

Finally, he broke the silence. "There," he whispered. He flipped on the flashlight, which shone red onto the sand, then pointed to a dark shadow inching onto the shore from the water. "The light beam has to be red so we don't confuse them."

Charlotte whispered back. "Confuse who?"

"It's a loggerhead sea turtle. She's coming ashore to lay her eggs." He aimed the beam toward the turtle. "This is a protected beach. They come here every year." He turned, his eyes lit with pride. "This is what I wanted to show you."

Charlotte was entranced.

"Watch," he said. "Quietly."

Using her flippers, the loggerhead pulled herself onto the beach. This was no small task, considering she weighed nearly two hundred pounds, which, on land, must have felt like a thousand. She was so intent on her mission that she appeared to have no knowledge of Charlotte and Jack watching her every move.

Charlotte shivered, and Jack moved like he was going to put his arm around her shoulders, then seemed to think better of it. The loggerhead pulled and pulled until she reached a spot safe from high tide. First, she used her front flippers to flick away the sand. Then, turning around, she used her rear flippers, sending sprays of sand to either side of her reddish-brown shell. She took no rest breaks, just dug and dug.

"She's digging an egg chamber," Jack whispered, his breath warm on her ear. "She'll lay about a hundred eggs and then come back in a couple of weeks and do it all over again."

"Really?" Charlotte turned to him, unintentionally rendering them face-to-face. Jack was the first to turn away.

It was dark now, except for the small amount of light coming from the crescent moon and Jack's flashlight. The turtle was still working, her pale yellowish bottom shell disappearing against the sand as she moved her rear deeper into the hole. Charlotte sucked in her breath when the loggerhead stretched her large head forward and, one by one, delivered mushy white eggs the size of ping-pong balls into the hole she'd just dug. Charlotte leaned forward to get a better look, accidentally touching Jack's shin.

Once finished, the loggerhead covered her eggs with sand and lugged herself back to the freedom of the ocean. Jack followed her with the flashlight until she disappeared under the waves.

Something about the mother turtle leaving into a deep, dark sea triggered an intense wave of grief in Charlotte. She wanted her mother back desperately. At least now it was easier to remember the mommy she used to have: the one whose lap was Charlotte's favorite seat, whose smile made everything okay, whose touch was more comforting than a favorite blanket. Yet, it was the painful images of Anna Grace's slow dying process that plagued her.

So many regrets.

Charlotte hugged her knees and breathed in the salty air. It seemed like every time she let the pain in and worked through it, the next time the thoughts came, the ache was a little less.

Once the cancer had spread to her mother's brain, the wise and strong Anna Grace could be found only in glimpses. But Charlotte refused to give up hope. They kept going with treatment, even when it meant administering chemo directly into Anna Grace's brain through a port. With each appointment, a piece of her mother would disappear. On the day she stopped talking, Charlotte made the decision to keep going with her treatment. The doctors approved it and, damn it, some mother was better than no mother at all. She would not be the one to give up. They would beat this thing. They had to.

It wasn't until her mother was wheeled out of a chemo session with her head tilted backward, her eyes floating in her head, and her mouth gaping open, that it hit Charlotte. They'd lost. The most loving thing she could do for her mother now was to take her home and help her die comfortably, with dignity. She'd tortured her enough with treatments—too many treatments, too much suffering. She called in hospice and went to work keeping her out of pain.

Charlotte bit her trembling lips together and cut her eyes

toward Jack. He seemed to be deep in thought, too. She dug her toes into the sand and punished herself by remembering more. It was her due for refusing to accept fate, for letting it all go on too long.

There had been a rare moment of lucidity in the midst of those wordless days, when Anna Grace reached out and said, "I'm sorry." Sorry for what? Sorry for dying? The next few days were pure hell: the "fish out of water" breathing, the mix of both dread and fervent desire for the whole thing to be over. She stroked her mother's arm and gave her permission to go, when in her heart she needed her mother to stay, to comfort her through the devastation like she had done when her father died. She swore to her mother that her legacy would live on, that it was okay to rest now, that her battle was finally over. She'd find a cozy spot in heaven and they'd see each other again someday. She was so very, very loved.

In her final moment, Anna Grace's arms reflexively pulled up when another breath was due but wouldn't come. A tense few seconds followed before her body relaxed forever. The silence had grabbed Charlotte, pulling her deep into a black pit of loneliness. She'd held onto her mother's arm until it became cold.

She was alone. She had no more family to count on.

"We'd better head back soon," Jack said, just as Charlotte's grief threatened to explode. "It's not an easy drive in the dark."

Charlotte fought to settle herself. Her breathing was upset and staccato, so she let out every bit of air in her lungs before she asked, "How'd you know the turtle would be here?"

"They come back at the same time every year. There were several more down the beach."

"There were?"

Jack nodded slowly, like he knew she was struggling but chose not to acknowledge it.

What else didn't he say?

Chapter Ten

SUNDAY AFTERNOON BROUGHT with it sunny skies and an unusually cool breeze. Charlotte finished her baking and preparations and procrastinated on writing Virginia's thank-you card again by going for a drive. She'd heard about abandoned tobacco barns, withered clapboard general stores, and rusting cotton gins that dotted the countryside. She pulled on a fresh pair of jeans and a white tank top, grabbed her digital camera, and could hardly wait to get some beautiful shots of the empty old buildings.

Her cell phone rang just as she remembered that she couldn't go on a drive—her car was still in the shop. Darn. She dug for her phone in her purse. It was Will, asking in his relaxed, I-don't-really-care way if she'd like to have dinner with him. Just his voice set her nerve endings ablaze. Her brain told her to say no, that it would be rude to lead him on, especially since Jack was so much more her type. But Will had been so nice to tow her car for her, *yes* slipped from her mouth before she could catch it.

What a weekend it was turning out to be.

Will wanted to pick her up, but Charlotte insisted she'd

meet him there. She could always borrow Birdie's land barge. That way, she wouldn't be stuck with him if the date turned out to be a disaster. He didn't sound happy about it but agreed, and told her to meet him at the marina. Charlotte loved seafood, but she couldn't remember the marina having a restaurant. At least she remembered to ask him what to wear and was relieved when he said jeans and a T-shirt. Long pants were important, he said, because they'd be walking into the woods and they might run into ticks, chiggers, or the Lowcountry's monster mosquitoes. Apparently, that's what a girl got for agreeing to go on a date with a cowboy: ticks, chiggers, and giant mosquitoes. Seriously. No wonder she hadn't seen the restaurant. It must've been hidden in the trees.

People did weird things in the South.

That night, Charlotte drove to the marina, which was really just a big metal building and four long docks of boat slips filled with everything from fishing vessels to sailboats. To the right of the docks was swampland, and on the left was a forest dense with pines. Several shrimp boats trolled in the distant deep water. Charlotte parked and stared trans-fixed as clumps of sea oats and water millet swayed in the breeze. Will knocked on her window, and she jumped like a fish on a hook.

He laughed. "You ready?"

She stepped out and locked the door of Birdie's maroon Cadillac. "So, where is it we're going, exactly?" A group of men nearby were dumping buckets of blunt-nosed dolphin-fish and striped amberjack into huge bins of ice. Hopefully, the restaurant would have a special fresh fish of the day on the menu.

"We're gonna catch our supper." Will led the way to his truck, not far away.

"Fishing?" The last thing she wanted to do was put something squirmy on a hook when they could just buy a fish from the fishermen right there.

"Sort of."

"I refuse to shoot anything. I'll tell you that now." She'd never been more serious.

"No shooting involved." He grabbed a grocery bag from the back of his truck and pulled out a package of raw chicken, throwing it into an old red ice chest on the ground. He put the lid on the ice chest and wiped his hands on his jeans before walking around to the driver's side door.

"Looks like that chicken's already been caught," Charlotte said.

Will smiled and handed her a bottle of bug spray he'd retrieved from the front seat. "Here, put this on."

"Oh, yes. Monster mosquitoes."

"And ticks and chiggers and horse flies and no-see-ums," he said. "I figure even one is too much for you, so we'll take some precautions."

"Great." Bugs that bit, and killing your own dinner. Perfect. Couldn't he tell she was more of a candlelight dinner kind of girl? She vigorously sprayed every exposed area of skin.

Will pulled the old, wheeled ice chest past the fishermen's building and behind what looked like a bait shack toward the woods to their left. Charlotte followed, and eventually stopped asking where they were going long enough to admire the scenery. She was getting used to the salt marshes and reedy grasses of the Lowcountry. Will was a knowledgeable guide. She learned about pluff mud and rice fields, Spanish moss, and alligators that could run up to thirty-five miles per hour on land. "Don't worry yourself," he said. "I'll boost you up into a tree if we find one."

"So happy to have a plan." She smirked, thinking about scaly creatures with huge teeth, bugs, snakes, and God only knew what else lurking about. It was all so prehistoric.

Looking down the footpath at the dense undergrowth and massive trunks of trees, it seemed impossible that the forest could open to the vacant sky of an ocean or lake or river. She couldn't imagine what kind of fish might live in the middle of a forest. The filtered light of the sun seeped through the canopy of longleaf pines and oaks. Spanish moss hung like old lace above her head. If she put her hand straight up, she could touch it. Judging from the light, it could have been any time of day, but it was approaching dinnertime and Charlotte had skipped lunch. Her stomach was empty and complaining.

Pine needles crunched like corn chips beneath their feet,

heightening Charlotte's awareness of the sounds around her: a blue jay squawking his displeasure, the rustling of leaves, and occasional unidentifiable whooshes and crashes. The deeper they walked into the woods, the darker it got. She was grateful Will was there with her. He was a knowledgeable guide, and she found his deep voice soothing. She followed along behind him trying hard not to stare at his backside as he wheeled the ice chest along the bumpy path. Everything about him was firm and strong. They'd been walking for ten minutes when Charlotte smelled it, the subtle swampiness of the salt marsh. It reminded her of the musty humidity inside the Pirates of the Caribbean ride at Disneyland.

Soon, foliage got greener, and in a couple more minutes the canopy of trees opened to the sky and they were standing on the edge of a small, brown creek. It wound its way out of the forest and into the expanse of the reedy marsh. Will looked proud of himself, and Charlotte couldn't help but like him. "What kind of fish do you plan to catch in a foot of dirty water?"

"It's not dirty. The color comes from the cypress roots."

"If you say so," Charlotte said, trying to come to terms with the fact that she might actually eat something that came out of a brown creek.

Will chuckled and opened the lid of the ice chest, wrapped a piece of twine around a raw chicken leg, and handed it to her. She took it with two fingers, holding it away from her body. She knew all about food safety, and handling raw chicken was only to be done under the most sterile of conditions. Will laughed and tossed his twine-attached chicken leg into the creek with a splash. Charlotte imitated him exactly. She felt a tug, and he told her to slowly and carefully pull up the twine. Clamped to the chicken by its large front claw was a sizable crab. It was beautifully blue with bright orange tips on the claws. She shrieked and giggled while Will brought a net underneath it and shook the crab into the ice chest. "You caught a sook," he said. "That's a female crab. The jimmies don't have the orange claws."

Charlotte was nearly giddy with excitement. She touched Will on the arm. "This is fun. Thank you." It wasn't that he said or did anything. It was a subtle expression on his face. He was relieved.

"You're a pretty good crabber, for a girl," he laughed.

"Thank you. You're a pretty good teacher, for a boy." She smiled sweetly.

"I thought you needed to experience a crab cook the way it's supposed to be done," he said.

"This is way better than a bunch of them piled up on a table." The more crabs she pulled in, the more proud and adventurous she felt. She was in synch with Will, in synch with nature.

An hour passed by like only ten minutes. Never in her whole life had she felt like she could survive without restaurants or shopping or indoor plumbing, but here in the forest of Lowcountry, South Carolina, she felt capable, invincible.

Her chicken leg came untied and landed in the creek, so she grabbed another one and tied it to the string herself. "Did you bring some wet wipes or hand sanitizer?" she asked. Her heart inadvertently leapt when he made eye contact with her. He was just so *manly*. She shuddered.

He chuckled as if she'd lost her mind. "No. Need some?"

"Well, yes." She held up her dangling chicken leg. "Raw chicken. Salmonella. Not good."

"Don't suppose I could convince you to rinse your hands in the creek."

She might've been willing except for the fact that there were creatures in the creek with very large pinchers. "Not a chance."

"All righty, then." He pulled his T-shirt over his head and tossed it to her. She caught it, much to her own amazement, because her body had just ignited at the sight of his bare chest and arms.

"I—" She wanted to say, *I can't use your shirt* but couldn't speak the simple words. Instead, she gaped at him, and the ardent look on his face made her feel exposed, like he was privy to her thoughts. She wanted him to hold her, to put her head against his chest. She wanted to run her hands over his stomach. Despite the embarrassment, she couldn't look away. His eyes bored into hers.

In one long stride, he had her in his arms, her feet off the ground, his lips pressed against hers. The world spun in brown and green and water and heat and skin. She was breathing through her eyes or ears or lips or maybe it was his mouth, his lips or chest or back or no breath at all. Nothing mattered but his body, his nearness, his smell. No mother, no father, no Virginia, no Jack. Just Will and Charlotte. Just them.

He put her down, hugging her head against his chest. "Charlotte," he breathed. "I'm sorry."

"Don't be." She was just as much at fault.

Moving away, he put on his shirt, no concern for chicken juice. She didn't care either. He grabbed his piece of twine and tossed the chicken leg into the creek again, ignoring her. She knew why. The moment they just experienced together was so intense, he was clearly fighting for self-control. She moved to stand beside him, paying attention to her breathing, calming herself. Will pulled in a greedy, chicken-loving crab while Charlotte moved her eyes down the length of the muddy creek, focusing on where it disappeared into the marsh.

Just like the ocean swallowed the marsh, the South with all its quirks and beauty was swallowing her. California was beautiful but arrogant. The South was humble in its splendor. A cricket chirped nearby and she focused on the sound, still trying to quell the desire that'd taken over her body. From the corner of her eye, she watched him, his every movement serving only to make her blood run hotter.

"I hope I didn't scare you." He spoke in the direction of the creek.

"You didn't," she replied, picking up a chicken leg by the twine with her still-shaking hand and tossing it into the creek. What scared her was how passionately her body responded to his.

They caught fifteen crabs before Will took her and the big ice chest to the building next to the parking lot where she'd seen fishermen dropping off their catch. He shook the hand of a calloused, wrinkly old man before leading her to a kitchen in the back. Charlotte immediately washed her hands. Will opened the industrial-sized refrigerator and handed her a cold beer, taking another one for himself. Then he took a small bag of groceries out of the ice chest and pulled out shucked and halved ears of corn, round red potatoes, and kielbasa sausage. He put it all in the largest pot Charlotte ever saw. It almost took up two burners on the stove.

"All right, now, you don't have to do this part, okay?" Will said, grabbing a crab from the ice chest. "I promise you, it doesn't feel a thing." She watched, both horrified and exhilarated, as Will used a small knife to pry open the belly and pull the guts from the crab. He explained how the ice anesthetized them, made it so that they couldn't move their claws to pinch. When he put the second crab into the pot, Charlotte requested the knife. The shocked look on Will's face was priceless.

She took a swallow of beer, shuddered, and pulled an immobile crab from the chest. Using the small round knife to lift the apron, she pulled out the more unsavory parts underneath. Even though she hurt for the crab, it put her more in touch with the area, the Earth, the universe as a whole. There was something empowering about shucking the crab they were preparing to eat. Will found another knife and worked quickly and easily, finishing two crabs for her one. She couldn't help but notice how well they worked together.

The pot was boiling now, and all the crabs had been added, one by one, to the mélange. A little more crab boil seasoning and it was time for another beer. He opened one and handed it to her. It was cold and savory.

They sat around a long pine table for several minutes, the smell of crab boil mingling with the fishy, salty air. Will took her hand and held it underneath the table. "You fit in this place just fine, Charlotte Sinclair."

If only that were the truth.

After several minutes, he got up and walked toward a stack of old newspapers in the corner, grabbed a couple, and laid them out in the middle of the table. Then he picked up the heavy pot, his biceps round and taut, and poured the hot water into the sink, steam roiling in billows. "Watch out." His thigh brushed her arm as he moved in front of her to dump the whole pot of crab, sausage, corn, and potatoes on top of the table. There was no silverware to be seen, just a roll of paper towels. Clearly, this was eat-with-your-hands, lick-your-fingers, throw-all-manners-out-the-window food.

Just as a crab cook should be.

Will yelled for the men working outside the kitchen and turned to her. "Hope you don't mind sharing. These guys might be a little rough, but they're here when you need 'em. I don't see 'em often, but someone always ends up cookin' when I do. Usually we make our Lowcountry boil with a mess of shrimp, but they're not as much fun to catch." Several of them sauntered inside to help themselves to the food. Charlotte could barely understand what they were saying, their accents were so thick. Most were midnight dark and wrinkly from years spent in the sun. They laughed, and she laughed, the atmosphere full of good smells and good moods. She grabbed a bright red cooked crab from the table, and, following Will's lead, cracked one of the legs in half and pulled out a piece of meat. It was sweet, tender, and salty.

But Charlotte needed to get home. Mornings came early at the teahouse. Will walked her to Birdie's car. She opened the driver's side door and turned to say goodbye when he stepped directly into her personal space. He took both her hands in his. "Thank you for showing up tonight. I wasn't sure you would."

"I had fun," she said, avoiding his eyes, hoping he couldn't feel her pulse racing through her palms. "Thanks for teaching me how to crab."

"Charlotte"—he tipped her chin up with a finger, forcing her to look him in the face—"I forgot my manners back there." She could barely breathe. "I'm sorry. I should have asked." He was very serious, his face inches from hers. "Would it be all right if I kissed you?"

Not trusting her voice, she nodded. His dimple was the last thing she saw before succumbing to the warmth of his lips.

It was a miracle Charlotte made it home in one piece. She couldn't remember stopping at a single STOP sign. She may have been driving in the wrong lane, for all she knew. Her mind was completely consumed with Will Rushton. He did something to her. Something that made her toes curl and her face heat up like a bonfire. But they were moving too fast and she knew it. Attraction was dangerous if you didn't employ your brain.

And Krista had warned her about him. The truth was, she didn't really know him, and Krista had lived in Crickley Creek her whole life. Then again, Birdie had lived in Crickley longer than Krista, and she flat-out said Krista was wrong. Either way, it was time to use her logical mind and not her crazy emotions. Yes, Will made her knees weak and her head fuzzy. But he was also brash and sarcastic. She was under too much stress as it was. She didn't need to be the little woman to his big man. She would never stand for that if she weren't so lonely.

She locked the door to her loft and headed straight to the shower. When she pulled her shirt over her head, she smelled him on it. Holding it to her nose, she breathed in his scent until she felt like an idiot. *Get hold of yourself, Charlotte.*

Yes, this was getting dangerous.

Chapter Eleven

MONDAY MORNING, PASTOR Ashby Crane came into the store looking like a crooked little smile had been drawn on his face in permanent marker. Customers returned the smile, but no one spoke to him. He ordered a small hot tea and sat himself in the darkest corner of the store. Charlotte had heard that his sermons were enthusiastic, but the man himself seemed to be as quiet as he was tall. He appeared happy, alone with his prayer book and his tea, so Charlotte didn't bother him.

Birdie burst through the front doors, glanced at Ashby, and went straight for Charlotte. "All right, Miss Charlotte," she began. "We have business to discuss."

She braced herself. Whenever Birdie put a "Miss" in front of "Charlotte," she was substituting manners for force. It was a sign Birdie was determined to get something.

"Yes, *Miss* Birdie?" she teased. "What is it?" Maybe Birdie was about to reprimand her for not sending Virginia a thank-you note for the print.

"I'm just gonna come right out and say it. No use beating around the bush, right?" Birdie said.

Charlotte held her breath.

"Seeing as I am your best and most regular customer, I believe it is high time you put my name on your menu." Glaring at her, Birdie straightened her back like she was prepared to argue until she got her way.

"You want me to write your name on the menu?"

"Don't go acting like this is some big ole deal. Your menu is written in *chalk*." Birdie's lips pursed defiantly. Charlotte made the same face right back at her. "*Miss* Charlotte," Birdie began.

Charlotte was laughing now. "Oh, don't *Miss Charlotte* me, Birdie. You can have your name on the menu."

Birdie's face brightened.

"What did you have in mind? Shall we name a drink after you? Maybe instead of ordering a cup of Earl Grey, people could order a cup of Birdie Mudge?" She giggled.

"Laugh it up," Birdie said, forcing a college-ruled piece of paper covered with large, loopy handwriting into Charlotte's hand. "I was thinking more along the lines of this formula here. It's a drink like no one's ever experienced before." She pointed vigorously at the paper. "I guarantee you it will be a best seller because it has twice as much caffeine as anything else you serve. I call it the Early Birdie Special."

Charlotte's interest was piqued: three shots lightly roasted robusta espresso, one snack-size Hershey bar (will melt in the hot liquid), one-third cup Coca-Cola, one-fourth cup whipping cream, one pinch cinnamon.

"I want my name written in purple chalk, and I'd like it right there at the top of the menu." She pointed to the large, black chalkboard hanging on the wall behind the service counter. "That way, more people will order it." In her puffed-up state, she walked behind the counter, helped herself to a cookie and marched toward the front door, stopping only to point at Ashby and say, "And that's how you do it, Ashby Crane. Score one for Birdalee."

They added her name to the board that very day, and a mere two days later, Birdie's creation was a hit. Which might have something to do with the fact that Birdie was in the store all day on Tuesday, not-so-subtly persuading customers to buy her drink. Generally, everyone liked Birdie's liquid energy, many of them grabbing a hot ham bun or an apple blossom to go along with it.

Naturally, Birdie's newfound talent for drink-inventing seriously irked Scruggs. He told Charlotte that he was making it his goal to get his name on the menu, too. Above Birdie's. In red chalk. There was nothing he looked forward to more than Birdie leaving on her much-anticipated singles cruise to the Caribbean. To be free of her for a week was going to be more of a relief than passing all of his finals. Birdie, of course, was planning to partake of every drink on the islands as research for her next invention.

"I said to myself, Birdie, you just might have a future in the drink business. I'm gonna do my research and sell my idea to Co-Cola."

"Whatcha gonna call the next one?" Scruggs retorted. "Old Biddy?"

Birdie shot a *shut-up* look at him and threw a napkin at his head. "When you get your name on that board, we'll talk business. Until then, you need to shut your pie-hole."

Jack and Will both came into the store every day for the next two weeks. Jack usually showed up around seven A.M. wearing a suit and tie and toting his laptop. No matter where she was or what she was doing, Jack always tracked her down to ask about her day or her health or how the store was faring. He seemed to genuinely care about her answer. Then he ordered his black coffee and pastry, headed to his table by the window, opened his laptop, and shut out the world. He acted as if their evening on the beach never happened.

But today was different. He asked Charlotte if she would accompany him to a dinner party at his mother's house tomorrow night.

"Really?" she asked. "This is something your mother is hosting?"

"Yes," he chuckled. "Don't worry. You'll be with me."

Well, it would be a good opportunity to thank Virginia in person for the dogwood print, now hanging in her bedroom. Plus, Jack was the type of boy she always pictured herself with. He was far safer than a testosterone-filled ladies' man like Will. He was more like her, the quieter, more serious sort. "Okay," she said. "It's a date."

Charlotte spent the rest of the day ping-ponging between guilty and giddy. Finally, she would get to know Jack better, but she might lose Will in the process. She didn't want that to bother her, but it did.

Will usually stopped by midafternoon, a bit dusty in his work clothes. His presence filled her world for the few minutes he was there every day. She'd been successful at slowing things down, holding him at bay with excuses that wouldn't allow the two of them to be alone. He could be under no illusion that they were dating. But each time he came into the store, they both lit up like stars entering the atmosphere.

She opted not to tell him about her impending date with Jack.

That night, alone in her loft, Charlotte was in good spirits, despite the pounding in her head and the ache forming in her muscles. It was easy to ignore those small annoyances when she felt like she was making good, logical choices. She had picked up her car from the body shop the night before, and it turned out Will was right, Jimmy was the best in the town. The car looked almost new and drove the same as before the accident.

The next morning was Thursday, and Charlotte was extraordinarily tired, her head felt hot and her hands clammy, but she didn't want to miss seeing Jack. He'd mentioned having a court date at eight, so she knew he'd be stopping in for a quick breakfast before heading into the office. She had her back to the counter, cleaning out an empty pitcher, when she was grabbed from behind in a bear hug.

Will.

"What are you doing here so early?" she asked. How much time before Jack showed up?

"Heading out of town for materials. Thought I'd stop by and get some grub for the road."

"You're calling my all-natural pastries grub?"

"Yep. Best frou-frou grub in town."

Charlotte playfully hit him on the chest. She turned, grabbing a white paper bag printed with the store's logo, and prepared to fill it with goodies when Jack walked in. Her heart skipped a beat. His face held an expression she hadn't yet seen. What was it? Anger? Surprise? Will seemed to notice it, too.

"Hey, man," said Will, walking around the counter toward Jack. "Good to see ya. Been a while." He patted him on the back.

Jack seemed to shrink. "Yeah. How've you been?"

"Good. Good," Will said. "You?"

"Fine."

There was an uncomfortable pause. Both men looked to Charlotte, who was busy watching them.

"So, how's Ruth Marie?" Will finally asked.

"She's fine."

Ruth Marie? Charlotte searched her memory. It had to be the girl at Virginia's party; the beautiful blonde on her way to the bathroom when she first met Jack. The one he ran after. Plus, Ruth was the name he said at the beach. She kicked herself for never asking about her.

"Glad to hear it," Will said. "Tell her I said hi." Patting him again, he turned to face the counter as Charlotte finished bagging the pastries.

She handed Will the bag. "On the house," she said and looked to Jack. "Can I get you some coffee? Don't you have that big case today?"

"Yes, please," he said. His face showed no emotion. "It's going to be a tough one."

Charlotte began Jack's coffee and put together a bag of goodies like she'd done for Will: a hot ham bun, lemon poppy seed muffin, banana, and several chocolate mints. She could hear the guys talking about that year's Army/Navy game and speculating as to Army's chances. Grateful they weren't talking about her, she walked around the counter and handed them their drinks and Jack his bag of food. "This ought to be enough to last you awhile."

Jack looked confused. Usually, Charlotte gave him his muffin on a plate. "Thanks," he said, glancing toward his usual table in the corner.

"Thanks, hon," Will said, giving her a strong side hug that smashed her head into his chest and bicep.

"You're both welcome," she said.

The men walked out the door together.

As soon as they were gone, the slight dizziness she'd been

feeling since the night before increased in strength and shot straight to her head. She forced herself to walk to a nearby empty table and sat down, laying her head on her arms. A wave of nausea hit hard, like an unintentional ride on the Tilt-a-Whirl. Controlling her breathing, she tried to get her stomach under control. For two minutes, she hyperventilated and sweated while her stomach turned inside out. Now she knew why she'd been tired and achy. She'd rather have a broken leg than the flu.

"Krista? Scruggs?" she said weakly. "I'm going upstairs."

They looked at her strangely. Charlotte rarely left them alone during the morning rush. "You okay?" Krista asked. "You look a little green."

"Mmm-hmm," she said, holding her stomach. "I'll come back down when I feel better."

It felt like climbing Mount Everest to get to her loft. She immediately fell onto the couch. "No, God. Please. Not the flu." But she knew what was coming: body aches, fever, hyperventilating, desperate wishes for an end to the nausea. She lay curled on the couch, her knees folded into her chest like a newborn baby.

Not only did she not have time to be sick, she had no backup, no one to take care of her. Her eyes drifted to her bookshelf and the firefly jar. "You're supposed to be here, Mother. I need you to take care of me." She hated crying; it never solved anything, but this time, she couldn't hold back the sobs. In her weakened state, self-pity won out. She sobbed until she slept and when she opened her eyes, she was curling a box of tissues in her arm. She didn't remember getting up to get it.

Chapter Twelve

"YOUR HANDS ARE cramping," Jack said, walking into her den, holding a glass of water. He'd come back to the store late that afternoon, following his court appearance.

"How'd you get up here?" Charlotte squeaked, heart thumping. Her tingly hands were stuck at ninety-degree angles. Somehow, she managed to change into her pajamas and was now lying on the couch, so sick she was sure she looked several shades of green.

"Scruggs told me you were sick. He let me up."

"Oh," Charlotte said. If she could move from the couch, she'd use every last bit of energy to kill Scruggs. "I'm sorry I won't be able to make it to the party."

"It's no problem," Jack said, staring at her hands.

She held them up, arms moving freely, hands immovable, bent at the wrist. "Weird, huh?"

He sat next to her on the couch, taking her frozen hands in his.

"See, I have this thing where I can't throw up," she explained between heaving breaths. "So I get panicky and anxious, which makes me breathe," she panted, "like this. I don't know why my hands do this. Maybe too much oxygen." She moved her arms as if she were trying to get her fingers to wiggle.

He smiled as if he understood and gently moved her hands around at the wrist. "Relax, Charlotte. Just relax." He held her right hand, massaging her thumb, making slow circles down to her palm. She calmed her breathing and focused on her hands. He moved to her index finger and repeated the rubbing. She tried to relax them, still seized but less numb; the tingling began to subside as blood flow increased. His face was soft and peaceful as he moved his hands up to massage her arm from the elbow down.

Then another wave of nausea hit.

"Ride it out," Jack said, placing her hand gently on the couch. "Control your breathing." He rubbed her back and breathed with her. If she weren't so sick, she would have laughed. It was like having a Lamaze coach. "You can do it. This will pass."

Charlotte held on to his words, forcing herself to slow her breathing until the wave receded. She lifted her eyes to the firefly jar. *Did you send him, Mom? Did you send him here to take care of me?* With effort, she sat up, embarrassed to look the way she did, to be out of control of her appearance, much less her body. Certainly, whoever Ruth Marie was, she probably never looked so unkempt. Charlotte considered trying to get dressed, but there was no way her body would let her walk the ten feet to her bedroom, much less put on fresh clothes. She was stuck looking awful. Jack picked up her left hand and resumed his gentle, circular massage. She fell back onto the couch, too exhausted to worry.

Two hours later, Charlotte awoke alone in her bedroom. She barely remembered Jack escorting her there, tucking her in. Everything was hazy. Had he really been here, rubbing her hands, or had it all been a dream? The sound of voices came from the den. It was Jack, and there was a woman too, speaking in a singsongy lilt. Her stomach lurched.

Virginia.

Jack's reply came in a deep whisper, then the sound of his footsteps, and the door to her loft opening and closing. It was absolutely not possible that she was now alone in her own home with Virginia Buchanan. Her eyes stayed fixed on her bedroom door. She saw Virginia's tall shadow first. A second later, the woman herself stood in Charlotte's doorway.

"Oh good, child. I was hoping you'd be awake," Virginia cooed sweetly, walking over to the bedside and patting her on the arm. "I'm glad to see you're feeling better."

Charlotte wanted to say, "Not better, just awake," but she held it in.

Virginia looked around the room and visibly twitched at the sight of her dogwood painting hanging on the wall above Charlotte's bed. "Where'd you get that?"

Charlotte studied her. Did she really not know? "From you."

Virginia looked like she just ate a bug. "I would never!"

Oh my God. How could he? "Jack gave it to me. He said it was from you." The tension in the room was practically vibrating.

Virginia looked shocked for a millisecond before she regained her composure. "I will deal with Jackson, then." That was fine with Charlotte. In that moment, she was happy to throw him under the bus. "I'm afraid I'm here with some bad news, honey."

Afraid, my ass.

"It's just that I can't stand to see you get yourself into an unfortunate situation." Her lipstick traveled upward into the wrinkles on her pursed top lip. "You see, Charlotte"—she walked over and patted Charlotte's arm—"my Jackson is going to marry Ruth Marie Wallace. It's been this way for years, everyone here knows it. I have no idea how word never got to you."

Charlotte moved her arm away and sat up taller against her pillow.

"No need to get upset now," Virginia said. "This is not about you. This is about what is best for Jackson." She strode to her dogwood painting and checked the signature in the corner.

"I'm not upset," Charlotte said. "I just don't know why we're even discussing this." Or how Virginia had the audacity to come into her bedroom and speak to her that way.

"It's simple." Virginia took a step backward with a stone-carved smile still on her face. "You need to stay away from my son."

Charlotte swung her legs off the side of the bed, her strength suddenly returning. "Are you kidding me? I think you need to talk to your son. I'm not the one who started any of this."

Pointing a perfectly manicured finger at Charlotte, Virginia's face turned vicious. "Now, I've been very nice to you, despite all you've done to me, and right now, you *will* promise me you will leave my son alone."

"What on earth are you talking about? You have not been nice to me and I've done absolutely nothing to you."

"Make me that promise." Virginia's hands clenched like she wished they were around Charlotte's neck.

"You do know that your son is a grown man, right? Go talk to him."

Virginia didn't budge. "I am not leaving until you promise me."

Charlotte heaved herself out of bed to a standing position. "Who do you think you are? I don't have to promise you anything."

Virginia remained motionless, her eyes squinting with fury.

Charlotte walked in her crumply pajamas to the bedroom door and held it open. "You need to leave."

"You have no idea how things work in these parts." Virginia stepped out the door, visibly shaking. "I will not allow some easy California tart to bring shame upon my family. Do you understand? You will *never* be one of us."

"Get out!" Charlotte screamed with every ounce of energy she had left. Virginia was already walking haughtily toward the front door.

Charlotte waited until she heard the door to her loft shut firmly, then locked it and dragged herself back into bed, pulling her soft down comforter over her head.

Twelve hours later, Charlotte awoke with a start. Jack was on a chair beside her, his eyes closed, mouth hanging open. The clock read 7:00 A.M. It was Friday. She sat up, panicked, startling him out of sleep.

"You okay?" he asked.

Her head spun with the sudden movement, forcing her to lie back down. Jack Buchanan was the last person she expected to see sitting in her bedroom. "What are you doing here?"

"I took the day off to make sure you were okay."

"Okay? No, I'm not okay." Her voice was hoarse. "How could you leave me alone with that"—Charlotte struggled with the sheets that had become knotted around her body— "that ridiculous mother of yours?"

"Damn it all to hell. What'd she do?" He jumped up, his hands in fists. "Damn that woman. I knew it. I knew I couldn't trust her the minute Mrs. Duckworth insisted on seeing me. I finished up her case a year ago." Shaking his head, he said, "Mrs. Duckworth, Mother's *friend*. I should've known it was a setup."

Charlotte wiped her swollen eyes and brushed her hair from her face.

Jack sat next to her on the bed. "I'm so sorry, Charlotte. I only meant to leave her with you for a second."

"You lied to me." Charlotte moved away from him toward the middle of the bed. "That painting," she pointed, "was not from her." She took a deep breath. "And you never mentioned you were engaged."

Jack shook his head. "Shit," he whispered. "I'm not engaged, Charlotte. Ruth Marie and I have been taking a break. Mother had no right to say that to you."

"What's that supposed to mean? A break? How long is a break?" She wanted to throw something at him, both for herself and for Ruth Marie.

"I've been with her a long time, and she really is a good person, so it's all a bit of a process." Appearing to gather his wits, he morphed into Jackson Buchanan, lawyer. "And I'm sorry about the painting. I was trying to smooth things over."

"I don't get how you could think that giving me something of hers without her knowledge would help. You didn't just give me the stupid art, you gave me a lie." She hated how her voice sounded shrill with emotion.

"I just didn't want you to hate her," he said. "She usually not so awful, and I thought that if you were open to giving her another chance, she'd see what a good person you are."

"You are taking the painting back. I don't want it."

"Please, Charlotte. It's yours. Think of it as a peace offering from me."

"I don't want your peace offering." She stood, wobbled, then took it off the wall and handed it to him.

"Think of it as a son's attempt to make up for what his mother lacks." He tried to hand it back to her. "That picture represents hope to me, the hope a son has for his mother to be a better person. The hope that people can change. The hope that a girl he cares about might like him, too." Jackson placed it on the floor by her bed. "Plus, I figured Mother would like you by now. I mean, you're a really great person. I don't know what her problem is."

Charlotte climbed back in, exhausted. "Your mother tried to make me promise to leave you alone."

"I'm so sorry, Charlotte." He laid his hand on her arm, the same arm that, hours earlier, Virginia patted. "There's no excuse for her behavior." He took a deep breath. "I'll take care of it."

"I don't know how you plan to do that." How did a person handle a woman who had absolutely no regard for others, who thought she was superior and had no clue when she was crossing a line? "I mean, the things she said to me were—" Charlotte couldn't find the words to describe the beating she took. "They were not normal and not okay. Does she think this is the 1800s? She can't tell me who I can date."

"No, she can't." Jack moved his eyes to her face. "I'm sorry, Charlotte. I like you. There's something about you..."

Maybe her mother's death and her move to Crickley Creek were all to get her to this very moment. Or, maybe she was just feverish.

Jack stood, his back toward Charlotte, staring at the picture of Anna Grace and Charlotte's stepfather on the wall. "The night I first saw you at Buchanan Manor, you were wearing that gold dress. You looked like an angel. It was like I knew you from my dreams." He turned to face her again. "Like you had finally shown up and I didn't even know I'd been waiting for you. Please, Charlotte. Don't listen to my mother."

She nodded, caught up in the moment. Jackson Buchanan wanted a relationship! "Okay," she said. "Okay."

She'd made a choice. Maybe dating Jackson Buchanan would cement her inclusion into Crickley Creek society. More importantly, maybe it would bring her closer to the life her mother used to have—or should have had. Plus, she liked him.

Yet even though Jack was right here, sitting on the edge of her bed, it was Will who remained the lock screen in the back of her mind. Will, who'd been so diligent, so patient with her. Will, who had accepted her excuses but gently persevered. Her lungs squeezed tight as she remembered his smile from yesterday morning when she handed him his breakfast at the store.

"Oh my God! The store!" She jumped from the bed. "I have to get dressed." A surge of dizziness forced her to sit back down. "I have to take a shower." She covered her eyes with her hands until the dizziness passed. "Krista's not working today. Scruggs is supposed to do storytime for the kids. He can't do it all alone."

"Charlotte," Jack whispered.

"All those kids are going to show up and Scruggs won't be able to read to them."

"Charlotte."

"Who's going to run the counter? Oh my God, I have to get down there."

"Charlotte," Jack insisted. "Don't worry about the store. It's covered." He leaned her gently into the pillows and pulled the covers to her chest. "Scruggs and Mother have it handled."

Charlotte relaxed into the bed, until the word sunk in. "Mother?" She threw the covers to the side and jumped up again. "Oh God, no."

He grabbed her by the shoulders. "Relax." He tried to ease her into bed again, but she was immovable. "From what I hear, they're doing a pretty good job."

"Why would she do that?" she asked. "Why on earth would she help me when she just made it perfectly clear that she hates me? I don't want her help."

"She doesn't hate you."

"Are you kidding? After the shock-and-awe campaign she

just launched at me? What do you call it? Because I call it hate."

"I call it the Southern way."

"I'm getting sick of all this *Southern way* stuff. I'm supposed to believe that people in the South just feel free to barge in when someone's sick and—"

"No, that was just Mother being Mother. I'm telling you that if someone needs help, we help. That's how it's done here." He looked proud. "As a matter of fact, I'm sure there's a waiting list of Junior Leaguers itching to get behind that counter and serve up some coffee. Your business has probably improved since word got out you were sick. We all love a person in need."

"I don't like this. I'm not comfortable with this at all." She bent over, pressing her face into her pillow. "This makes absolutely no sense."

"People around here like to help."

"Not people like your mother," Charlotte said. A person either liked someone or they didn't. If they liked them, they helped them, if they didn't like them, well, then they left them the hell alone.

He took the pillow from her hands. "How's your stomach? Are you feeling okay?"

"Better. I'm a bit confused, pissed off, and tired but better." Lifting her hands, she wiggled her fingers.

Jack made toast and tea for breakfast and, for lunch, he heated chicken noodle soup from the assortment of soups and casseroles dropped off by various friends of Virginia's and Birdie's. Charlotte was finally able to eat comfortably. She never asked him about Ruth Marie, and he never brought her up. Charlotte figured that she wouldn't push just yet. There was time to talk about all of that later.

Sharing the afghan, the two sat together on the couch, watching the local news. They talked about politics, current events, and her favorite subject: books. She discovered he had a fondness for Jane Austen, which she considered a rare and attractive quality in a man. It felt natural to have him around. He fit in her home like an old comfortable chair fit next to a reading lamp. The only thing that could spoil the moment would be Virginia showing up again, but Jack assured her she wouldn't. Charlotte took a deep breath and snuggled into his side.

An urgent phone call for Jack interrupted her happiness. She listened to the low murmur of his voice from the kitchen, not as deep as Will's, but still masculine. The sound of his footsteps moving around the kitchen was somehow comforting, a welcome relief to more than a year of loneliness.

After several minutes on the call, Jack walked out with the news she had been dreading. "I've got to run home for a shower and head into the office for a while. I'll check on you later, okay?" Charlotte reluctantly nodded. She didn't want to appear ungrateful for the time he'd already sacrificed.

Jack put a fresh glass of ice water and a plate of saltine

crackers within reach on the coffee table and placed her cell phone next to the glass. "Call me if you need anything." Then he kissed the top of her head and walked toward the door.

"Thank you," Charlotte called after him. She heard her door open and close, and his footsteps grow softer as he moved down the stairs.

Chapter Thirteen

B LESSEDLY, SATURDAY ARRIVED, and with it, Charlotte's energy. She took a hot shower, scrubbed every remnant of the flu from her skin, and shampooed her hair twice. She brushed her teeth for a full three minutes before dressing in a pair of fresh leggings and her favorite vintage Indigo Girls T-shirt. It felt good to be out of her jammies. Next, she set out to disinfect the loft. Lysol and bleach were the order of the day. She sprayed and scrubbed and wiped and mopped. Just as she stuffed her sheets in the washing machine and set it to the sanitary cycle, she heard the doorbell ring. Hopefully, it was Jack.

She could see a tall shadow and the outline of a cowboy hat through the glass. A rush of guilt hit her like a flood. When she'd finally been able to get out of bed long enough to check her cell phone, there were two messages from Will. She hadn't called him back yet. She unlocked the door.

"Hi, Will."

"Hey, hon. How ya feeling?" His presence filled the store with energy.

"Better, thanks. Come on in." She expected a hug in

greeting; instead, he kept his thumbs in the front pockets of his jeans. Maybe he sensed that she'd made a choice. She pulled a chair from a table by the window and offered it to him. "Sorry if I smell like bleach," she explained. "I'm trying to catch up on everything I neglected while flat on my back." Glancing around the store for the first time, she noticed it was perfectly clean and tidy, everything in its place.

Will pushed back the chair she'd just pulled out and instead led the way to "their" table by the stairs. "Do you mind?" he asked before pulling out a chair for her. Taking off his hat, he sat down and picked up a packet of sugar, turning it over and over in his hands.

Charlotte sat across from him, unable to shake the guilty feeling.

"I've been trying to visit you for the past two days," he began. "Your guard dog wouldn't let me through."

"Guard dog?"

"Yeah, Scruggs kept turnin' me away. Thinks he's your bodyguard or matchmaker or something." He looked abashed. "I'm glad you're okay."

"Yeah. Me, too. I'm sure Scruggs just figured I was in no condition to have visitors." Truth was, she had no idea why he let Jack visit but not Will.

Will put down the packet of sugar and hesitated. "So, I'm guessin' you heard."

"Heard about what?" She hoped nothing had happened to Birdie on her cruise. Or maybe Virginia had a heart attack? Someone else crashed their car into Virginia's creek?

"About Jack and Ruth Marie."

"That they're taking a break?" Did Will know she was waiting for Jack to come see her that very moment?

"I thought you already knew." He looked at his hat like he should put it on and leave. "I shouldn't be the one telling you this. I thought Jack would've told you by now."

"Told me what?"

Will rubbed his square chin with his large, calloused hand. "That they're getting married."

Charlotte shook her head. "No. They're not. Virginia wanted them to get married, but they're not. They're in the process of breaking up."

"They made the announcement this morning. Jack just called me to be a groomsman."

She felt the color drain from her face. Back on the dizzying Tilt-a-Whirl. She sat, staring at Will. "It can't be." He must be wrong, somehow. He had to be.

"I didn't mean to upset you. My reason for comin' out here was to straighten some things out, not to tell you about the wedding."

Didn't mean to upset her? Surely, that had to be his ulterior motive. Why else would he race right over to her as soon as Jack called? Her temples pounded. *Jack was getting married. Jack was getting married. How could Jack be getting married?*

"Now is probably not the right time," he said sadly. "But

I think I got the answer I needed."

"I need to go to bed. I think I'm having a relapse," she sputtered.

He stood up and pulled out her chair. "I'll help you."

"No," she said firmly, walking to the front door. He followed and stood silently while she unlocked it. "Thanks for coming by." It was his cue to leave, but he remained where he was.

"Have a nice night," she said, inadvertently sounding sarcastic.

He moved to leave, then turned back around. "Just one more thing, Charlotte. Why?"

Oh, please just walk out the door so I can call Jack. "Why, what?"

"Why'd you lead me on if you've been interested in Jack this whole time?" He didn't look mad—he looked frustrated.

"I never led you on," Charlotte said. But it wasn't the truth.

Still, why would he choose that moment to make things worse? Selfish ass. He was the one who kissed her. He was the cocky showoff, the player, the one who probably had at least four other girls on the side. He was the one Krista had warned her about.

"Maybe y'all call it something else in California, but out here, if you kiss someone the way we—" He hesitated. "It's just not nice to mess with a guy's head."

"You're accusing *me*? We had one date, and last I

checked, I wasn't wearing a ring." Anger spread like a hot wave over her body. She was fully aware that Will didn't deserve it. Still, she wanted nothing more than to push him out the door. She had to get him out of here so she could gather her thoughts.

"Don't get defensive. I'm just trying to talk to you here."

"Your version of talking feels an awful lot like an ambush to me."

"Listen, I'm not trying to put you on the spot." Boy, was he ever good at acting misunderstood and disappointed.

"For your information, I can date whoever I want, without having to notify you."

"Did I say you couldn't?"

"No, because you don't get to tell me what to do." She tried to close the door in his face, but his foot was in the way.

"I sure as hell don't." He stepped backward onto the sidewalk and she locked the door with him standing there, looking irate. *Whatever.* In that moment, the only thing she needed to do was clear things up with Jack.

Grabbing her cell phone from the table, she ran upstairs, scrolling down to Jack's name as she went. When the phone told her to leave a message, she nearly cried. "Jack? What's going on?" She couldn't bring herself to say the words *you're getting married?* "Call me. Please."

Chapter Fourteen

"WHY IS IT that as soon as I leave, all the good stuff happens?" Birdie demanded, barging through the front door almost a week after Jack's big announcement.

"Nice to see you too, Birdie." Charlotte was busy refilling the fresh cream, taking advantage of the lull in customers. "How was your trip?"

"My trip was full of lecherous old men lookin' for someone to take care of their decomposing bodies." Standing like a large red and purple fireplug, Birdie appeared younger and, frankly, healthier than Charlotte had ever seen her. "Single's cruise, my butt. They promised handsome fifty-somethin's, but all I got was the walking dead on a ship. Now, stop what you're doing and tell me everything you know about Jack and Ruth Marie." Birdie was about as subtle as fireworks.

"Oh God, Birdie," said Charlotte, leaning her back against the cooler. "So much has happened since you left." Jack hadn't called or come in. And even though Will still came by the store a few times, he spoke to her only once, and it was just small talk. Charlotte was still looking for an opportunity to apologize. She had overreacted and regretted every thoughtless word that had come out of her mouth. Well, most of them anyway.

Charlotte gave Birdie a blow-by-blow of what happened a week ago. Birdie was so wrapped up in the story that it was a good thing there were no customers—she wouldn't have let Charlotte get away to serve them. By the time Charlotte got to the part about Virginia helping in the store, Birdie fanned herself and pretended to swoon.

"Virginia *worked*? Here?"

"Yeah, it's the strangest thing. I can't figure it out."

"Oh, bless your heart, Charlotte," Birdie said. "Where is your sense? Don't you go thinking Virginia is your friend, now. That's dangerous territory there, child."

"I don't think she's my friend. I just can't fathom why she'd do that for me. I know it's the Southern way, but come *on*."

"Look, darlin'"—Birdie put on her *I pity you* face—"let me just lay it out for you." She cleared her throat loudly. "You have no idea what you're dealing with."

"Exactly!" Charlotte nodded vigorously. "You're absolutely right, Birdie. I don't have the first clue what in the heck the people around here are thinking. I truly don't get any of it."

"Child, it's not you." Birdie grabbed Charlotte's hand and pulled her to a nearby table, muttering, "Good Lord, we've been standing a long time. I have got to sit myself down." She scanned the store for Krista and Scruggs before plopping herself into a chair. Charlotte followed suit. Once satisfied they would not be overheard, Birdie began.

"Now, Virginia is some sort of umpteenth generation from the South, and there is only one way she knows of behaving. You wouldn't know this because you didn't grow up here." She looked at Charlotte as if this fact alone should mean something. "You think that because she helps you in your store or says you're *sweet* or *nice* that she's on your side, that she likes you."

"I don't think that at all," Charlotte said. "I know full well that Virginia would rather I take the next plane back to California."

Birdie flitted her hands in front of Charlotte's face like she was swatting away a swarm of invisible flies. "Hush up and listen. I'm about to tell you something important." She leaned in close, making Charlotte's nose itch from her heavily applied Giorgio perfume. "Southern women have their own language. To an outsider, it sounds like English." She laughed at her own joke, then quickly became serious again. "Truth is, there's a whole other language going on underneath those words we say out loud."

"Considering Virginia has never once said something nice to me, I'm not sure where you're going with this, Birdie."

"Charlotte, you need to know this stuff if you're gonna survive out here, so listen up." Birdie scanned the room again and whispered, "A good Southern lady will never say something that can be gossiped about, so she speaks in code. You can't exactly complain when somebody calls you *sweet* or *precious*, now can you? You'd be the one to look bad." She studied Charlotte's face as if she were looking for a sign of comprehension. "Honey, *sweet* can be like slamming the door of the sorority house in your face. And *sweet little thang* is even worse."

Charlotte's eyes narrowed. "I'm sure that not everyone speaks in code, Birdie. Plus, I'm a pretty good judge of character. At least, I used to be."

"Bless your poor little heart. You just don't get it, do you?" Birdie smirked and lifted her eyebrows as if to say, *See what I just did there?* "All right then, let's talk about Virginia comin' in and working in your store. You remember what I just said about saying one thing and meaning another? The same goes for actions. See, a good Southern lady will go out of her way to do something for somebody, even if she really can't stand that person."

"That's crazy."

"Oh, no, honey, it's smart, because she knows that socially, she just earned herself some equity."

"So, you're telling me that Virginia worked at my store, despite the fact that she hates me, so she would look good to other people?"

"Now, I haven't talked to her yet, but I'd bet good money that Virginia was earnin' herself some room for bad behavior by helping you out when you needed it. Think about it. I can just hear her saying, *Now, why would I ever do such and such a thing to poor Charlotte? Remember when I took over her store for her when she was sick?"*

Charlotte must have looked upset. "Look, honey, don't take it personally. Ginny's been the turd in the punchbowl for a bunch of folks. And just like she did with your mama, she picked you out special, right from the start."

"Really, Birdie? In real life, people who hate you don't get behind your counter, fix people drinks, and plot evil against you the whole time. It just doesn't happen."

"It does in the South." Birdie made a *you'll see* face. "What exactly did Ginny say to you?"

"She tried to make me promise to leave Jack alone."

"What else?"

"Um." Charlotte strained to remember if Virginia used any words like *sweet* or *precious* or *bless her heart*. "She said something about trying to be nice to me after all I did to her." Just saying the words made her want to punch something. "I did nothing to her, by the way."

"Mmmm." Birdie shook her head. "Well now. She didn't even bother herself with beating around the bush, did she? This may be worse than I thought."

"Come on, Birdie. You're being a little melodramatic, don't you think?"

"I have never been inclined toward the dramatic, Miss Charlotte."

It was a good thing Charlotte wasn't sipping something;

it would have come out her nose. "So, what do you suggest I do?"

"First," Birdie leaned in, "watch your mouth. You've got to play to her game. Don't say anything about her that might get repeated." She scratched her head. "Now, normally I'd say you have to kill the woman with kindness, paste on your biggest smile and compliment the heck out of her. You know, *your shoes are lovely, Mrs. Buchanan, I love your hair, Mrs. Buchanan, that is a wonderful point you just made, Mrs. Buchanan*, but I don't know." Birdie leaned back and used both hands to scratch what must have been a massive head itch, then she hit the table with both hands.

"Stay the hell away from her. Yes, ma'am. That's the best thing to do." Birdie's hair stuck out in twelve different directions, which somehow helped to illustrate her point.

"That will not be a problem," Charlotte said. "I do not plan to put up with any more of Virginia's stupid Southern shenanigans. I am done with her. She does not scare me."

"She probably should scare you, at least a little."

"I don't care."

"I'll try to run interference as best I can. But for God's sake, don't let her do anything else for you. You can't let her help you."

What a strange predicament. Strange people. Strange way of thinking. "Birdie? Why would you be friends with that woman if you believe all of what you just said?"

"She's been my friend since preschool, honey. Just like

your mama. Too late to change it now."

"I'm sure my mother never behaved like that."

"Let me tell you, child, your mama knew firsthand that if she wanted to get anywhere with old society, she had to be good at playing the game." Birdie leaned back, her point made. "Listen. Most folks here'd be happy to give you their last egg for your birthday cake, but there's a group of 'em who just plain don't know any other way to be." She shrugged as if she weren't one of them. "Honest, Charlotte, they'll never let you in, so you might as well give up trying."

Charlotte didn't need Virginia Buchanan's blessing to belong in Crickley. If Anna Grace loved it here, her daughter would, too. There was nothing Virginia could do to change that.

"It's not your fault, darlin'. You're just not from these parts, is all."

Charlotte was getting tired of hearing that.

Scruggs slapped a wet rag on the table beside them. He shot Charlotte such a look of understanding, she knew that he was well aware of subtext.

She also knew in that moment that Birdie was right. She may be done with Virginia, but she wasn't finished playing the game.

"Now, as for you, young man," Birdie raised her voice to Scruggs. "Why on God's green earth would you let Jack Buchanan take care of our Charlotte?" Scruggs ignored her and walked away. To Charlotte's amazement, Birdie jumped up and did a jiggly sort of jog after him. "Come here, you!" she huffed. Scruggs stopped and turned around, hands on hips, eyebrows raised.

"Now." She pointed a thick finger at him. "Explain."

Scruggs stood eye to eye with her. "Look, Miss Bird. That place was a germ stew. I'm willing to sacrifice one man for the cause, but not two. Not to mention, I wasn't about to let Prince Charming see our Charlotte all undressed and goopy."

"What do you mean?" Charlotte asked.

"Will was persistent, but I saved you." Scruggs grinned. "I let the lawyer up instead."

"*You* could have watched her." Birdie stuck her finger in his chest.

Scruggs swiped Birdie's hand away with a napkin. "I have finals coming up. Can't risk getting sick." He turned to Charlotte and mouthed the word, *sorry*, then pulled a bottle of hand sanitizer from his apron. He squeezed a glob of it onto his palm, offered some to Charlotte, and purposefully excluded Birdie.

"You can bite my bottom, Mr. Screw Loose," Birdie said.

"Now that's just nasty."

"Cut it out, you two," Charlotte said, secretly enjoying their banter. There was comfort in words spoken directly, words without subtext.

The next morning, Charlotte woke up antsy, ready to get out of her loft and into her store. There was no sign of Jack or Will, and that probably wouldn't change. Birdie came by midmorning for her usual treat, only this time she bought herself a stack of romance books so tall, she needed two bags to carry them out. She stopped only to torture Scruggs and then disappeared as quickly as she arrived. It seemed all the customers left with her. And since both Krista and Scruggs were scheduled to close, Charlotte took the opportunity to sneak away for a drive. She wanted to get out and take some pictures, explore the area, and see if she could feel her mother's presence somewhere.

As she drove into Birdie's and her mother's old neighborhood, the homes became smaller and the yards less maintained. But rather than appearing old and rundown, there was a clear revival going on. Shells of homes were actively being added on to. Most likely, as the residents grew old and moved on, the heirs were beginning renovations. Charlotte loved how Southerners revered their history. They didn't let go of things easily.

She was quickly coming up on the home her grandparents once owned, the one she never saw as a child, the one she had to research to find. She slowed to a crawl and stopped in front of a low-slung red brick house built during World War II. It was considered modern at the time. Charlotte rolled down her window and took a picture from the comfort of her car. She stayed awhile, hoping to feel something. When a car came up behind her, she waved it around and watched it park several doors down, next to an old white truck. She used the zoom on her camera to see if it was Will's.

It was.

Will stood on the front lawn, angrily pointing his finger in the face of a young man. The boy was probably twenty or so, with a look of abject terror.

At least now she knew. Krista was right. Will was an ogre.

Her knuckles turned white as she squeezed the steering wheel. She didn't want Will to see her, so she put the car in gear and drove toward downtown. Clearly, she'd made a mistake by trusting both Jack and Will. But it hadn't gone very far. It was survivable.

Chapter Fifteen

T HE SECOND TIME Charlotte heard about the Logger-head Festival was when a ponytailed Girl Scout came into the store, asking to hang a flyer in the window.

Scruggs yelled from behind the counter, "Hey, MacKenna!"

The Girl Scout turned. "Hi, Mr. Scruggs."

"I believe I'm in need of some Thin Mints."

"We don't sell 'em till February."

"Aw, you're killing me. My life ain't complete without eating me some Do-Si-Dos." He winked at her.

MacKenna giggled. How did everyone in town manage to know each other, even the children?

"Thank you, ma'am," said the girl, who immediately taped the paper to the window before running off to ask the same question of the next place of business. Charlotte stepped outside to read the flyer. The day was bright and crisp. The delightful feeling of summer on its way buoyed her spirits. She'd been lonelier than ever since Jack stopped calling and coming by. He hadn't so much as sent a text since that morning in her loft three weeks ago. It was time to get out of her own head and back into life.

She turned her face toward the warmth of the sun and smiled into its rays before turning to read the sign.

23RD ANNUAL LOGGERHEAD FESTIVAL

MAY 23

11 A.M. – MIDNIGHT

GREEN BEACH PARK

FEATURING THE BIG STOMPIN' DADDIES!

WATCH THE MISS LOGGERHEAD PAGEANT

COMPETE IN THE OYSTER-EATING CONTEST

ENJOY THE KIDDIE PARADE, LIGHT PARADE, AND TALENT SHOW

$10 PER PERSON, BEER AND FOOD NOT INCLUDED

SEE Y'ALL THERE!

Charlotte nearly laughed out loud. If she hadn't already seen a loggerhead, she might think the festival had something to do with felling trees. Other towns had shrimp festivals or oyster festivals; leave it to Crickley to have the Loggerhead Festival. It sounded like they'd all be snacking on endangered turtles.

And it seemed like something her mother would have loved.

A loud engine noise startled her, and she spun around to see who it was. It came from the biggest and oldest white Dodge pickup truck she ever saw. She recognized it immediately. Will stretched to the passenger side, manually rolling down the window.

"That's noise pollution!" she yelled, mad at herself that she sounded excited to see him. He smiled, and goose bumps spread along her arms.

"I see you got the flyer," he said, waving her over.

She reluctantly walked up to the truck. "Sounds like a pretty big deal around here."

"It is. Wanna go?"

"You mean with you?" *Yes*, her heart pounded. *No*, her brain argued.

Will chuckled. "Yes, with me."

"On a date?"

"Do you want it to be a date?" he asked.

Charlotte tried to choose her words carefully.

"Hold up now," Will interrupted. "Before you answer, would you hear me out for a second?"

She agreed, grateful to have a moment to strengthen her resolve to say no. She'd seen for herself that he was mean. She absolutely should not get involved, no matter how lonely she was.

He put the truck in Park in the middle of the street and leaned across the bench seat toward her. "I need to apologize for what happened that night I told you about Jack and Ruth Marie." He paused.

Was that it? The shortest, most insincere apology ever?

"I should have been more sensitive to your feelings," he said. "That was a rough night, and I'm sorry I didn't make it easier for you. Sometimes I have trouble with all that emotional stuff. Mama says I can be like a bull in a china shop, the way I run people over. I don't mean to."

She'd never seen him look contrite before. Her resolve was melting as fast as ice cream on summertime asphalt.

"It doesn't have to be a date if you don't want it to be. Maybe we can start over as friends."

The car behind him honked. Charlotte waved at the car, mouthed *one minute*, and turned back to Will. "I probably shouldn't have been so upset about it," she said.

His face relaxed. "So, is that a yes?"

"No." Yet she was tingling with excitement, damn her.

"Is it, maybe, opposite day today?"

She couldn't help but smile. "Friends." What was the harm in having a friend? She needed friends. Maybe she could even be a good influence on him, teach him not to yell at people.

The car honked again, and Will waved his arm through the open driver's side window, indicating for them to drive around. She watched the way he moved with confident, easygoing mannerisms, like time was to be savored, not raced against.

"I'll take it." Will slapped his hand against the steering wheel as if it was a teammate and they'd just made a play. "I'll call you." He put the truck into gear and drove away slowly.

Charlotte stepped back and watched him leave. When

his tailgate disappeared around the corner, she bounded back to the store. What a beautiful day.

Krista was near the door as she walked in. "How's Mr. Rushton?"

"Great." Oh, how she wanted him to be great.

"Look, I don't mean to be rude." Krista twisted her white-blonde hair into a perfect bun on top of her head. "But you know he's a cheater and a liar, right?" She didn't wait for an answer. "I mean, I've already warned you about him once. Guess I've got to come right out and say it now."

Charlotte stopped dead in her tracks. "Krista, it's not that I don't believe you, okay? I'm just trying to figure him out for myself."

"I'm sorry," she said, biting together her perfect pink lips, "but you've got to trust me. Will Rushton only cares about himself. He will destroy anyone in his path to get what he wants. You need to be careful."

"How do you know this?"

"I watch people," Krista said without compunction. "But it's not just me—everyone knows it."

What Charlotte really wanted to do was sock Krista in the nose. "Well, Birdie doesn't think so. She speaks very highly of him."

"Birdie's old school. She doesn't know how things really work, how people are nowadays." Krista put her hands in the front pockets of her apron, her bun lilting to the side. "Birdie has barely set foot outside of Crickley Creek—except for a cruise or two. I may have been here my whole life, but at least I *want* to leave."

Scruggs walked by, grazing Krista with his protruding elbow, somewhat knocking her off-balance. "What the heck, Scruggs?"

"Oh, I'm sorry Krista, did I interrupt something?" He raised his eyebrows and put his hands on his hips, Scruggs style. "You might want to carefully consider what you say about people. Will Rushton might be the bee in your bonnet, but he has done a lot of good for this town."

"Oh, please." Krista looked perturbed.

Charlotte shooed Scruggs toward a waiting customer.

"You might oughta stay away from him," Krista got in the last word.

At the rate Charlotte was being told to stay away from people, she would soon be avoiding half of Crickley Creek. "Thanks for the advice." She moved past Krista toward the bookshelves in the back. The last thing she wanted to do was argue with her employee. She needed her and wanted her to be happy working here.

Charlotte had unpacked half a box of books when she heard a deep voice from behind her say, "Hey, boss." The beer belly and bright orange hunting cap gave him away. The man who gave her the shivers, the one who set Will on edge, was right behind her. He smiled in a lecherous, sweaty sort of way.

"Hi." She put on a smile. "How can I help you?"

"I already got me my drink." He held up a large soda cup from a nearby gas station.

"Okay then. Enjoy your day." Charlotte turned toward the bookshelves, pretending to be confident in her task at hand. He followed. She adjusted some books, read the spines, checked the order. He was entering her personal space.

"Nice place you got here," he drawled.

"Thanks." She kept at her work.

"You read all these?" His belly grazed her back.

She was stuck between him, the bookshelf, and a chair. "No."

He pulled a book from the shelf over her head, treating her to a whiff of his underarm. A scantily clad femme fatale with half-torn dress was on the cover. "I like this one. Kinda looks like you." He put the book in front of her nose, positioning his unshaven face close to her ear. His breath reeked of whiskey. "You're mighty pretty. They make 'em all like you out there in Cali-forn-i-a?"

Charlotte shoved the chair aside with a loud scraping sound and walked quickly to the center of the store.

He stayed on her heels. "You scared or somethin'? Why you leaving? Rude, don't you think?" His voice got louder. "Are all y'all California chicks rude?"

Scruggs and Krista suddenly appeared next to her as Charlotte turned to face the man.

"Leave her alone," Scruggs said, puffing out his chest.

Krista put her hand on the man's arm and whispered for him to be nice, this was where she worked. He let out a guttural laugh, uttered, "whatever," and, thank God, turned toward the door. He hadn't gone two feet before he turned back to Scruggs and growled, "I'll stomp a mud-hole in your ass you ever do that again, boy." Viciously, he threw the book he'd been holding. It hit Scruggs on the arm.

"Get out!" Charlotte yelled, pointing to the door.

Waffles pushed open the door from the back patio, running toward the man and yapping furiously while Krista ushered him out.

Charlotte turned to a stunned-looking Scruggs. "You okay?"

He picked up Waffles and held her tightly to his chest. "I haven't been this pissed off since Emma Bishop dumped me for a Sigma Chi." They both watched as Krista shoved the man through the open front door and off the curb outside.

It took several minutes before she came back looking like a hit possum. "I'm so sorry," she said to Charlotte.

"You know him?"

"Yeah. He's my cousin, Randy."

It was hard to imagine such a distasteful human as a relative of beautiful Krista. "Does Randy have a problem? What in the heck was that all about?" Charlotte was about two seconds away from calling 911.

"No. No." Krista scratched the side of her nose and sniffed. "Randy's just going through a hard time right now.

Judging from his irritability and general discontent, I'm pretty sure he's been suffering with depression. Anyhow, I told him not to come back."

"The damned Hassell clan. A bunch of hotheads. Except for you, Krista, of course." Scruggs, like a worried father, was now walking the inside perimeter of the store, checking outside the windows to make sure the bastard was gone. He was still holding a yapping, angry Waffles.

Charlotte's body shook. "Tell Randy that if he ever comes near my store again, I'll call the police."

"My family isn't as bad as everyone around here says." Krista was red-faced and breathing heavily. "But I don't think calling the cops would work on Randy."

"Why?"

"He's just not afraid of much, is all. But don't worry, I'll handle him." The light in Krista's eyes had dimmed, replaced by something hard and resigned. It appeared as though Krista had experience handling wayward family members.

"I hope so," Charlotte said.

Chapter Sixteen

CHARLOTTE CLOSED THE doors to Tea and Tennyson, locking them behind her. She paused for a moment, taking in her store from the outside, then placed her hand flat against the old red brick warmed by the evening sun. That weathered brick had survived nearly a hundred years. Now it was hers. *Her* piece of history. The warmth spread like melted butter from the brick into her arm. She felt in her core how proud her mother would be that she'd built this life for herself. That she did it, she was running the tea and bookshop she'd dreamed of for years. It wasn't perfect, but it was working.

A slight breeze blew her hair into her face, and she swore she smelled the faintest aroma of honeysuckle.

Charlotte smiled and leaned her back against the warm brick while the setting sun went to work creating a neon pink and orange swath above the downtown buildings. Will would be here any minute. She'd been waiting for weeks and was anxious to get started. Birdie was great, but she really needed more friends, and Will had been nothing but nice during the weeks since they made plans.

At exactly six o'clock, Charlotte heard the familiar rumble of Will's truck. She stepped to the edge of the sidewalk, and he pulled the truck in front of her. When he hopped out, he looked like the cowboy she'd first met in jeans and boots, only this time, he wasn't wearing his Stetson. He wore a blue button-down shirt and his hair was shorter, contrasting the white skin of his scalp with his tanned face. He looked like an oversized little boy whose mother dressed him up for church.

"Hey, why're you waiting out here?" He chuckled. "I do know how to ring a doorbell."

"I wouldn't want you to strain yourself," she joked. "Anyway, I like it out here. It's a nice night."

"It *is* a nice night," he said, opening the passenger-side door for her. "Let's get this date started."

"It's not a date."

Will slid his thumbs through his belt loops and stood solid in front of her, like a John Wayne statue. "Are you riding with me in my truck?"

"Yes."

"Am I buying you dinner?"

"I don't know," she said, raising her eyebrows.

"Of course I am." He laughed, muttering, "You California girls thinking you're gonna pay on a date's just not right. What kind of men they got out there anyway?" He put his hand on the small of her back. "So, it's a date."

"I think I should have a say in this."

"You do." He pressed gently, leading her toward the truck. "You're coming with me, right?"

"Yes."

"Good. I've been waiting a long time for this. Let's go."

Charlotte climbed in, and he shut the door and jogged around to the driver's side. "Friends," she said. "We're just friends."

Will had to have heard her, but the only reaction she caught was a slight deepening of his dimple. On the twenty-minute southeast drive to the park, he was chattier than usual. He asked questions about her college years in California and even shared a story of when he and Jack were at the Citadel. "Great place to be from," he said. "Tough place to be."

The last thing she wanted was to run into Jack at the festival. A hundred and fifty different scenarios of how she'd react when she saw him again had played out in her mind since he left her life what felt like months ago. She had begun to let him in, begun to open her heart, and he abandoned her without so much as a backward glance. He wouldn't even give her the respect of an explanation. Damned Buchanans.

The only information Charlotte had about Jack was what Birdie shared about the impending joyful wedding happening the next week. What a strange show of concealment, with Birdie acting like Jack never so much as breathed in Charlotte's direction, like Charlotte had no reason on God's green earth to be upset. Birdie just flapped around dress shopping and gift buying, gushing loudly over flower choices and wedding dresses. When she brought her fellow Junior Leaguers into the store a few days ago, most of the talk wasn't centered on their next service project, but about how beautiful a bride Ruth Marie would be, how her parents must be so proud that Jackson was finally marrying her, and what kind of gift Virginia was going to give her new daughter-in-law. The family silver? The china?

But every time Charlotte asked Birdie why Jack hadn't called or come in, or why the wedding was planned so quickly, Birdie's lips shut tight as a vault. "Oh my soul, Charlotte," she said. "Let it go. You're gonna drive me to drinking if you keep it up." Virginia must have convinced her long ago that Ruth Marie was a better choice than Charlotte. Either that, or Ruth Marie was pregnant. Those things happened.

Will made the turn onto Green Beach Road. As they neared the ocean, the cooler air coming in for the night mixed with scents of pine and seawater. Breathing in deeply, she exhaled, trying to clean the negativity from her brain.

"You back?" Will asked.

"Huh?"

"Back from your mental vacation?"

"Oh," she said. "Yes. Sorry."

"Everything okay?"

"Fine, thanks. Just thinking."

"Well," he began. "Thinking is good."

Charlotte laughed. "Yes. Most of the time." Thankfully, he didn't pry.

Following the rustic signs to the nature trail, Will made a right into a large dirt parking lot clearly marked with Loggerhead Festival signs. Volunteers in Day-Glo orange used flashlights to direct the crowd. He parked his truck between a badly aging Chevy and a brand-new BMW. He opened his door, then turned to Charlotte, who was pulling on the passenger door handle. "Sit tight. I'm getting that for you," he said. She watched as he took long strides around the front of the truck and opened the door for her.

"Thanks." She slid out.

They followed the signs to the trailhead. Music played in the distance, but trees obscured the source of it. Charlotte realized the party was actually deep within the woods.

"Welcome to the Loggerhead Festival," said a rugged-looking female volunteer with long black hair pulled into a braid.

"How far do we have to walk?" Charlotte asked.

"Only 'bout a quarter mile, shug. There's a road over there on the backside if you don't want to hike it." The lady pointed to the left where a truck appeared to be driving into the forest. "This is the fun way, though. Y'all bring some spray?"

"What is it with all the bug spray around here? It can't be good to rub chemicals all over your skin," Charlotte said.

"Oooh," the volunteer joined in, "you gotta get over that, honey. Unless you plan on being dinner."

Charlotte pulled her sweater sleeves down as far as they would go, checking the air for mosquitoes. She hoped the chill of the fall evening would cut down on the insects.

"We'll fix you up," Will promised.

Following Will as he led the way along the trail, Charlotte was grateful that, although fading, sunlight still filtered through the thick forest of pines. Small beams of light from the flashlights of the volunteers stationed along the trail helped more and more. Will stopped before a small bridge spanning the short width of a creek and turned toward her, offering his hand. Together, they walked over the wooden slats. His hand felt large and dry. Funny how she had become accustomed to his hugs at the store, but holding his hand was like going from friends to lovers in the tiniest of moments it took skin to touch skin.

Chapter Seventeen

WILL AND CHARLOTTE strolled along the uneven dirt trail over logs and rocks. Twinkle lights haphazardly hung from the trees and various sizes of fake turtles lay scattered along the path. Loggerheads, she presumed. Garlands made from empty beer cans and shrimp nets spotted with plastic sea life draped the trees. Lanterns hung in the branches along with all shapes and sizes of glass bottles, which clinked together in a tinkly symphony. Charlotte gasped when she saw small flashes of light. "Are those fireflies?" she asked. They were everywhere, blinking their welcome.

"Naw. Those are just lights. They'll be coming soon, though," Will said.

She couldn't help but feel disappointed. She'd lived here since January and hadn't seen a single firefly.

"I'll show you some." He squeezed her hand. "We can spend lazy nights on my back porch. I've got tons living in my woods." That sounded nice, but also a little presumptuous.

Something lay ahead, judging from the noise of people

talking. She strained to see what it was. About twenty yards away stood an old log cabin, currently in use as a first aid station. Will, still holding her hand, pulled her up the steps into the cabin. It was brightly lit and smelled of wood, mold, and rubbing alcohol. A lovely older woman, impeccably dressed in dark navy jeans, a light blue button-down shirt that matched her eyes, and a perfectly styled brown bob, turned to greet them.

"Mama," Will said. "I'd like you to meet Charlotte."

Holy crap. Charlotte froze.

"Charlotte, this fine woman right here is my mama, Allison Rushton." Will dropped her hand and casually rested his arm around his mother's shoulders.

Mrs. Rushton first wiped her hand on her jeans, then extended it toward Charlotte. "So nice to meet you. Did my boy drag you in here just to say hello to me?" Will's mother looked accusingly at him before smiling widely at Charlotte.

"No." Will raised his arms as if he were innocent. "We have a legitimate reason for being here."

Charlotte looked at him, confused.

"We need bug spray," he said, pulling Charlotte to his side. "Okay, and also, I wanted y'all to meet each other."

"This son of mine," said Allison, "is obnoxious." She punched him playfully in the arm and walked to an old wooden table to grab a bottle of Avon Skin-So-Soft. The antique-looking cluster of diamonds on her left ring finger sparkled brilliantly under the fluorescent lights. "Here y'all go." She tossed the bottle to Will before turning to help a partygoer.

Will poured some of the oily liquid into his cupped hand and rubbed it on his arms and neck. It smelled powdery and herbal, not like chemicals at all. It was a very feminine fragrance, which Charlotte thought was funny.

As if he knew what she was thinking, he said, "It's the best thing for keeping off the mosquitoes." He poured more and turned to face her. "Roll up your sleeve and give me your arm."

"I can do it." She reached for the bottle.

Will caught Charlotte's arm with one hand. He grinned at her while he spread the liquid from his hand onto her skin, his rough tanned hands so manly against the creamy, delicate skin of her arm.

"Can't waste good stuff," he said. "You wanna do the other one?"

Charlotte stuck out her other arm, goose bumps rising in anticipation of his touch. He worked his way down to her fingertips and hesitated, then placed her hand by her side and turned to exhale. The sexual tension in the room went from a five to a ten in the span of a second. Picking up the bottle, he held it as if ready to pour its contents in her hand. "You, uh, need to do your neck too," he stammered.

Charlotte made a cup with her hand, accepted the liquid, and quickly massaged it into her neck, staring at the ground as she did it.

Shouting their goodbyes to Allison, they got back on the trail. Lights as bright as daylight shone through the trees ahead, illuminating a space larger than a football field. It was a huge grassy clearing with the Atlantic Ocean and a full moon as a backdrop, and it appeared as though every resident of Crickley Creek was here.

The peace of the woods exploded into the chaos of a crowded party. The talent competition was underway on a stage to their left, and various beer and food stands dotted the perimeter. Arts and crafts concessionaires hawked their wares, and kiddie bounce houses had lines twenty children long. A booming voice announced that the band would begin in less than half an hour. Once it began, the party would probably shift to a more adult crowd.

"So, the way I see it," Will said over the din, "we should go ahead and get ourselves a spot near the stage now, then pick up dinner after the first set when we need a break and can sit for a bit."

Charlotte saw too many holes in his plan to keep quiet about it. "Or, maybe we can eat now while I'm hungry and the lines aren't too long? We can still take a break if we need one, and I'm okay if you are with not being too close to the stage." Really. Loud country music screaming at her from a speaker taller than Will did not appeal.

He looked amused. "How is this date going to work if you don't stick with my plan?"

She smiled sweetly and shrugged.

"So here's what we're going to do," he began. "We're going to eat now, then find a spot somewhere not too close to the stage, and take a break whenever the heck we feel like it. Got it?"

"Got it." She giggled.

Will used his height to look over the top of the crowd and list their dinner options. He bought them two large paper cones filled with cooked shrimp and found a bench to sit where they could watch the crowd interact: groups of people talking and laughing, families chasing after small children, women looking exasperated, men looking drunk, and teenagers moving about in packs. Every so often, a friend of Will's walked up to shake his hand. Will introduced one of them as Mike Compton, his foreman and brother of Mayor Sonny Compton. Mike was short but far less heavy than his brother, the mayor. He had deep wrinkles around his eyes, a quick smile, and a firm handshake. Charlotte liked him immediately and, for men who were surely put through all kinds of stress together on the job, Will and Mike seemed genuinely happy to see each other.

Will threw their empty paper cones in a big blue trash can just as a loud guitar riff ripped through the air. The booming voice of an announcer began the build-up to introduce the band. The crowd howled their approval, and with a loud click, all the lights shut off. Blinded by the sudden darkness, Charlotte reached for Will. She found his bicep as he leaned down to help her up, and her head hit against his chest. She stood into his embrace until her eyes adjusted and lights came up on the stage glowing and blinking in red, white, and blue. He kept his arm around her as they wound their way through the crowd to the front.

The Big Stompin' Daddies ran onto the stage, burning up the night with country rock music. Charlotte stood in front of Will, shielded by his size from the crowd for two loud songs, until the band switched gears and played a style of music that raised her mood to joyous. The jumping and screaming of the crowd turned into spinning and jiving. She couldn't help it, the sound made her body want to move.

"They're shagging," Will spoke into her ear. "It's like a slow shuffle with Southern soul." He spun her around. "A Lowcountry specialty." Grinning, Charlotte followed his lead. "Do kind of a slow jitterbug and you'll get it," he said.

"I have no idea what a jitterbug is," she yelled over the music, wiggling just a little.

Will leaned in, still swaying with the beat. "Don't y'all dance in California? This is beach music."

Charlotte watched the couples spinning and shuffling. "It's kinda like swing dancing!" she yelled up to Will. "But there's not enough room."

He pulled her close, holding her hands to his chest. She tried to step back to find some space for movement, but he held on tight, moving her back and forth and round and round with the beat. Soon, she fell in step and closed her eyes, allowing the music to transport her while he held the crowd at bay. It was a chilly night, and his body was warm and solid. She nestled in. The band played a version of Kenny Chesney's "When the Sun Goes Down" and she felt on her cheek the vibration in Will's chest as he hummed along with the tune. He spun them both around, and she opened her eyes.

Her heart stopped. *Jack.*

She could see him clearly, only a few people away, dancing with a tall, beautiful blonde. *Ruth Marie.* Where Charlotte was on the shorter side of five foot four, Ruth Marie stood at least five ten. And where Charlotte had long, brown hair, Ruth Marie's was light blonde and cut into a chic bob. They danced comfortably together and seemed very much in love.

Hurt and anger burned from her stomach all the way up to her throat just as Jack caught sight of her and their eyes locked. He steered Ruth Marie into the crowd, away from Charlotte and Will, but Ruth Marie turned her head and looked directly at Charlotte. It felt like she'd just been caught stealing. Ruth Marie's face said it all. She knew there had been something between Jack and Charlotte. She knew, and it hurt her.

Charlotte pressed her head into Will's chest, giving Jack and Ruth Marie a chance to disappear into the crowd. She no longer felt like dancing. "Can we sit for a minute?" she shouted up to him.

He nodded and led the way through the crowd to a

bench on the outside of the field. Charlotte sat and pulled off one of her new black shoes. She purposefully did not wear heels, making a conscious choice of cute, comfortable flats, forgetting they were new and not yet broken in. A large blister had popped, leaving a raw spot on the back of her foot.

Will sat beside her. "You're gonna need a Band-Aid if you plan to do more dancin'. Sit tight for a second and I'll run down to the cabin and get you one."

"I hate for you to have to do that," she said. *I'd hate for Jack and Ruth Marie to see me here alone.*

"It's no problem. Gotta get you back in shape; this night's just starting." He winked at her before popping up and jogging away. "Be right back."

Maybe if Ruth Marie weren't so beautiful it wouldn't hurt as much. It's not like Charlotte and Jack were ever an actual couple anyway. They never even kissed. She hugged her knees and watched the crowd. Clouds covered the moon, and aside from the colorful lights from the stage and the glow from surrounding concessions, it was completely dark. Hopefully, Will wouldn't be gone long.

Without warning, the bench she was sitting on lurched wildly, forcing her to throw down her legs to steady herself. A large-bellied man chose the spot beside her to sit and finish a yard-long beer. He reeked of cigarette smoke and body odor. She raised her eyes to his face. The first thing she noticed was his filthy, bright orange hunting cap.

"Hey," Randy said with a drunk Southern drawl.

Chapter Eighteen

S HE THOUGHT ABOUT getting up and running, but the seething contempt on his face made her afraid he'd chase after her.

"You ain't gonna answer me? I said 'hey' to you." He lifted his upper lip in a dog-like snarl.

"Hi," she replied.

"I seen you out there dancin' like you got it all going on. Shaking yer ass, thinking yer hot shit." Spit leaked from his bottom lip. He licked it and took a long pull of his beer. "Here's a little piece of information for you. You's nothing more than a piece of shit. And pieces of shit don't get to tell me where I can and can't go. You got that? If I want to go to your stupid-ass frilly little store, I will goddamn do it."

"I don't even know you," Charlotte said, shaking.

"Here's what you got to know. I can mess up you and your boyfriend faster than stink. Ya hear me? You just go ahead and tell that boyfriend of yours that he ain't gonna have a life till he gives back what don't belong to him. You tell him that. Bitch." He tossed his empty beer in the direction of the trash can. Then, by the grace of God, the monstrous man got up, nearly heaving Charlotte off the other end of the bench, and stomped into the crowd.

She shakily put on her shoe and stood on wobbly legs, forcing them to move forward, desperate to find Will. Half running, she moved in the direction she thought he'd gone, looking for a sign leading to the first aid cabin. Every minute that passed made her more anxious to find him. She was in the middle of the crowd with no sense of direction. Bodies were pressed in all around her, none of them familiar. Her heart beat so quickly, it felt as if it might fly out of her throat.

She turned around and walked back in what she thought was the direction of the bench. Maybe Will was there, waiting for her. She heard someone call her name and turned toward the sound. A vile gang of rednecks, led by Randy, leered and waved her over. Most of them were of the same round build, and they all appeared to be the same amount of drunk. "Heeey, baby," one of them slurred. "I'm gonna get me some of that," said another. The gang walked toward her. Fear gripped her by the torso and thrust her forward. Tripping over her own feet, she skidded on her knees in the dirt. She surveyed the damage: two skinned knees, complete with little rocks and dirt mixed into the blood. Someone reached down to help her up. She couldn't hear what they were saying, but she understood when they pointed toward the edge of the field. Yes, she would go straight to the first aid cabin.

The pain was beginning to set in when she arrived at the wooden building. An enormous man wearing an orange vest greeted her by the steps. "Looks to me like you need a little tending to," he said.

She nodded.

"Come on, honey." He offered her his arm. "You've already met my wife. And my son."

Charlotte did a double take, noticing his broad shoulders and cookie-colored hair. He was built like Will, only heavier in the middle.

"Name's Kelly Rushton."

Kelly was not the name she expected for such a masculine man. "Nice to meet you."

He led her into a large room where he sat her in a chair and examined her knees. She studied his face up close; his eyes were wrinkled like he would enjoy a good joke, and his nose was strong and straight, like Will's.

"I'm sorry this happened to you, honey." He tore open a sterile wipe and gently cleaned the dirt from her scrapes. "Will should be here soon. I'm sure one of the volunteers told him I found you. He's probably running around this place, looking for you like a bloodhound on a scent." Kelly dried the wounds and meticulously placed an extra-large bandage on each knee. "Be right back with some ice. Just stay put." He smiled at her, running his hand over the back of her head. It was such a fatherly gesture, Charlotte almost cried. She sniffed and looked up just as Will came through the door.

"What happened?" Kneeling in front of her, he was still taller than she was in the chair. His hands hovered over her bandaged knees.

"Are you alright, honey?" Allison asked from behind him.

"Fine. Just lost my footing." Charlotte smiled weakly.

Will picked up her foot and took off her shoe. "I never got that Band-Aid to you." He sprayed antibacterial cleaner on her raw blister and dabbed it gently with a sterile pad, then stretched a Band-Aid horizontally across the wound. It felt better immediately.

"Thank you."

Kelly came back with two Ziploc baggies full of ice. Will placed her legs on a chair and gently set the bags where her skin was beginning to swell.

"You got some good scrapes there, darlin'," Kelly said before taking his wife's hand. "Let's give 'em some time," said Allison. "We've got customers up front."

"Charlotte," Will said. "What in the hell happened?"

She gave him the rundown. When she mentioned what Randy Hassell said to her, Will's face darkened, his lips a tight line. Realizing she'd never told him about her run-in with Randy at her store, she filled him in on that, too. He clenched and unclenched his fists.

"Goddamn it." He nearly knocked off a bag of ice as he stood. "Dad!" Kelly lumbered his way back to the room.

"Watch Charlotte for me, please. I've got business."

"Watch Charlotte?" She jumped up, her knees catching fire as her voice rose. "Watch Charlotte? Where are you going?"

"To teach a boy some manners."

She tried to grab his arm. "You're going after him? To do what?" But he was already out the door. "Will!" She spun around to his father. "Don't let him go!" Panic rose from the pit of her stomach. "There's a group of them. They'll kill him."

Kelly led Charlotte back to the chair, counseling her in a paternal tone. "Nobody's gonna be killing anybody. Will knows how to take care of himself. This has been a long time coming." Pressing the button on his walkie-talkie, he said, "Ricky, get some boys together to watch out for Will, all right? He's on the hunt for Randy Hassell." Charlotte got the shivers.

Kelly gently patted her on the shoulder. "Don't you worry a thing about all this, all right? None of it's your fault. Will'll be just fine."

She wanted to yell, "How do you know?" How could Will fight all of those horrible drunken men? Her stomach burned. The only hope was that the volunteers would find him and help.

She could barely keep herself seated.

Chapter Nineteen

T WENTY MINUTES PASSED, and there was still no sign of Will. Shouldn't someone call the police?

Without a word, Kelly stood and left the other room. He returned shortly with Will's mother and two stunningly beautiful young women. One had auburn hair, straight and long. She was petite, but a glimmer in her eye made Charlotte think she was tough for her size. The other girl was tall with curly blonde hair and full pink lips that shot her a quick smile. Kelly introduced them as his daughters, Natalie and Brooke. None of them appeared concerned that Will was currently hunting down an aggressive group of drunk men. Charlotte forced a smile, but she wanted to scream. Somebody needed to *do* something.

Finally, Will came back without a limp or a black eye, appearing completely unscathed. As a matter of fact, he held a plate of funnel cakes, which he handed to her. Not only was he not dead, he had brought dessert. She was speechless.

Allison patted her son on the back and motioned for Natalie and Brooke to follow her out the door. Then she smiled as if to say, "See, we told you everything would be okay."

Charlotte didn't feel like everything was okay. She fixed her gaze on Will. "Did you talk to him?"

"Naw," he said, taking a bite from the plate Charlotte now begrudgingly held. "Couldn't find him."

"Couldn't find him?" Charlotte felt her anger growing. "Do you know how worried I've been? Do you think maybe you could have come back sooner or called or something?" Her voice rose, the plate of funnel cakes shaking with her emotion. "I thought those guys would kill you." She was breathing faster now. "And you wouldn't listen to me! I asked you not to go."

He wiped the powdered sugar from his mouth with the back of his hand. "So, you do care about me."

"Stop it," she said. "Just stop it. I'm so mad at you right now, I could beat you up myself. For all you know, Randy could have had a gun."

He kneeled in front her, his face within inches of hers. "I didn't mean to worry you." He was smiling, damn him.

She pushed him away, inadvertently throwing the funnel cakes to the floor. "Why is that guy after me? Why is he after *you?*"

"Don't worry about it, okay?" Will bent and swept the funnel cakes onto the plate. "It's business stuff."

"Don't tell me what to worry about." Charlotte stood. "If it's *your* business, why is he harassing *me?*"

"My guess is that he's using you to get to me." Will became serious for a moment. "He knows—" He looked away, changing gears. "Don't let him bother you."

"Okay. Sure. Because it's that easy."

He moved his hand toward hers. "No. Of course not. You're right."

She knocked his arm away. "Don't agree with me." She tried hard to keep her voice from showing her fear. "Tell me why he hates you so much."

"He's gotten himself into a mess, but don't worry, I've got it handled."

Charlotte threw her arms in the air. "You're not going to answer me, are you?"

"I am answering you." Will moved forward tentatively, reaching for her hand again.

She stood painfully and stormed past him toward the door before turning around to face him once more. "I see what you're doing. You did something to make him mad, didn't you? Who's really the bad guy here, huh, Will? Is it the drunk redneck or the big businessman who's gonna take care of things behind the scenes? Who sounds more dangerous to you? The dumb one or the smart one?"

"What are you talking about? Don't make this into something it isn't, Charlotte. I was mad enough to fight him, but after a bit of walking around looking for him, I decided I didn't want this to ruin our date. Okay? Anyway, it wouldn't be a fair fight." He laughed at his joke.

"Do you really think this is a time for joking? That man is dangerous, and I'm beginning to think you are, too."

"I'm about as dangerous as a kitten." He grinned at her a little too eagerly.

"Oh, please, Mr. Trained-to-Kill Army Officer. Don't treat me like I'm stupid. You're just as dangerous as he is, and he was probably first in line at Walmart this morning, buying ammo because he knew you'd be here. Or maybe because he knew *I'd* be here."

"Charlotte, calm down. I would never let Randy Hassell hurt you."

"Are you trying to be macho? Because that crap doesn't impress me. I'm not some little girl ready to swoon because you're trying to defend me."

"No, you're not. You're different, that's for darn sure." Will walked toward her again and Charlotte moved backward two steps, almost out the door, too furious to allow him near her. Will stopped at the door, looking at her sadly. "Stay. We can talk this out."

"I don't know what I was thinking, coming here. I'm going home now."

"So, it's okay if you defend your mother, but not okay if I defend you?"

Charlotte glared at him. How dare he bring her mother into this.

"Look," he said. "If you want to leave, we'll leave, alright? We can go for a drive. I know of a great little roadhouse with pool tables and 80s music."

"God, you're just like a politician, the way you keep trying to shift everything to go your way."

"I'm not trying to do anything, aside from get more time with you." He reached for her, waving her toward him. "Just come on, okay? Come with me…we can work this out."

She was angry and scared and her knees hurt. There were too many what-ifs and questions about who to trust. She no longer knew who anyone was, including herself. She turned and limped down the steps.

Will followed her to the bottom. "At least let me give you a ride home," he yelled after her. She kept walking.

She was almost to the parking lot when Allison ran up beside her. Her voice didn't hold even a hint of anger. "I'm gonna have to insist that I drive you home, honey. I know it's none of my business, so I won't even talk to you about it if you don't want me to." Charlotte slowed down but kept walking. "Will has got that Rushton stubbornness about him. Gets him into trouble."

Charlotte could call for a ride. She didn't need her hand held.

Allison spoke softly, like she was picking up a conversation with a friend. "Will'll always be my sensitive little man. These days he's wrapped in big man packaging, but inside he's really very sweet. Stubborn, but sweet."

Charlotte didn't want to hear that.

Allison continued, "I want you to know that if you need to talk, I'm not gonna be upset by anything you say. I love my boy, but I'm under no impression that he's perfect."

"Right now," Charlotte said, "I can't even form a clear thought. I mean, I was expecting a regular date, and instead I saw someone I really didn't want to see, got scared out of my wits by a crazy redneck, skinned my knees, lost my temper, and now I'm going home with my date's mother." She turned to Allison. "No offense."

"None taken, darling."

Will's mother was comfortable to be around. Which only served to make Charlotte feel guilty. "I'm really not a high-strung sort of person. Tonight was just too much. Completely insane. This stuff doesn't happen in real life, but here I am living it."

Allison led the way to her older model white Lexus sedan in the middle of the large dirt lot filled with hundreds of vehicles. The car beeped, and Allison opened the passenger-side door. "It'll all look better in the morning."

"I hope so." Charlotte sat nervously while Allison closed the door and climbed into the driver's seat.

"If you'd let me take you back to our house, we have some homemade caramel pecan ice cream made special by Kelly, the original stubborn Rushton. He keeps it on hand for those times when he messes up and needs to appease me." Allison cut a look of shared secrets at Charlotte and drove out of the parking lot onto Green Beach Road. "Men can be clueless sometimes. They don't mean to be, they're just not tuned to our same channel."

"Ice cream sounds good," Charlotte said. "But I think

I'm going to opt for sleep. Thank you, though."

"Okay, honey. I'll get you home."

Charlotte rubbed the tan leather of her seat, looking out the window for several minutes until she spoke her thoughts out loud. "Ever since I moved here, I've felt like a tourist in my own country. The problem is, I don't have a home to go back to." The forest on their right ended abruptly, and Charlotte found herself looking out at the Atlantic. The moon bounced light off the water, and small dunes protected the beach.

"You may not know it, but you belong here just as much as anyone," Allison said. "Some people may like to pretend they've cornered the market on heritage, but it's really all just smoke. Every day, you're here building your business, your friendships, facing challenges, helping people, what you're really doing is carving out a little spot for yourself. Next thing you know, people are calling you by name and you can't imagine living anywhere else." She patted Charlotte's hand. "You belong here, honey. Take my word for it."

Charlotte stared out the window, wishing she could believe it.

"You know, you're the only girl my son has ever gone out of his way to introduce to us," Allison said. "I just plain ol' get a good feeling about you. You're no pushover, that's for sure, but after all these years of living in this town with all its characters and foolishness, I've learned to trust my gut. Listen to yours, Charlotte. It'll tell you what to do."

If only it were that easy. A rock had been lodged in Charlotte's gut since the day she'd arrived in Crickley Creek. She suspected there was one in her heart, too.

Chapter Twenty

B Y SUNDAY MORNING, Charlotte was spent, her mind exhausted from reliving Saturday night in an endless loop. For something that started off so well, how did it end so badly? In the middle of her tenth mouthful of Ben and Jerry's Cheesecake Brownie ice cream, she heard the unmistakable roar of an old pickup passing by on the street outside her loft. It was the third time she had heard the sound of his truck outside her window. He'd already left her an apology message on her phone and made it clear that the ball was now in her court.

Good riddance, she told herself, but felt no relief. He was a complication she didn't need. She would continue to tell herself that until it sank in.

Once again, she was starting over. The only people important in her life now were Birdie and Scruggs. Maybe Krista, but Charlotte was too annoyed to count her. It was high time Charlotte knew the truth about Randy and Will, and she was counting on Krista to tell her.

Monday morning, Scruggs came in first. Charlotte gave Waffles a kiss before opening the back door to the patio.

When she turned around, Krista had arrived.

"Krista? Could I talk to you for a minute?"

She put her purse behind the counter and looked at Charlotte strangely. "Sure. What's up?"

Scruggs stopped in the middle of tying his apron and raised his eyebrows at them both.

"Oh, stop it, Scruggs." Charlotte waved him off. "Get back to work."

Krista followed her to a table in the far end of the room where Charlotte offered her a seat and sat down across from her. "Krista," she began. "I'm coming to you as a friend, not as your employer, okay?"

"Oh-kaaay," Krista said, looking pale. "What'd I do?"

"You didn't do anything. This is about your cousin."

"Oh, Randy." Krista sat back in her chair, crossing her arms.

"That boy's like a tick without a dog," Scruggs commented from behind the front counter.

"Mind your own business, Scruggs," Krista yelled across the store. Waffles barked from the back patio.

"I want you to know that I trust you. I know you have a close family, and I respect and admire that. Actually, I'm jealous of that." Charlotte smiled with effort. "I don't want to get too personal, and you need to know that none of this will affect your job here. It's just that I'm finding myself in the middle of something."

"What?"

"Randy threatened me at the Loggerhead Festival. Scared the hell out of me, to be honest."

Krista's mouth fell open as she let out a deep sigh. She pointed to Charlotte's bandaged knees peeking out beneath her sundress. "Did he do that?"

"Not really. That was an accident." Charlotte's wounds still ached. "Krista, tell me what's going on with Randy and Will. Randy's bringing me into it now. Whatever *it* is." She hoped she was coming across as sincere and nonthreatening. "Please. I need to know what I'm dealing with."

"I'll tell you," she said. "But I don't think you're gonna want to hear it."

Scruggs walked over and pulled up a chair.

"Are you on drugs?" Krista snapped. "This is a private conversation."

He sat himself down and crossed his arms defiantly.

"Scruggs," Charlotte said. "Come on."

"Fine," he said. "I guess my opinion means nothing around here." He pushed the chair away loudly and sulked off.

"Alright, here's the truth," Krista said. "Fifty-somethin' years ago, my granddaddy started building homes. As a matter of fact, a Hassell built most of the tract homes in Crickley Creek. Nearly all of us worked for the company— all my boy cousins, my uncles, some girls, too. Randy took over—"

Scruggs, now behind the counter, threw out, "asswipe."

"Good God, have you got bat ears or somethin'?" Krista growled at him before shaking her head and turning back to Charlotte. "Anyway, Randy took over after his daddy retired, which was just about the time Will Rushton came back to town. You see, all these years, the Rushtons and the Hassells have had an agreement that the Rushtons would handle the commercial stuff and we would do the homes. But Will is greedy and wasn't gonna let that be. No ma'am, he moved back and started taking away our business. Just like that."

Scruggs turned on the espresso machine and began cleaning the frother, the loudest part of the machine.

Krista raised her voice. "Now, half of us don't have work since Rushton Construction took our business. My brother can't see the doctors he needs, I'm having to work here..." Her eyes became moist, and the sound of the frother overtook them.

"Scruggs!" Charlotte shouted. "Do you mind?"

He shut off the machine.

"Krista, I'm so sorry that happened to your family, and I'm sorry for Randy. I hate that Will stole his business. But I need to make something clear, okay? I am not with Will. I have no part in whatever it is he's doing. He's not my boyfriend." Charlotte put her hands together as if she were begging. "So, can you please ask Randy to leave me alone? I didn't do anything to him."

"I'll ask," she said, standing, adjusting her apron. "He's just upset is all. And sometimes when he's upset, he acts up a bit. Things have been real hard on him lately. They've been hard on my whole family." She started to walk away, her shoulders slumped.

"Thank you, Krista. I just want him to stop scaring the bejeezuz out of me."

"I'll try my best," she said without turning around.

Scruggs yelled, "Y'all are wasting your time. Men like him won't listen to a word you say." Charlotte and Krista turned to look at him, all puffed-up and righteous, holding a carton of half-and-half. "The way I see it, you have two choices: You can either get someone to stand outside that door with a shotgun all day and all night or pay someone from across the tracks to get it handled. *If you know what I mean.*" Wink. Wink.

"Scruggs," Krista said. "Since when are you freakin' Don Corleone?"

"Ya gotta fight evil with evil." He shrugged. "Just sayin'." He poured the cream into a stainless dispenser and added, "At the very least you need to get yourself a dog. I'd let you borrow Waffles but for her nerves. I'd have to get her doggie Xanax and that just won't do."

Customers were entering the store, so Charlotte got up from her chair to greet them, feeling like she was totally losing her mind. Instead of feeling relieved, she was more worried than ever. Randy scared the hell out of her—not only because he was physically revolting, but because there was something unstable about him. Something scary. She pasted on a smile for her customers. Logically, she knew Randy's anger wasn't totally without merit. Will hadn't honored an agreement. It may have been an agreement made with a handshake by their grandfathers, but in Charlotte's mind, that showed a definite lack of integrity on Will's part. It was the small-town version of what she saw often in California: money could turn a good person bad. She moved forward to greet her next customer. A tall, blonde woman returned her smile.

"Charlotte?" the woman asked.

She knew this face.

"I'm Ruth Marie Wallace, Jack's fiancée."

The name struck Charlotte like a frying pan to the head. In a daze, she noticed Ruth Marie was offering to shake her hand. She took it, forcing herself to make eye contact. The girl's eyes were a blue so light, they were too pretty to be useful.

"Hi. I'm Charlotte." *Oops.* "Well, you already know that." *Ah, hell.* "Welcome to Tea and Tennyson."

Ruth Marie was holding a shiny square envelope in her perfectly manicured, skinny white hands. She held it out to Charlotte. "I realize this may seem strange," she began.

No kidding.

"Jack and I would like to invite you to our wedding." She placed the envelope in Charlotte's reluctant hand. "We really hope you can make it."

Charlotte stared at her, dumfounded, before pulling out

the gold-and-white invitation. Ruth Marie stood still, waiting. "It's this weekend," Charlotte blurted.

"Yes." Ruth Marie shrugged. "I'm so sorry for the late notice."

She didn't know what to say. Her mind was busy analyzing every word Ruth Marie said, looking for subtext, for some awful hidden meaning lying beneath. "Are you sure you want me there?"

"We both do." Ruth Marie reached out and touched Charlotte on the arm. Her fingertips felt like ice on Charlotte's hot skin. What in the hell did a touch on the arm mean? Was it Southern for "If you show up, I'll rip every hair from your head," or could it possibly suggest "Yes, this is real and I'm truly this nice." Someone needed to write a rule book.

"Okay," Charlotte said, more as a wary consideration than an acceptance of the invitation.

"Great! See you there." Ruth Marie nearly jumped toward the door. "Oh, and I love your store." Her voice sounded like a child's.

"Thank you," Charlotte remained glued to the floor, holding tightly to the invitation in her hand.

As soon as Ruth Marie walked past the front windows, Scruggs ran to Charlotte's side. "Well, well, Cinderella. You just got invited to the ball."

"She's Cinderella," Charlotte said. "I'm the ugly stepsister. Excuse me." She walked around Scruggs. "I have to call

Birdie. Now."

Twenty minutes later, Birdie swooped through the front door, flying straight to Charlotte and grabbing her by both arms. "Aw, honey. I should have come here sooner. All this secret stuff has been killing me. Burning a hole right through my stomach."

"I knew it!" Charlotte led Birdie to the stairway. "I knew you were holding out on me."

"I had to," Birdie said, struggling up the stairs behind Charlotte. "I am a good person and good people keep their traps shut."

Once inside her loft, Charlotte pointed Birdie to her couch. "Sit."

"Fine." Birdie delicately placed her bottom on the cushion.

Charlotte plopped down next to her and glared at Birdie's flushed face with a look meant to convey, "Start talking. Immediately."

"Oh, don't make me come right out with it. Ask me some questions or something. Let a girl at least *try* to keep her word."

"Fine, Birdie. Why did I just get invited to Jack's wedding?"

Birdie shifted and stretched her neck. "Honey, if I knew, I would tell you. Honest, I would."

"Birdalee Mudge! I am going to strangle you."

"Oh, please."

Charlotte held up her pointer finger. "Why is Jack marrying Ruth Marie?" She held up a second finger. "Why have you always been on *her* side?" She held up a third finger. "And what secrets have you been keeping from me?"

"Hold up now, Charlotte," Birdie said, taking Charlotte's three fingers in her hand. "I am not on her side." She held Charlotte's hand in between her own. "Is that what you think? Come now, sugar. Put your thinking cap on. You can figure this out."

Charlotte pulled her hand away. "You think I haven't been trying? One minute, he wants to date me and the next minute, he's getting married. It makes no sense." She was exhausted from all the energy she'd spent thinking about it.

Birdie bore a hole into Charlotte's face with her eyes. She drew out her words just like she was trying to draw out an answer. "Something happened the day Jack left your apartment. What do you think it was?"

"I don't know." Charlotte threw up her arms in exasperation. "Was he in an accident?"

"Oh, don't be a ninny."

"Well, then stop making me guess. Just tell me."

"Oh, for heaven's sakes, Charlotte. She's pregnant. When Jack got home from tending to you, Ruth Marie told him she was pregnant."

"I figured that when I heard the wedding was so soon. Still…"

"Bless his bones," Birdie said, shaking her head. "Jack's a good man. He's doing the right thing." She reached for

Charlotte's shoulder. "I wasn't on her side, honey. It's just that Ruth Marie is a good girl and doesn't deserve to be destroyed by this. Virginia made me promise not to tell a soul."

"But don't you think I should've been the one person you told? And why didn't *he* tell me? He could have saved me a lot of wondering."

"That, I can't speak to. But I do know he was feeling pretty puny about the whole thing. He's not used to making mistakes, that boy. We've all just been trying so hard to protect Ruth Marie's reputation."

Charlotte leaned back into the cushions, her chin on her chest. "I still don't get it. In this day and age you don't have to get married."

"Maybe it's that way in Los Angeles, dear heart, but not here in Crickley."

Charlotte could've guessed that part. "I just don't get why Ruth Marie invited me."

"Look, she's been loving that boy a long time. Maybe she's holding her enemy closer, like that old saying."

"Well, I am absolutely not going."

"Oh, hush with that. Of course you are. You get a hand-delivered invitation from the bride, you are obliged to go." Birdie stood up from the couch. "We'll go together." She offered Charlotte her arm for a hoist from the couch. Charlotte took it and stood. Birdie patted her on the back. "Now let's go get me a cookie 'fore I faint from hunger."

"Let's both have about twelve of them," Charlotte said.

Chapter Twenty-One

I CAN'T BELIEVE *I'm doing this.* Charlotte pulled her favorite light yellow silk organza dress over her head. She straightened it and looked in the mirror. It was a classy vintage tea dress that brought out the green in her eyes and flattered her small figure without attracting too much attention. She hoped to blend in so well at the wedding that Jack wouldn't know she was there. She applied a light pink gloss to her lips.

How would she feel watching Jack make a vow to another woman?

"He was never yours to begin with," she said out loud to her image in the mirror. One last look and she was on her way out. She paused at the bookshelf, kissed her fingertips and pressed them to the firefly jar. "Here we go, Mom."

Downstairs in the store, Charlotte pulled together a gift basket of goodies: a hardcover cookbook, a variety of teas and coffees, two mugs, Italian biscotti and a simple wedding card without too much heartfelt sentiment. She didn't want to come across as phony. She signed it, *With sincere wishes for a wonderful life together. Charlotte Sinclair.* Just as she finished, Birdie pulled up in her maroon Cadillac.

Rain on your wedding day was said to symbolize good luck. Charlotte hoped that was the case for Jack and Ruth Marie, but it still felt wrong somehow. Not to mention, she'd brought her cashmere sweater but hadn't thought to bring her raincoat.

Charlotte tuned out Birdie's yammering as they crossed the bridge to Katu Island. She remembered the last time she was there with Jack. The beach, the sunset, the turtles, stories of his childhood, alligators eating marshmallows. Birdie's tires crunched along the road, the rain already forming puddles in the gravel. Just like the rainy day she met Will. She might be mad at him, but she had to admit she missed his hugs. There was something about him that made her feel like everything would be okay, like he would keep her safe.

She shook her head. What a stupid notion. Nothing had been alright with Will. He was mean and greedy and she wanted nothing to do with him. Or his dimple. Or his slightly crooked bottom teeth. *Dammit.*

Birdie didn't notice. She was still talking to the air around her as she drove past the entrance to Virginia's house and turned left onto a narrow road. At the end of the lane was a small church that, according to Birdie, had been built by some ancient Buchanan forefather. She parked her Cadillac next to a tree and they both climbed out. Charlotte looked around the grounds of the small, white, steepled church surrounded by now-familiar live oaks draped with

Spanish moss. Behind it, a gently rolling lawn led to the ocean. The vast greenness made her want to run barefoot to the sand, skip the wedding entirely, and relax to the sound of the waves.

Pulling her sweater over her shoulders, she linked her arm through Birdie's. It wasn't raining anymore, and she understood what the locals meant when they said, "If you don't like the weather, wait an hour." The white double doors were swung wide open, revealing a large room lined with twelve rows of wooden pews and an aisle in the middle leading to a small altar. Every empty space was filled with hundreds of white flowers, white candles, and white paper lanterns. The effect was a stunning, glowing ambience. A groomsman asked, "Bride or groom?" and Charlotte panicked.

"Groom," Birdie interjected.

Charlotte started toward the last pew in the back of the church. But Birdie had a different plan. She pulled both the groomsman and Charlotte to the second row from the front. Charlotte took the interior seat, allowing Birdie the aisle, hoping to use her as a shield. To Charlotte's right, standing in a group with the other groomsmen in the front of the church, was a very familiar head and broad shoulders. Will. Her heart lurched and she looked down, trying to hide her face.

The string quartet played a rendition of "I Love You, Truly" while Crickley's elite made their way to their seats.

Charlotte didn't belong here. She looked back to see if she could sneak out and wait for Birdie in the car. But it was too late. The groomsmen took their cue and formed a line by the raised altar, facing the audience. Pastor Ashby Crane stood in the middle. Out of the corner of her eye, she noticed a door on the side of the church to her right. It opened and Jack walked in. He looked directly at her, like she was the only person in the church, smiled warmly and walked the short distance to the altar. When she turned her head forward, she noticed Will watching her from the stage. His brow was furrowed, and he looked uncomfortable in his formal wear. Charlotte grabbed onto Birdie's forearm. She just needed something real. Someone stable. Birdie patted her hand distractedly.

When the last of the attendants were in place by the altar, the music switched abruptly to the traditional bridal chorus from Lohengrin. Ruth Marie and a tall, good-looking man, presumably her father, appeared at the back of the church. She was ethereal, with an expression of absolute certainty as she glided down the aisle in a simple form-fitting white satin scoop-neck gown. Not an unintended bump could be seen. Her short blonde hair was curled and decorated with perfectly placed rhinestones and pearls, covered by a fingertip veil and short blusher draped over her glowing face. From her hands spilled a bouquet of white lilies and roses. Her eyes never left Jack.

The ceremony took all of ten minutes. Afterward, the

guests drove to Buchanan Manor and formed a line to congratulate the bride and groom, who stood in the foyer flanked by Ruth Marie's parents and one perturbed-looking Virginia Buchanan. Charlotte held tight to Birdie's arm. It never occurred to her that there might be a receiving line, and the thought of coming face-to-face with Jack and Ruth Marie made her want to hit something. Bracing herself, she moved slightly behind Birdie, enough that she felt somewhat hidden. Birdie never stopped yapping at the woman in front of her.

By the time they were only one guest away, Charlotte's heart was pounding so hard, she was afraid she wouldn't be able to hear what they said for the whooshing in her ears. She glanced down the line at Ruth Marie, accidentally catching her eye. Damn. She couldn't sneak away now. Ruth Marie's expression stayed fixed in an obliging smile toward the person in process of congratulating her. A few minutes later, it was their turn.

"Mr. and Mrs. Wallace, Mother, Ruth Marie, you all know Ms. Birdalee Mudge," Jack said by way of introduction. Birdie shook hands with Ruth Marie and the Wallaces, winking to Virginia. "And this is Charlotte Sinclair." Jack shot Charlotte a look of gratitude.

Really? He was looking at her as if she had already forgiven him. *How dare he?*

"Glad you made it," Ruth Marie said through her perfectly painted lips and sparkly, straight teeth. Instead of shaking Charlotte's hand, she pulled her into a gentle hug.

Charlotte half-heartedly returned the hug before pulling away. She stuffed her confusion and forced a smile. "Thanks. Me, too."

Ruth Marie leaned in to whisper in Charlotte's ear as if they were old friends. "We have lots to talk about. We'll find you later." *She must be earning equity for something big.* There was no good reason for her to be that nice. Charlotte then shook Ruth Marie's parents' hands and turned to Virginia, only to find her distracted by another guest.

The whole encounter left her off-balance. Frowning, Birdie took her by the arm and led her into the kitchen where they squished themselves into the butler's pantry to keep out of the way of the help. "You're shaking like a willow tree in a windstorm," she said, holding Charlotte by the shoulders. "What on earth did Ruth Marie whisper to you?"

"Something about having a lot to talk about."

"What could Ruth Marie possibly have to talk to you about? And on *her* most special day."

"I should be asking you!" Charlotte was exasperated. "I have no idea. The only thing I know for sure right now is that I shouldn't be here."

"Sugar honey iced tea," Birdie cussed. "Stay here." She moved past her like a frazzled mother hen. "I gotta go find Ginny."

Charlotte stood bewildered in the kitchen for a few

minutes before grabbing a glass of red wine and moving herself to the sunroom. As soon as she walked in, she wanted to turn around and walk back out. Will sat in a wicker chair in the corner, chatting animatedly to a buxom blonde who reminded Charlotte of Barbie or a cheerleader or a stripper or all three mixed together. As soon as he caught sight of her, he half stood from his chair, but then sat back down and reengaged in his conversation. Charlotte turned around the way she'd come, walked too quickly through the door, and with a bump, ran directly into Virginia. The contents of Charlotte's wineglass landed squarely on the front of Virginia's dress.

Virginia yelped like an angry peacock and fixed furious eyes on Charlotte. Charlotte gasped. *Oh good God. No.* She stood frozen, horrified. In a flash, Will was beside her. From the corner of her eye, she saw his arm jerk forward. Virginia screeched again. Louder this time. Did he? *Oh my God, he did.* Whatever had been in Will's glass was now covering Virginia's bodice and dripping down her leg. Charlotte slapped her hand over her mouth. She hadn't meant to laugh, but it was all so absurd. It couldn't truly be happening. Will was apologizing to Virginia, offering to pay for her dress, behaving like a gentleman who would never, under any circumstances, purposefully drench a woman.

"Oh my word, oh my word. Lord have mercy, Lord have mercy." Birdie rushed to Virginia's side, ushering her toward the back staircase. "We'll fix it. We'll fix it." Charlotte laughed harder that Birdie was saying everything in twos. "Your hair still looks good. You still got your hair, honey," Birdie desperately reassured Virginia as the two of them escaped. The attention had been successfully removed from Charlotte.

Charlotte had trouble controlling herself. She was laughing like a crazed maniac. Remembering a nearby powder room, she jogged for the door, jumped inside, and locked it. Catching her breath, she looked around the hunter-green and maroon bathroom. An oil painting of British gentry on a foxhunt hung above the toilet. She nearly howled again. Who did Virginia think she was?

Forcing herself to breathe through her nose, she dabbed her eyes with a tissue drenched in cold water. Finally, after several minutes, the exhale to end the madness broke loose and the laughter stopped, leaving a pit in her stomach the size of a granite quarry. Truly, she was cursed. Had that really just happened? Her life was completely out of control. Nothing in Crickley made sense, and everything she did went hideously wrong. She wanted to go home. She hated Virginia and Jack and Will and the stupid island and the stupid house and...

"Nothing's as bad as all that." It was her mother's voice. "Pull yourself together, love. You've got things to do."

Charlotte sniffed and stood up straight, grimacing at her red face in the mirror. She took a few deep breaths and sat on the closed commode, clearing her mind and focusing on her breathing. When her face was a normal color again, she stepped outside. She had to find Will and thank him, then force Birdie to take her home.

Will was easy to spot. He was in the hallway, attached to the blonde Barbie look-alike. Well, maybe not attached. She had her hand on his bicep in a flirty, territorial way, tipping her large chest toward him. Charlotte wanted to gag. What Will did when he threw his drink on Virginia was incredibly selfless, but she wasn't about to thank him in the middle of his burgeoning big-breasted association. She turned and walked in the opposite direction.

The party was in full swing by the time Charlotte saw Birdie again. She'd been forced to give up her search when she was waylaid by Mayor Compton and was now his guest in the grand dining room having a piece of chocolate groom's cake. He was holding court, deep into a lengthy lecture on the virtues of gaming casinos, when Birdie and Virginia walked in. Virginia wore a light blue dress similar to the one she'd worn at the crab cook. Both women looked very seriously at Charlotte. She tried to hide her discomfort with a large bite of cake and feigned interest in the mayor's story.

"Charlotte, may we have a word with you, please?" Virginia asked, interrupting the mayor without apology.

"Of course," Charlotte said, feeling like she'd just been summoned to the principal's office. The other guests went on about their business as if nothing had happened. On legs made of Jell-O, she crept behind them up the stairs to Virginia's bedroom, apologizing the whole way for spilling wine on Virginia's beautiful mother-of-the-groom's dress. When she stepped into the room, she was shocked to see Jack and Ruth Marie already there, sitting on the bed. Birdie walked to the reading chair, and Charlotte and Virginia remained standing.

Through the open entrance into the bathroom, Charlotte could see Virginia's ruined dress draped over the sink. It was as if they'd found the murder weapon and were about to confront her with it. Were *all* of them going to yell at her?

"Charlotte, dear," Virginia began, pacing. "We have something rather difficult to talk about."

"I'm so sorry. Please let me pay for the dress."

Jack stood. "Don't worry about that, Charlotte. This has nothing to do with the dress. To start out, it's my mother who owes *you* an apology." He shot a look at Virginia that told her she'd better behave.

Charlotte didn't want an apology from Virginia. She wanted to leave.

Virginia stared back at him. "Jackson. I believe you meant to say that Charlotte owes *me* an apology. She owes Ruth Marie an apology, too, for that matter."

Crap. Here we go.

"No, Mother. I meant exactly what I said."

"It's okay," Charlotte said. "I'm sorry. Really, I am." She was sorry—for ever being interested in Jackson Buchanan.

For moving to Crickley Creek. For coming to their damned wedding. For everything.

Jack shook his head at Charlotte. "Don't apologize." He moved to stand beside her, facing his mother. "You know damn well what you did, Mother."

"This must be about the rudeness," Birdie interjected. "Uh-huh. Yep, it's true, Ginny, you picked her out special the minute she got here."

Virginia glared at her and pursed her lips. "I did not pour wine on her dress, and I certainly did not try to seduce any son of hers. We are here to discuss Charlotte's actions."

"No, Mother," Jack said. "That was an excuse to get you in here. The truth is, you've been behaving badly, and you know it."

Virginia turned her narrowed eyes to her son. Then, quick as a flash, her face softened and her lips curled upward sweetly. "Y'all are hurting my feelings, now," she purred. "It's not fair to accuse a person in a group like this. Jackson, you and I will talk on our own." She moved toward him with a phony smile, her eyes demanding him to obey her, her voice singsongy and high-pitched. "Come on now, son. We'll talk in the office."

"Sorry, Mother. Every person in this room is here for a reason."

She stopped dead in her tracks. "No, son," she insisted, her voice an octave lower, her accent more pronounced. "You and I will speak privately." She moved toward the door. When Jack didn't follow, she turned and shot him a look hot enough to boil tar.

"Mother, you will walk back in here, shut your mouth, and listen."

Charlotte thought she was about to witness the spontaneous combustion of Virginia Buchanan. The woman practically vibrated. "You will not speak to me that way, young man."

"Yes, I will, Mother, and you will stand here and you will not interrupt."

Virginia's face burned deep red, and her lips visibly shook as she considered her options. Finally, she thrust forward her chin and stayed.

Charlotte stole a glance at Ruth Marie, who sat on the bed with a look of concern on her face. Jack turned to Charlotte, taking on the countenance of a prosecutor. "Let me back up a little, okay?"

She crossed her arms against her chest, anxious to figure out what the heck was going on with this screwy family and why she had to be a part of it.

"Alright then. Charlotte, do you remember how your hands seized up when you were sick?"

"Yes." Whatever. Did he need some big thank you for pretending to care about her when she had the flu? He wasn't going to get it. Hell, no.

"Well, the same thing happens to me," he said, holding up his hands for inspection. "Aside from myself and my dad, you're the only other person I've ever met whose hands seize up when they're nauseated."

What? She thought she was the only hand-seizer on the planet. Anyway, that was a nice piece of information, but pertinent *how*? She wished he would get to the point already.

Jack turned to the group. "Okay, I think everyone here would agree that my mother's been especially rude to Charlotte ever since she got here, right?"

"I have been nothing of the sort," Virginia began. "I will not stand for—"

"Fine, Mother," Jack interrupted. "Then you may sit."

Virginia, crimson, defiantly remained standing.

"You know, Mother," Jack said, "that from the minute you saw her, you were downright mean and vindictive. I saw how you treated her at the crab cook. I've heard you talk to your lady friends about her." He pointed at her. "You flat-out lied to me when you told me Mrs. Duckworth needed to speak to me."

Virginia put her hand to her chest as if she were physically wounded by his words. Stabbed in the heart.

Birdie mumbled, "This ain't looking good."

Virginia opened her mouth to protest; Jack motioned for her to close it. "You told Charlotte to stay away from me."

"I would never—"

Oh, yes you would.

"There is no excuse for your behavior, Mother."

Virginia huffed furiously.

Jack turned to Charlotte and carefully touched her arm. "You okay?"

"I think so." She'd be better if they'd let her leave now that the great truth about Mrs. Duckworth had been revealed. Unless there was more. For a crazy mind-spinning second, Charlotte thought maybe Jack was standing up to his mother in order to win her back. But that wouldn't happen on his wedding day. And his wife wouldn't be smiling.

Jack's voice still sounded like a lawyer's as he said to her, "You know that photo of you with your mom and dad in your bedroom? When you were sick, I had a lot of time to look at it." He paused. "Do you know why your mother left Crickley?"

"Well, like Birdie once said, she had too much potential to stay in a small town. She needed to spread her wings."

Birdie sat nervously picking at the hem of her skirt.

"Hmm," Jack said. "I got to wondering about why she left, so I got on the computer and found a copy of your birth certificate." He moved to the Buchanan family portrait hanging large above the stone opening of the fireplace and stood silently beneath the portrait of himself as a boy with his mother and father.

"There's no father listed on it."

The silence Jack allowed felt contrived, like those planned pauses trial attorneys used in order for the impact of their point to sink in. At the same time, a strange internal force began drawing Charlotte to the painting just as Jack stepped away from it. With a feeling of dread, she walked over, stood on her tiptoes, and squinted up at it.

Jack whispered, "Who's your biological father, Charlotte?"

"David Sinclair may be my stepfather," Charlotte said with more passion than she intended, "but he's the only one who matters." She tore her eyes away from the painting long enough to look straight into his.

"But he's not your biological father, is he?" The question was posed gently, but she wanted to punch him anyway.

"My mother always said he was a soldier on leave, a moment of weakness that ended in me. She didn't know his last name." Charlotte felt like she was on trial. "It doesn't matter, though. My dad is David Sinclair." As though drawn by a magnet, her eyes moved again to the tall man with brown hair and green eyes pictured a few feet from her head. Why hadn't she noticed it before? She inhaled deeply and couldn't release it any more than she could tear her attention away from the painting.

Bill Buchanan looked just like her. Jack's father looked just like her.

Virginia broke the silence. "Well, Bill's dead. And anyway, she couldn't possibly be his; the Buchanans haven't given birth to a girl since before the War of Northern Aggression. It simply can't be."

Charlotte's mind spun, connecting the dots.

"You reminded me of someone," Ruth Marie shared in

the midst of a reverie. "It took a while, but I finally figured it out. You reminded me of Jackson." Jack smiled proudly at his wife.

"Oh, precious girl," Birdie said, cooing her way over to Charlotte. "I'm so sorry." Birdie stood beside her, stroking her hair, *poor baby*ing her over and over. Charlotte pushed her hand away.

"Was this another one of your secrets, Birdie?"

Birdie scrunched her face. "No!"

"How could you not have known, Birdie? You were my mother's best friend."

"Well, I did think maybe you looked a little like Bill." She crinkled her nose and widened her eyes enough to succeed in appearing repentant.

"And you never said anything? How could you let things get this far?"

"Last I checked, I was not the information superhighway, for heaven's sake." Birdie put a hand to her forehead, sputtering, "And don't even think about blaming me for you and Jackson, because I was gone! I went on the cruise and that goll-danged Scruggs let Jack into your apartment and—"

"Birdie," Ruth Marie interrupted softly. "I don't think any of that is important now. Charlotte has a half-brother."

"Oh my God," Charlotte said, turning toward Jack. Oh. My. God. The lips she dreamed of kissing. The arms she longed to cuddle in to. What might have happened. What almost happened. He was her *brother*. She felt like a hot iron just pierced her heart. She would have to mentally scrub out every remnant of all the fantasies still too fresh in her mind. Thank God they never happened. She could barely catch her breath. She looked at Ruth Marie, who smiled carefully at her. No wonder Ruth Marie didn't hate her. Charlotte wasn't a threat at all.

"There is absolutely no truth to any of this." Virginia seethed in a strangely detached way, watching the scene as if it were a movie. "That girl is not my husband's kin. She is no part of this family. You can't prove it, and I won't allow it."

Jack moved before her. "She is, and you know it."

"I do not know it, Jackson." She pointed a finger into his chest. "Neither do you."

He took a step back. "Don't lie, Mother. You knew it from the moment you saw her. You knew she was Anna Grace's daughter and, as soon as you laid eyes on her, you knew she was a Buchanan, too. That's why you were nothing but awful to her at the crab cook."

Birdie fell back into the floral chair, legs straight out, a look of distress on her face.

"It was your hatred for Charlotte that gave you away, Mother. You knew the truth, and now, so do we."

"I will not have my good name sullied by some ridiculous person from, of all places, California. You," Virginia growled at Charlotte, "will leave this house immediately."

"She has just as much right to this house as we do," Jack said.

"Good name?" Charlotte pulled her shoulders back and took a step toward Virginia. "I would be a much better Buchanan than you."

"This family needs someone like her," Jack said.

Virginia's jaw dropped. Then she turned on the heels of her dyed silk shoes and walked proudly from the room.

Jack turned to Charlotte, taking her hands in his. "I'm so sorry, Charlotte. I'm sure this felt like an ambush, but I had to tell you this way."

Charlotte pulled her hands away.

"Look," Jack continued, "with all that's happened, either you wouldn't come or Mother wouldn't come if I tried to plan something. Ruth Marie came up with this idea, and it seemed like the only way. Plus, Mother won't do anything stupid if there's a crowd around." Jack turned to Birdie and Ruth Marie. "Y'all know she's heading down to the reception right now, acting like nothing's happened." Both girls nodded.

"I can't believe it," Birdie uttered. "Anna Grace gave up everything." She heaved her body out of the chair and walked to Charlotte, pulling her into a hug. "Are you okay, precious girl?"

She was simultaneously devastated, excited, and furious. "No. I'm not okay. I just found out who my biological father is." Her voice got louder and her sentences faster. "He should've known that I exist, at the very least. But he's dead." She sat on the chair Birdie just abandoned, her head in her hands. "He should be here to love me. He should be here to apologize to my mother. And he should be here to throw Virginia from an airplane over the South China Sea."

Birdie laughed, then smacked a hand over her mouth.

"And you," she pointed to Jack, "should have told me this sooner." She exhaled loudly. "And Mom. I hate being mad at her when she's not here to defend herself." Her voice cracked. "Why didn't she tell me? Did she give up everything because of me or because of him?"

The room was silent. Birdie contorted herself into a crouch so she could lay an arm over Charlotte's hunched shoulders. "Darlin', at least you have a brother."

Charlotte looked up at Jack, taking in his long legs, narrow waist, and broad smile.

He was her brother.

Chapter Twenty-Two

J ACK AND RUTH Marie eventually left to attend to their guests, and Charlotte tried to get Birdie to take her home. If Virginia came upstairs and physically tried to remove her from the house, Charlotte couldn't be responsible for what she did or said. But Birdie was far too revved up to leave, so Charlotte resigned herself to staying a little while longer. She took the opportunity to pump Birdie for information, and learned of the high school romance between Bill and Anna Grace and the jealousy Virginia harbored. The Buchanan and Parker families had been large South Carolina landowners for generations. Both claimed war heroes and old money—two things highly prized in social circles. Virginia and Bill were virtually promised to each other since birth by their families.

"You know, Virginia don't take kindly to losing," Birdie said. "Much as I love her, that girl was determined to win one way or another." She pursed her lips at the memory. "Your mama was beautiful, but she was only a first-generation resident of the South, and she had no money to speak of. Poor girl hardly stood a chance."

The knockout punch that won the fight was when Anna Grace earned a scholarship to the College of Charleston. She was leaving, and Bill would be staying to learn the family business. Bill and Virginia married quickly that summer, giving birth to Jackson seven months later. By then, Anna Grace had moved. But not to Charleston as planned. She'd gone to California.

Birdie looked like she was about to pop a brain vessel from thinking so hard. She was silent. Too silent. She stood and straightened her dress with a pull and a shimmy. "Hold up, Charlotte, I'll be right back."

Alone again, Charlotte stared at the portrait of Bill, Virginia, and Jack. She was part of that family. Impossible. She looked intently at Bill. They had the same green eyes, high cheekbones, and straight nose. Jack had his eyes, too, only the shape and definition of his face was completely Virginia's. She tried to imagine herself painted into the picture but couldn't quite see it. She didn't know those people.

She had to get out of here. Immediately.

She ran, nearly sliding down the back stairs, out of the sunroom, onto the vast green carpet of grass sloping down to the Atlantic. She wanted to run straight into that ocean; maybe a shock of wet and cold would blast all of the confusing emotions from her body and render her blissfully numb. Instead, her feet led her around the house to Birdie's car. It was, thankfully, unlocked. The passenger seat was cold, and she curled into it.

Charlotte nearly fell out of the car when Birdie opened the door she was leaning against. "Unless you were planning on a repeat of the day you met Will Rushton, I figured you'd come to my car rather than tryin' to walk to town. See, Ashby. I told you so." Birdie gripped Pastor Crane by the arm. "I have something to tell you," she said guiltily. "And Ashby's here because he used to be friends with Bill, and because I need me a little support." She squeezed his hand before transferring her hand to Charlotte's knee. "Honey, I promised your mother that I would never breathe a word about you to anyone. It was her secret to share, not mine."

Ashby looked at Charlotte sadly. "Please forgive Birdalee. This has been very hard on her."

"Pssshhhh," Birdie spat. "I deserve whatever she throws at me. I should've told her sooner." She put her face close to Charlotte's. "I never should have left on that cruise when it looked like Jack was taking a liking to you."

"Ya think?" Charlotte said, flabbergasted that Birdie would let things get this far.

"I am so, so, sorry," she began, her face scrunched up like she was trying to squeeze out a tear. "I tell you, I was just about fit to bust that day at Virginia's crab cook when you were talking to Jack. Mighty God in heaven, I had no idea what to do." She patted her heart like he was having palpitations. "But I've been holding on to this god-awful secret so long that I just kept my grip tight on it. Just like all those times that I wanted to tell your daddy about his daughter but never did."

Daddy? What a strange feeling to have Bill Buchanan attached to that word.

"I swear, this is the reason my hair is turning gray. I blame it for my crow's feet, too." Birdie teetered, then fell onto her rear. "Help me up, Crane." Ashby heaved until Birdie was back on her feet, huffing and puffing.

Ashby filled in while Birdie caught her breath. "Bill loved your mother. There was no doubt about that. But he was a teenage boy just like the rest of them. And that Virginia, she was a game player, persistent as a danged horsefly and willing to lie and—well, let's just say *use what God gave her* to get her man. She thought she had him by rights."

Charlotte flinched when she caught sight of Middie walking toward them, out of breath. "Hey y'all. You really ought to get out of here. Mrs. Buchanan is on a tear."

"Middie, you just do your best to keep that woman in the house," Birdie ordered. "We're not done here yet."

"I'll do my best," said Middie, "but don't blame me if she finds you."

"Good Lord, that woman is a curse," Birdie said. "We'll be quick about it."

"Listen. It was Bill's parents who told him Virginia was pregnant." She stared at Charlotte as if waiting for a light to turn on. "Virginia went to Bill's parents before she told him. He had no choice but to do the right thing."

Charlotte shuddered at Virginia's unbounded selfishness.

"Bill was as torn up about it as an old roof in a tornado. He took responsibility, of course, but I can tell you his heart wasn't in it. And then, when Anna Grace took off to California without so much as a word, it was all he could do not to follow her. It was the baby, not Virginia, who kept him here." Birdie wiped at a nonexistent tear.

"Awful, I say." Ashby swept back what few strands of hair remained on his head. "I just hate reliving it."

"I tried so hard to get her to stay." Birdie flapped her hands toward her chest to emphasize her innocence. "But the stakes were too high, and I don't just mean her reputation. Let us not forget that the Buchanan and Parker families were real powerful in these parts back then. No telling what they would have done."

"So, they were both pregnant," Charlotte said, thinking out loud. "Virginia just told him first."

"Yep," Ashby and Birdie said in tandem.

"By the time your mama found out she was pregnant, Bill and Virginia were already two weeks into planning their wedding," Birdie said. "It was all anyone talked about. I tell you, Anna Grace looked like some sort of hollowed-out shell of a person. Her eyes were so puffy and dark from crying all the time, if I didn't know better, I'd have thought she'd been punched. She was only eighteen, Charlotte. She made me swear I'd never tell anyone, especially Bill." Birdie fanned herself.

Ashby's narrow face seemed to grow longer as he put his

chin to his chest, either reflecting on something or pulling himself together. When he looked up again, his eyes were moist. "Now, I didn't know this at the time, but your grandparents, rest their souls, sent her to California in order to give up the baby, to save her reputation. Charleston was just too close. That's how things were done in those days."

Birdie stepped partially in front of Pastor Crane and bent down for effect. "There is no way on God's green earth that Anna Grace would ever give away her baby, and hell if she'd come back and live in the shadow of Bill and Virginia. She was awfully mad at her folks for suggesting it."

"Yeah," Charlotte said, "but most families get over that stuff. I mean, most families forgive each other."

Ashby moved Birdie aside. "Whatever mistakes Anna Grace made are hers. Just like whatever mistakes your grandparents made are theirs. Your job is to do better than them. You have to make sure you don't pass on those generational sins to your children, God willing." He looked her straight in the eye. "You will never send someone you love away. You will never be that stubborn. You will never keep such a secret."

"Amen to that," Birdie said.

Charlotte sniffed. "So, Mr. Buchanan never knew my mother was pregnant."

Birdie fanned herself. "Y'all are makin' me sweat. There's just so much to it all. Who knows what those Buchanans would have done if they'd found out. I mean, heck, they might have been able to take that baby away if they'd wanted to. Right, Ashby?"

He nodded. "Those folks knew every judge in at least four counties."

Birdie abruptly turned toward the house, as if she heard a sound. Charlotte inhaled sharply, having been so caught up in the story that she almost forgot Virginia was still nearby. They all watched the front door intently for a few seconds. Finally, when Birdie was satisfied no one was there, she went on. "Think about it. As far as the Buchanans were concerned, Bill was doing what they'd always expected him to do; he was marrying Virginia. Everything was peaceful until the townsfolk did the math and figured out that Virginia had a full-sized baby after only seven months. Good Lawd, Ashby, d'you remember the scandal? Bless his bones, Bill just sat tight and acted like a happily married man. Did a good job of it, too. Fooled me."

"At the very least, when Mama found out she was dying, she should've told me about my dad," Charlotte said.

"She knew she wouldn't be around to pick up the pieces," Birdie said. "She couldn't allow Virginia into your life if she wasn't going to be around to protect you. I'm sure she thought it was better this way."

"But you, Birdie. After all the talks we've had. Why didn't you tell me right away? Why did you wait so long? How am I supposed to trust you? What else are you hiding?"

"Do I look like I can keep more than one big secret?

Good Lord, it nearly killed me." She patted down her wide skirt and turned, giving no time for an answer. "Alright, Ashby, you can go now," Birdie said, shooing at him. "I'm gonna take this child home before Virginia gets a hold of her again."

Charlotte was exhausted. More than anything, she wanted to crawl into her bed and sleep for a week.

Ashby awkwardly patted Charlotte on the shoulder. "Hang in there. God's got a plan for you."

So far, I'm not sure I like it.

Chapter Twenty-Three

BIRDALEE MUST HAVE been working the phones all Sunday, because Monday morning, business at Tea and Tennyson increased tenfold. Townsfolk who would never dream of walking into a bookstore came to get a look at Charlotte Sinclair, bastard child of Bill Buchanan. Most of them showed enough kindness to judge her surreptitiously, and left her alone to do her job. Others must have graduated from the Birdie School of Social Awareness—they came right out and asked about it.

Pamela LeBaron asked, "So, Charlotte, how're you feeling? I've been worried about you, what with finding out about your dad and all." She lifted her eyebrows and tilted her head in mock concern. "Why don't you tell me all about it?" There was Susie Herring, who asked, "So, Charlotte, what do you think about having a claim to Katu? Are you gonna get your rightful portion?" The Reichert twins, Holly and Noelle, danced into the store. "We know we haven't met you yet, but we just want to hug your neck! Congratulations! You're so lucky!" As if Charlotte just won entrance into the social class envied by the majority of Crickley Creek.

It was a rough couple of days. Charlotte knew Birdie hadn't meant any harm, kicking off the gossip chain. It would have happened anyway, just slower. This way, Charlotte would be the object of intense interest for a week or two and then everyone would move on to the next scandal.

Scruggs, however, was furious. He made no bones about it. In typical Scruggs fashion, when Birdie walked into the store, he snuck to the back door and let Waffles in. That dog loved to bark at Birdie as much as Scruggs loved to annoy her. Birdie finally got smart and threw the dog bits of her cookie, which Waffles ate with relish, forgetting to keep yapping. "Better than a hush puppy," Birdie beamed. "And it should make her good and gassy, too."

By the time Charlotte closed the store and went upstairs, she felt like she'd just endured the stockade. She listened to the messages on her cell phone—one from Will, checking to see how she was holding up. It was the second message he'd left, and she felt guilty for not returning the first one.

Even though she was furious with Birdie, she needed her. She would ask her to let everyone know that she'd return their calls later when life wasn't so complicated, when she could actually make it through a day without tormenting herself over what her mother never told her, what her father never knew, and what she'd dreamed of creating with a man who turned out to be her half-brother. Her chest tightened like a wrung-out dishrag. Would she ever recover from the possibility that something…something—she couldn't bear to even think the word *sexual*—could have happened with Jack? She felt cold all over.

The next message was from Ruth Marie, checking in from her honeymoon in Hawaii. "Jack would really like to talk to you," she said. "We both hope you're doing okay." Charlotte saved the message. It was like history repeating itself: Jack married the acceptable girl, the one he'd been expected to marry since he was old enough to date. At least, unlike Virginia, Ruth Marie was nice. Another day or two, then she'd talk to them. She wasn't ready yet; the seesaw of emotions still had her off-kilter and hypersensitive. She'd have Birdie contact them and explain that she'd be in touch soon. It would be terrible to have people think her rude on top of everything else.

Friday rolled around, and Charlotte was exhausted. She'd spent a lot of time near the back staircase so she could run up to her loft if anyone she didn't want to deal with walked in. Even Will was in the store several times, looking for her.

On Monday, she was wholeheartedly sad, bordering on depressed, but four days later, she was leaning more toward happy. After all, she'd gained a lot of what she'd been searching for. She knew more about her mother and more about herself. Slowly, the mysteries that defined her mother's life had been uncovered. There was peace in that. Plus, she had a brother now. With some time and luck, that might turn out to be good. Her dead father and angry stepmother, on the other hand, were an entirely different issue. Charlotte turned the sign on the front door to CLOSED.

Scruggs and Waffles went home, leaving Krista to put the leftover pastries into boxes. Every Friday, Krista dropped them off at a local church. Charlotte was almost finished straightening the bookshelves when she noticed Krista walking toward the restroom, talking on her cell phone with a serious intensity. She tried to give her some privacy and went back to lining up the books. Several minutes passed before Krista reappeared looking haggard.

"Krista, are you okay?"

"Yeah, I guess. Something happened, and I kinda need to get home quick."

"Of course," Charlotte said. "No problem. Go on home." She waved toward the front door. "I'll take the pastries to First Baptist. You just take care of yourself."

"Thanks," Krista said. But she made no move to leave.

"Are you sure you're okay? Do you want to talk?"

"Charlotte"—Krista wrung her hands and stared at the floor—"please don't hate me."

"Hate you? Never. You and Scruggs are the only reasons I'm in business." Hopefully, Krista recognized that she truly meant the compliment. "Don't worry about leaving me here. I'll handle the rest."

"Thanks." Krista smiled weakly. "It's not that. I guess I'm just upset. That was my cousin calling to tell me Randy's in jail. I'm meeting my aunt down at the station 'cause my mama has to stay with my little brother, Zach."

"Oh, Krista, I'm sorry to hear it." Even if she was relieved to know Randy was locked up.

"Yeah. I guess it happened this afternoon. Something about stealing from the business, which Randy says he didn't do." Krista wiped her nose with a fistful of tissues. "Stealing from the business is stealing from the family, you know."

Charlotte reached out and touched her shoulder. No one got to choose their family.

"I'm so tired of my family being the losers in this town," Krista said. "And Randy has all kinds of excuses for why the company was failing—most of them having to do with Will trying to take him down. But now that I think about it, it was probably more about Will whoopin' up on him on the high school football field or dating the prettiest girl in school or doing something or other that Randy was wishing he could do. Truth is, Rushton Construction got into the home-building business, and all of a sudden, everybody said they did a better job and that this town needed the competition and all. I've had to spend my whole life as a Hassell; you'd think I'd know better by now."

Charlotte felt her face burn hot.

"But," Krista said, "Randy got Jack to be his lawyer. I mean, Jack wouldn't defend Randy if he actually did it. Right?"

What? Jack was on his honeymoon. Had Randy tracked him down to Hawaii?

Krista apologized at least three more times before leaving

to see her cousin. Charlotte tried to make sense of it all. Why would Jack represent someone like Randy? Especially if Will was involved. It couldn't be possible.

Also, she might be wrong about Will. It wasn't like she'd never been stupid and pig-headed before. If she were honest with herself, she'd never given Will the benefit of the doubt and, even worse, was always quick to believe every bad thing said about him. Could it be that all the time she spent questioning his integrity was because of some vendetta Randy had about Will being a better athlete in high school? Or getting some girl? That would be ridiculous. That would make her ridiculous. She put the last apple blossom in the box next to a stack of organic oatmeal raisin cookies.

This time, she was going to get the truth.

Charlotte closed the store and walked to her car, carrying two large boxes of leftovers, reliving her date with Will at the Loggerhead Festival. He'd been patient with her when she accused him, not defensive like a guilty man would have been. How had she not seen that before? And he didn't make a single excuse. He must have known that she was too emotionally wound up to accept an explanation. Clearly, he had her figured out. At the time, it made her furious, like he had no regrets and no time to try to explain it to her—but maybe his answer had more integrity than she realized. He was taking responsibility for whatever his part was. He wasn't trying to blame someone else. He didn't beg her to stay, either. And while that hurt her feelings a little, she couldn't help but respect him for it.

Once in the driver's seat, she pulled out her cell phone and dialed Jack's number.

His voice came loudly over the phone. "Hey, Charlotte. You okay?"

"Yes. Yes, I'm fine. I'm so sorry for bothering you on your honeymoon."

"No problem, sis."

In the world of talkers, Charlotte was a condenser rather than expander. "I need to ask you about Randy Hassell. Krista just told me some stuff I want to verify."

Charlotte thought she could hear Ruth Marie in the background. "Verify away," Jack said.

"Is it true that you're defending him?"

"What? No, of course not. I don't even talk to Randy Hassell."

"I thought so. Can you tell me, did Will ever do anything to him?"

"Like what? Throw the ball to a better receiver? Fix the homes Randy screwed up?"

"I was afraid you'd say that."

She heard the tiniest of sounds, most likely Jack grinding his teeth. "Look here–Randy Hassell is a low-down, lazy crook. That boy used cheap materials and scrimped on darn near everything, charging folks too much for shoddy homes and refusing to fix them when they broke. He needed to be put out of business." He sighed loudly. "Lying bastard."

She leaned her head against the steering wheel and closed her eyes. "I'm such a freaking idiot."

"What are you talking about?"

"It's just that Krista told me some stuff about Will that I believed. Long story. Anyway, now I'm wondering if maybe I haven't been fair to him. I screwed it all up."

"I'm sure you didn't screw anything up. Will's a very logical, understanding kind of guy. He'll forgive you. And if you're worried about some story Randy Hassell cooked up about him, let me just go ahead and reassure you right now. I've been through hell and back with Will. We went to war together. I've seen him so dead dog tired he was hallucinating. I know who he is in his core, and I can tell you he's solid. There's no one I'd rather have my back than Will Rushton. And that's the gospel truth."

Jack paused. "This is what's been holding you back?" He chuckled. "Sister, git your skinny behind over to Will's house."

"Oh, please. That is completely out of the question." He was probably out with that big-boobed Barbie doll chick. "The last person he'd want to see is me." It was too late. It had to be. She'd been too much of a self-centered shrew.

Jack chuckled. "Charlotte. Aside from his family, I probably know Will better than anyone else." There was certainty in his voice. "Whatever it is you did, he'll forgive you."

"He shouldn't. I am officially the biggest loser on the planet."

"No, I already won that title." She caught the innuendo and appreciated it.

"No way. Uh-uh. I can't just show up at his house unannounced." She might not have reconciled the idea in her mind, but in her heart, she knew. She was going. "I don't even know where he lives."

"Take Bayfront Drive all the way down until you get to the most beautiful antebellum home. You can't miss it. It belongs to Will's folks. You'll take the gravel road to the left of the house all the way down to the water. The house on the water belongs to Will—built it himself. You'll know it when you see it."

"I don't know."

"Look. Will sided with you against my mother. He wouldn't risk being ostracized by society unless he was hoping for something long-term."

Charlotte sat shaking in her car. At the very least, she had to pull herself together enough to deliver the pastries to the church. One thing at a time. She looked at herself in the rearview mirror and smoothed her hair. Starting the car, she sat there until she felt calm enough to drive.

Chapter Twenty-Four

T HE JETTA SEEMED to drive itself. She couldn't say if she stopped at stop signs or held to the right side of the road. Her mind was completely overtaken with thoughts of Will. The day he rescued her from the island, something about him had drawn her in, a magnetism, an appeal, an allure so strong, the temptation beneath it felt somehow frightening. She wouldn't give him an inch because—because what? Because she was afraid of loving him? Or because she would have to give up control?

Just looking at him made her feel anxious. He had the power to hurt her by virtue of her attraction to him. His personality only added to it; how he challenged her way of thinking, made her laugh and didn't take himself too seriously. When he took her crabbing, everything she did seemed to please him. He'd loved showing her new things, like blue crabs hanging from a chicken leg, like tight abs and wide shoulders...

She gripped the steering wheel. *Stop thinking about that. You can't be in that frame of mind when you see him.* She forced herself to move her mind forward. Those delicious crabs, the bond he had with the fishermen. Those men didn't suffer fools. Why hadn't she taken that into account?

And that kiss.

Dammit, Charlotte. You are going to the man's house alone at night. You are going to apologize. That's all. She opened her eyes extra wide, trying to distract herself with scenery, but there was none, only asphalt and the double yellow line marking a two-lane road. It was dark, and there were no streetlights.

His lips. His body pressed against hers. She'd barely recognized herself during that scary, passionate, world-spinning, had-to-have-every-inch-of-him kiss. No one had ever come close to stirring up feelings that intense. Remembering made her heart beat like a rabbit's, so fast her vision began to blur. She squinted at the road ahead and forced herself to breathe slowly.

Inhale in. Exhale out. Breathe in. Breathe out. He could have taken it further. He could have thrown her into his truck, tried to get her to do things she would later regret. His hands could have wandered. But they didn't. She smiled at the thought of his face when she agreed to go to the Loggerhead Festival. His white teeth, his dimple. How big and strong his hand felt when he held hers in the woods.

She was the one who got mad when he tried to stand up for her, when he went off after Randy. And she was the one who got mad when he thought better of it. The memory of the powdered sugar funnel cakes on the floor of the old log cabin almost made her cry. She was the ogre. How could she not see that? He never raised his voice with her, only calmly tried to reassure her.

All this time she'd been blaming him and he was the one who should have been running the other way.

It was like she finally opened the door and all the truths she worked so hard to ignore ran through her mind, turning on all the lights.

A drive that took ten minutes felt more like ten seconds. She wasn't prepared to be here as she turned onto Bayfront Drive. What would she say? What if he told her to go away? Her heart was too hopeful, too contrite, to handle such a reaction. All the repressed feelings pulsed through her body. Even her fingertips had a heartbeat. She could barely endure the longing.

One way or another, tonight, she would find out where she stood with Will Rushton.

In the distance, Charlotte could see that the road ended in a cul-de-sac. Flanking a brick-lined driveway at the top of the circle were two rows of live oaks, and just like any movie-worthy Southern estate, at the end of the road was a veritable castle. No wonder Jack was astonished when she realized Charlotte had no idea where Will's parents lived. Their home was a tree-lined oasis, a house done more in the Federal style than Virginia's overstated Greek Revival mansion. The lights were on in the windows where black shutters were permanently fixed open as if to welcome guests or interested passersby. Like a mouse hole in a giant red brick wall, the single black front door stood highlighted by a semi-circular fanlight above. Wisteria, gardenia, and azalea wrapped the base of the home like a fancy cake plate. To the left was a smaller gravel driveway, just like Jack said there would be. Slowly, Charlotte turned the car down the drive, her head spinning along with her tires.

It was a surprisingly long drive to Will's house. The road turned from gravel to well-packed dirt as she entered the densely wooded forest. She drove slowly, keeping her eyes focused ahead. When the road began a slight decline and the trees cleared, she gasped. The moon shimmered off the deep water of the Atlantic, spotlighting Will's wooden cabin like a lighthouse. Nestled cozily in the woods, the reddish planks matched the trees and the wrap-around porch was like an invitation to stay awhile. The tall, pitched roof and perfect angles looked like work only Will could do. It hardly seemed real; like it was made out of candy and a witch would meet her at the door.

Charlotte pulled her car alongside Will's truck and turned off the engine. Opening the car door, she sat for a moment, listening for a clue as to whether Will knew she was here. The only sound was the distant whooshing of waves on the beach and the crickets, cicadas, and frogs singing their night chorus. *This is stupid.* She stepped out of the car. *He doesn't know I'm coming. I could get myself shot.* She slammed her door shut and stood motionless, waiting for Will to run outside with a shotgun. Too late to turn back now.

Bravely, she walked onto the veranda. There were potted flowers on either side of the front door. She giggled nervously at the feminine touch while her heart thudded against her chest, driving blood into her face as she knocked. Cooling her hot cheeks with her cold hands, she waited. After standing, trembling, for a full minute, she pressed the doorbell. The chime rang clearly inside the house, but she heard no sounds of movement. Nothing. Not the sound of a television or footsteps coming to the door. But his truck was here, and the lights on the other side of the house appeared to be on. He had to be nearby. She rang again.

Just as she turned to walk back to her car, she heard the sound of claws clicking, then scraping on wood. She turned around just in time for a fuzzy brown-and-white dog to jump up, desperately trying to stretch high enough to lick her face. Off-balance, she shrieked and nearly fell over. The dog sat, as if on command, his stubby tail thumping furiously against the wooden planks. Charlotte scratched his head and smiled at his furry face. Could it be? Will appeared from the side of the house, looking taller than ever from her vantage point. He stopped and stared at her.

"Your house is w-w-wonderful," Charlotte stuttered, her voice sounding strange to her ears.

One corner of his mouth smiled. "Thanks." The puppy ran circles around them. They remained silent, watching, until the dog finally sat again.

"Is that the dog from Katu?" Charlotte asked.

"Yeah." His cheeks looked as red as hers felt. "I named him Lucky."

He'd grown so much. "You rescued him."

"I bought him." He bent down and scrubbed the dog once on the back. "Virginia was never crazy about Bill's dogs; not sure why she's still having them bred. Anyway, she got her price."

Charlotte bent to scratch behind Lucky's ears. Did she have anything to do with him owning this dog? "Thank you," she whispered, perhaps too gratefully.

"Please don't thank me." Will sounded serious. Too serious.

She stood to face him.

"How can I help you?" he asked.

This was going to be harder than she thought. "I owe you an apology." His face relaxed a little, which gave her just enough courage to gush forth. "I was horrible and stupid and wrong. I totally misjudged you."

There was no smile. "Charlotte, stop."

"I knew in my heart you were not a bad person," she went on. "Really, I did. I think maybe I was trying to protect myself from any more pain in my life, and so I latched on to the opinion of someone else and made that my excuse for pushing you away. It was wrong of me."

"Charlotte." Will's voice was deeper and louder. "Stop."

She looked up at him, dazed, rewinding everything she'd

just said to see where she messed up. His next words stabbed her in the heart. "I'm not your consolation prize."

"Of course not," she stammered. "I was just confused."

"Yes, I believe that's true. I also think you are still confused. It's too soon for you to know how you feel about me. You just got a shock like none other, and now you're reaching for a life preserver." He stood tall and firm. "Look, I know how I feel about you, okay? And I know how I want you to feel about me. But you just went from zero to sixty in about a day. I'm not gonna let you, or me, get yanked around any more than we already have been."

"But that's just it. I realize how wrong I've been. Whatever games we were playing are over. That's why I'm here. To set things straight."

He bit his lower lip and, for the first time, she noticed he hadn't shaved, his hair was tousled, and he was wearing an old ARMY T-shirt in lieu of his usual button-down. "I need you to be sure." He looked like he needed a good eight hours of sleep.

"It's you," she promised, moving closer. "It's always been you, I just didn't know what 'brother' felt like until now. It was easy with Jack, comfortable. It's different with you."

Will took a step backward. "Jack or no Jack, you don't know me. You took little bits of information like, say, the fact that Randy Hassell hates me and I run a construction company and I can be a little sarcastic sometimes, and you added two and two together and got six. That person is not me."

"That's why I'm here. I talked to Jack and Ruth Marie tonight and, for the first time, I know exactly who you are." She felt her voice rise shrill in her throat.

"Charlotte, I've put a lot of thought into this, even talked to my mama and sisters about it, and here's what I've got: All this is too fresh for you right now. Surely, you can't even see straight for all you've been through recently. If I'm gonna call myself a man, I'm gonna have to back off and leave you alone."

She clenched her hands into fists. Tears burned in her eyes. She wiped at them madly.

"Listen, I'm doing my best to use my backbone instead of my wishbone, okay?" He shook his head sadly. "I'm trying to help you."

"I don't want you to help me. I want you to believe me." She was getting louder, stepping backward toward the porch stairs.

"Don't think for a second this isn't hard on me, too." He took a step toward her.

"What more can I do?" She stopped and threw her arms up. "I'm here, now, apologizing to you."

"Yes. And it's about damn time, too."

"So…"

"So, I'll wait you out. I happen to be stubborn enough to do it."

"This is not what I hoped for." Charlotte walked slowly

down the stairs and turned. "But if you need time, I'll give you time."

"No, *you* need time. And I'll give it to you."

She turned toward her car, mumbling. His heavy footsteps moved away, and Lucky's claws clicked behind him on the wood, then the front door shut. Her heart pulled with a longing she thought might kill her. She could barely manage to get the key into the ignition.

A sound came from inside the house, a loud knock, as if Will had kicked over a chair or punched a wall. She closed her door and drove home.

Chapter Twenty-Five

TEA AND TENNYSON was dark, full of sharp angles and creaking sounds. Lingering smells of coffee stuck in the air, this time stale and repulsive, not the welcoming smell of a warm morning brew. She dragged herself up the stairs, numb to her cozy apartment, numb to the yellow light in her bedroom. She went through the motions of washing her face, brushing her teeth, and putting on her flannel winter pajamas. Wind whistled through a crack in the seal of her bedroom window.

Not my consolation prize?

How could he say that? She shuffled to the kitchen, turning on lights, looking for duct tape to temporarily fix the window. She hadn't meant to choose Jack; it'd just worked out that way. The junk drawer had nothing better than Scotch tape.

I'm over it. I finally have my head on straight. Why can't Will understand that? Heck, I practically threw myself at him. Her cheeks flamed at the thought. And he'd turned her down. It was a sharp knife to her ego, a reminder that she had to protect herself. Only this time, she didn't want to.

She was ready to take a risk again. In her home office, she found a bottle of Elmer's glue. Squeezing hard, she spread it around the perimeter of the window like caulk. Miraculously, the whistling stopped.

If she could just get to sleep, things would surely look better in the morning. She snuggled into her soft mattress and pulled the floral covers underneath her chin, hoping the warmth and comfort would relieve her icy loneliness. Turning on her side and hugging her pillow, she tried to empty her head of thoughts of Will.

Sleep. Just sleep.

A vision of Lucky appeared beneath her closed eyelids. He was wagging at her arrival, nudging her leg with his nose, his brown-and-white face eagerly seeking her approval. She wanted nothing more than to snuggle into his fur and hold on tight.

Rain pelted her bedroom window, bringing with it the fury of a Southern storm, lightning flashing and thunder booming a mere second later. The window shook, and her glue sealant dissolved with the pounding rain, setting the wind free to whistle its victory through the cracks.

Charlotte gave up her bed and moved to the couch. The bedroom light illuminated the den enough to see, and frequent shocking flashes of white made the objects in the room shadowy and eerie. She shrouded herself in her mother's knit afghan, her eyes moving from the storm outside her big front window to where the firefly jar sat on the bookshelf. Despite the chaos outside, it sat calmly in the same spot as always, on the third shelf from the top, nestled in the corner by her favorite books.

Hopping up, she scooted in her blanket to the jar, picked it up gingerly, and carried it back to the couch. Turning it over on her lap, she examined every wing, every tiny head, every lovingly painted golden tail. Holding the cold glass to her lips, she kissed it, then unscrewed the cap and stuck her nose close enough to smell the tiniest hint of honeysuckle. The familiarity of the smell made her feel like a little girl, lonely and desperate for her mother.

"Mom, I'm trying to stop missing you so much." She placed the jar on her lap. "I messed things up with Will, and I need you here to talk to." A gust of wind sent rain beating into the front window, setting off a car alarm outside. She ignored it.

"I treated him like he was second best. I didn't trust him. I accused him of terrible things. And now that he's not sure about me, I've never been more sure about anything." She ran her finger across the raised word MASON, the same word that was on every jar of strawberry preserves her mother ever made. "I'm tired of being alone." She blinked back the tears brewing hot behind her eyes. "And I think I've spent too much energy on regrets." She carefully placed the jar on the coffee table by her knees. "I mean, I did the best I could at the time. And I know that you would want me to live my life and be happy."

She leaned back into the couch and looked up at the ceiling. The wind calmed, the bedroom window ceased its whistling, and the only noise was that car alarm sounding its siren on the empty street. Charlotte whispered, "We could have avoided a lot of this pain and confusion if you'd just told me about my dad."

With a crack and a percussion, the moment was gone and the cacophony outside began again. Eventually, the car alarm stopped and the wind died down. Charlotte flopped sideways on the couch and pulled the blanket up to her ears, staring at the jar on the table.

"I wish you were here." A weaker lightning flash cast a glow onto the firefly jar. The thunder never came. The storm was passing. She fell asleep.

Chapter Twenty-Six

L ATER THE NEXT week, Birdie entered the store like a meteor entering the atmosphere. She made a trail straight to the front window and oohed and aahed loudly over Charlotte's new display of classic books: Steinbeck, James, Faulkner, Austen, and, of course, poetry books by Tennyson. "The good dead ones," Birdie said.

She fingered the lace curtains framing the space, picked up a board printed in gold lettering, and announced, "I think Ms. Austen wrote this one for me. *It sometimes happens that a woman is handsomer at twenty-nine than she was ten years before.* Handsomer is such a nice word." Birdie replaced the card and picked up another. "*Under certain circumstances there are few hours in life more agreeable than the hour dedicated to the ceremony known as afternoon tea.* Now that Mr. James, he is a man after my own heart." She stuck the board back in place and picked up Charlotte's favorite by Sir Alfred, Lord Tennyson. She read, "*It is better to have loved and lost than never to have loved at all,*" and sighed happily. "I do love a good window treatment."

Charlotte was pleased to see Birdie flitting about. There

was something forgivable about the fact that Birdie had kept her mother's secret, even if she should have said something much, much sooner. Any piece of sunshine during that gray week was welcome. She hadn't called Jack to tell him that things blew up with Will. Ruth Marie left her a message, but Charlotte didn't feel up to returning the call. In the meantime, Krista refused to talk about Randy. Her hair and makeup were perfect, as usual, but she sulked around the store like a sloth. Adding to it all, the sky was overcast, the air wet, and it'd been windy the past two days. Charlotte hated wind. Bad mood was an understatement.

"How ya doin', sweetness?" Birdie asked Scruggs. Pigs must have been flying out of every pen for twenty miles.

He looked up from his coffee preparations, his eyebrows raised. "Ms. Birdalee."

"Don't y'all think it's just the most beautiful day?"

Scruggs shot Charlotte a *the lady done lost her mind* look. "Not really," Charlotte said. "It looks awful out there."

"Nothing an Early Birdie Special and some cookies won't fix." She snapped her fingers toward Scruggs.

Charlotte was intrigued. "What's going on, Birdie?"

"Oh, nothing to worry your pretty little head about. All is well with the Mudge household."

"Mudge household? You live alone."

"Yes. Yes, I do." Birdie walked closer to Scruggs and snapped her fingers again, this time about two inches from his nose. "One Early Birdie Special and three cookies, please."

Smirking with his whole face, Scruggs said sweetly, "How about a dead bird sandwich?"

"No thanks, I don't care for chicken." If she'd had long hair, she would have flipped it. Instead, she turned her head swiftly and her Aqua Net-sprayed helmet of hair went with it. Turning back briefly, she added, "Put a little extra sugar in that coffee drink, Scrappy."

He rolled his eyes and made a show of adding sugar to the drink.

Birdie put an arm around Charlotte, interrupting the customer who'd just come up to chat with her. "Excuse us," Birdie said to the patron as she pulled Charlotte away. She placed her nose next to Charlotte's ear and whispered, "So, has he?"

"Has who what?" Charlotte whispered back.

"Has Will been by to see you yet? I know you went to his house, because I saw his mama at the Piggly Wiggly, and she said she saw your car drive by. She said Will won't talk about it, but the boy's been downright grumpy for days." She opened her eyes as wide as Frisbees, clearly expecting an immediate answer.

"I'll tell you about Will if you tell me why you're in such a good mood."

"Why is it that you're concerning yourself with my state of well-being? I am just happy to be alive, alright? A girl is allowed to be in a good mood without people bugging the holy hell out of her for it." Birdie frowned. "Now tell me about Will."

"There's nothing to tell. We just need some time."

"Hmph." She glared. "Well, I'm sure you do. Um-hmm. You've got to get used to having a brother and all. Yep. But it's not like you kissed your brother or anything, right? I mean, Jackson told his mother and everybody else that nothing happened between you two. That should make things a *little* easier." Clearly, Birdie was more interested in confirmation of her statement than in trying to make Charlotte feel better.

Charlotte nodded. "Thank God nothing happened." She shot Birdie a look. "No thanks to you."

"Alrighty then." Birdie seemed relieved. "So, I might have bought all that 'I'm confused' hooey for a while. But it's been long enough. You and Will Rushton are perfect for each other, and what God hath brought together and all that crap."

Charlotte turned to face her. Might as well get it over with. "He turned me down, Birdie. Now that I'm no longer confused, he is." Her voice cracked.

Birdie rolled her eyes. "Oh, *please*, stop feeling sorry for yourself. I know you both better than you know yourselves. I'm gonna have a word with that boy." She winked. "You ain't seen nothing 'til you've seen Birdalee Mudge get things moving in the romance department."

"Please don't get involved, Birdie," Charlotte said. "The

last thing I need is for this to be like high school with you running over to tell him I like him and that he should like me back. Just leave him alone."

"Oh, relax yourself. I happen to be an expert in this particular area."

"Birdie, no." As much as she loved Birdie, her forcefulness was about as welcome as a hangnail.

"Don't underestimate me, child." Birdie squeezed Charlotte's shoulders. "Now, how're we gonna get that boy in here?"

"We're not."

"I can't believe he hasn't called you yet. How long's it been since you heard from him now? Four days?" She wrinkled her nose. "Shoot."

"It doesn't matter. I don't know what to say to him anyway." Charlotte tried to wrench herself from Birdie's grasp.

Birdie squeezed her tighter. "Look, honey, you just say whatever you have to. Win that boy over." She released her grip only to sweetly put her hand on Charlotte's cheek as Charlotte tried to step away. "Don't worry, sweetheart, I have a sixth sense about these things. He won't be able to resist you."

That tiny show of empathy was enough to throw her right back into sadness. But she smiled at her friend. "I hope so."

Charlotte returned to her customers and spent the rest of the day thinking about Will. She wanted a chance to apologize for getting defensive, show him she was actually a reasonable person, capable of having a difficult conversation without losing her temper. What was it about him that made her take everything so personally?

She needed to get to him quickly and apologize before Birdie made a bigger mess of things.

Chapter Twenty-Seven

THE CHIME ON the front door sounded past closing time. Darn it. Charlotte had let Scruggs go home and forgot to lock the front door. Just a few more minutes and she would be putting on her pajamas and slippers, settling down to watch some mindless Netflix drama. She turned to welcome the customer with a smile, which died on her lips.

"Hello, dear," Virginia Buchanan said.

Charlotte nearly slammed the door in her face. "Hello."

"I've come for a cup of tea."

She couldn't bring herself to be rude, even though the woman deserved it. Curiosity got the best of her. "Of course. Chamomile?"

"Sure."

Charlotte knew how this *CSI* episode would play out. Teashop owner found dead in the morning, a single gunshot wound to the head. No suspects. Virginia Buchanan living out the rest of her days, pretending she had absolutely no idea what happened. She could hear the drawl: *What a shame. Bless her heart, poor little thing.*

Virginia stood at the display table holding a boxed silver

tea diffuser. Charlotte quickly poured the hot water and dunked in the tea bag. "Is this sterling?" Virginia asked.

"Stainless steel," Charlotte said, holding out the cup for her.

Virginia set it down and took the tea. "I suppose the days of heirloom silver are gone. No one cares about their ancestry anymore."

"Oh, I don't think that's true." For heaven's sake, she just found out she had Buchanan ancestors. Of course she was interested.

"Families simply aren't what they used to be." Virginia looked wistful. "I would just love some company while I sip my tea. Would you be so kind as to join me?" She was already walking toward a table. Charlotte followed. They sat across from each other at a table for two near the front window. It was dark enough outside that, with the lights from inside the shop, anyone driving by would be able to see them clearly. Charlotte took comfort in that.

"Now," Virginia began. "I see no reason why we shouldn't be friends."

I can think of about a hundred. Charlotte didn't give her the satisfaction of a reaction.

"Of course, you know you are welcome to visit Katu any time you like. I'm sure Jackson can show you some of the more special areas." She reached across and patted the table in front of Charlotte. "I made a book one time of the photographs I took at our rookery. Such lovely birds, the colors are just remarkable. You might like to look at it sometime and learn all about the different species we are fortunate enough to provide a home for." She paused. Charlotte hardly heard a thing after the word "visit."

"Yes, thank you. Jack already showed me the loggerhead beach. It's beautiful." She fought to keep the disdain from her voice.

Virginia smiled tightly. "Yes." The word had two syllables when she said it. She sipped from her tea. "And you are welcome to go to that beach anytime you like. Of course, we trust you with our dear little turtles."

Dear little turtles? Charlotte nearly burst out laughing. "Are you trying to find out if I will attempt to get a piece of the island? Is that what you're here for?"

Virginia squinted and sat up straighter. "I would never presume such a thing. I am simply extending an invitation to you to visit my beloved island because it is my intention for us to be friends. That is all."

Charlotte bit her tongue.

"I am doing my best to honor your mother, my son, and my old friend Birdie."

The fact that she left her husband out of the list glared like a floodlight. Virginia continued to sip her tea, a look of satisfaction on her face.

"Did my dad drink tea?" Charlotte asked. She knew full well that she was pushing Virginia's buttons.

Virginia put down her cup, a bit too forcefully, and tea

splashed onto the table. "If you're speaking of Bill, he drank coffee."

"Was he a morning person or a night owl?"

"A morning person." Virginia adjusted herself in the chair. "He always rose before the rest of the house. Was out before breakfast, tending to something, almost every day."

"Did he like animals?" Charlotte had to suppress a smile. She was getting too much pleasure out of torturing the woman.

"Of course he liked animals." She huffed. "Alright, now, enough of this. I'm sure if he'd met you, the two of you would have gotten on just fine. Is that what you want to know? Bill liked coffee and books and pastries, just like most people. It does not make him your father."

Charlotte began to speak, but Virginia interrupted. "He also had perfect manners. No one could say he was not a gentleman."

"Did he know about me?"

"There was no reason for him to know about you."

"Did *you* know about me?"

"Miss Sinclair. If you are trying to imply that I am lying, I will not stand for it. I came here to be your friend."

"I believe you came here to find out if I was going to try to lay claim to something. And the answer is…I might."

Virginia looked uncannily like Cruella de Vil. "If you were ever to try something like that, my lawyers would be very pleased to help you relocate yourself somewhere far, far away."

"So, now you're threatening me." Charlotte was filled with righteous courage. The woman was so filled with fear and contempt, she'd orchestrated a whole tea-drinking scene.

Virginia stood. "You listen to me, little girl. You are not a Buchanan. You will never be a Buchanan." Her lips lost all color, and she adjusted her mint-green silk button-down as she took a moment to compose herself. With her head cocked and her fake smile reglued in place, she began again. "Now, I know this is a sensitive subject for you, but I'm not doing you any favors by not being completely honest. You are not Bill's daughter. I don't know what kind of trouble Anna Grace got herself into out there in California, but I can promise you that my husband had nothing to do with it."

"That's funny," Charlotte said. "Because your son, your friend Birdie, and Pastor Crane all think differently."

Virginia stared at her a second before she spoke. "None of that matters now, does it?" She smiled widely, her long bottom teeth making her look a bit like a rodent. "You can't prove a thing." With that, Virginia walked, ever so slowly, to the front door and let herself out as if casually leaving her own home.

Charlotte closed up shop and went upstairs. She had to admit, she was proud of herself for holding her ground. No matter how much she expected Virginia to be a selfish, hateful, wicked excuse for a person, it would probably always come as a shock when she experienced it. A part of her wanted to take Jack and get a DNA test to prove that Bill Buchanan was her father, just to get back at Virginia. Sweet revenge would feel so good after all that woman put her through.

She put on her pajamas in a daze, heated a Lean Cuisine in the microwave, turned on the TV, and plopped onto the couch, eager to push the evil things she wanted to do to that woman out of her mind. She talked to the firefly jar between bites of sesame chicken. "Virginia Buchanan made your life miserable, didn't she?" Charlotte chewed. "You were trying to protect me." Which only further proved that Bill had to be her father. She knew it in the depths of her soul.

Proof or no proof, nothing Virginia could say or do would ever change the fact that Bill Buchanan was Charlotte's father.

Chapter Twenty-Eight

CHARLOTTE PAIRED HER favorite little black dress with a short vintage beaded jacket and three-inch Jimmy Choos. It was Friday night and Birdie was coming by to take her to Chaucer's restaurant for what she called "a little bit of fancy spoiling." Charlotte felt like an old Hollywood movie star, curiously excited to spend some one-on-one time with Birdie despite the fact that they'd probably end up talking about Virginia the whole time. Maybe she could steer the conversation more toward Jack or Will. Jack was filling the role of brother so nicely. Clearly, what she had thought was attraction was an innate knowledge that they were somehow connected. Like on a spiritual level, they sought each other out, shared DNA screaming to be discovered.

The phone rang and Charlotte leaned over to pick it up. She didn't recognize the number.

"Hi, Charlotte, honey. This is Allison Rushton." Her voice was sweet and kind, yet there was an edge to it. She sounded worried. "I'm so sorry I didn't call you sooner, I had a bit of trouble finding your number."

"Is everything all right?" Charlotte asked.

"Is Will with you?"

"No."

"Well, there's been a little accident on a job site." She paused. "And now we can't find him."

Charlotte went cold. "Oh, my God. Where do you think he is?"

"We were hoping he was with you." Allison's voice was strained. "There was an explosion at one of the homes he's building out on County Road 41. We're out here now. We don't know what caused it." There was a pause. "One of his men didn't make it. Mike Compton. He's gone."

Panic rose in Charlotte's chest. *No!* The nice man she'd met at the festival? "Where are you?" Charlotte asked. "Do you want to come here? We can use the store as a central location to look for him."

She yelled something to Kelly, then spoke into the receiver, "That'd be great. Thanks, hon. We'll be right over. His sisters will stay at his house in case he goes home."

"Okay, good." Charlotte hung up and fell onto the couch. She sat, stunned, for a few minutes, then pulled herself together enough to send both Birdie and Jack a text. It was like she was having an out-of-body experience. Will wasn't really missing. It was all a bad movie. It couldn't be her life.

JACK AND RUTH Marie pulled into her parking lot at the same time Charlotte unlocked the front doors for Will's parents. Jack ran over, and Ruth Marie caught up quickly. After hugs, no words were spoken as they all came inside. Kelly walked around looking blankly at the bookshelves, while the rest of them sat at the table nearest the front door.

"I can't believe it," Allison said, clutching a tissue to her bright red nose. "I can't believe this is happening."

"He'll be okay," Charlotte said, desperate for any words that might help. "I know it."

"Yes. He's okay. He has to be." When Allison choked on the words, Charlotte found herself unable to breathe. "But Mike," Allison cried. "He has a family. Oh my God, oh my dear God."

Kelly strode over and gently lifted his wife from her chair, placing her on her feet. He hugged her face into his chest, soaking her fear and grief into his body. Charlotte watched as Allison relaxed into him and her crying tapered off.

Without warning, Birdie shot into the store like a squawking macaw, all colors and feathers flying. "Okay, y'all, I'm here and I brought snacks." She held up a bottle of tequila and a giant box of Moon Pies. "I figure we'll need these. Who wants to go first?"

Jack walked up to her and took the snacks. "This may not be the right time, Ms. Birdie."

"Ain't no better time, Jackson." She walked over to Kelly

and Allison and immediately began spewing questions at them. She wanted every last detail of what they knew about the accident and where Will might be. Of course, the end result was always the same: Mike was dead, and no one knew where Will was.

The front door opened again, and Pastor Crane walked through. "Oh," Birdie said. "And I brought a pastor, too."

Charlotte felt nauseated, and this was without any Cuervo or Moon Pies. It was the agony of an innocent person's death and a burning need for answers. She went into a cold sweat, felt the color drain from her face, and began to hyperventilate. While Ruth Marie got her some water, Jack tried to help her breathe slowly while massaging her hands to keep them from seizing up. Allison rubbed her back.

Birdie glared at Charlotte. Jumping from her chair, she grabbed her arm and pulled her away from her caregivers. "You're coming with me, young lady."

Too shocked to protest, Charlotte had to kick off her high heels to keep up as she was led by the elbow into the ladies' room. "Look, child," Birdie waved a finger in front of Charlotte's face. "This is not about you. His family is trying their damnedest to keep things together and you are *not* helping." Fiercely pulling two paper towels from the dispenser, she threw them at Charlotte. "Now, wipe your face, put your big girl panties on, get out there, and deal with it."

Charlotte wet the paper towel and pressed it against her swelling eyes. She'd always been told to embrace her emotions, let them flow freely. But, as much as she hated to admit it, maybe Birdie was right. Maybe she should try to be strong for everyone else. She could always break down later.

With a new resolve, Charlotte looked in the mirror, fixed her hair, stood straighter, and did as Birdie commanded.

Two more hours passed before Will finally called his mother. He'd been with Mike's body at the hospital, but he was home now, safe. He made it very clear, however, that he didn't want any visitors.

"What about Charlotte?" Allison asked. "She's here, too."

Charlotte heard him say, "Don't let her get anywhere near me." Her heart dropped as she slumped into her chair.

She'd just gotten all the answers she needed.

"I have news," Jack announced. He'd been standing in a corner on the phone for the past several minutes.

"Randy Hassell was just arrested." The room became silent. "He was found walking down the county road without a shirt on."

"He wasn't wearing a shirt?" Charlotte asked. The image of Randy's sweaty beer keg of a belly unveiled for public viewing was repulsive, to say the least.

"Well, that's something Randy is known for. I don't know why, but every time that man gets drunk, he takes off his shirt."

"So, did they arrest him for indecent exposure?" It didn't really make sense. Generally, going shirtless was not a punishable offense for a man.

"Public intoxication." Jack looked serious. "But that's not all."

"Did they link him to the explosion?"

"Yes, ma'am. Allegedly, Randy was babbling on and on about it."

"He did it on purpose?" Ruth Marie asked too loudly.

"From what I understand, Randy would be bragging about it one minute and screaming about it the next. Looks like he didn't know Mike was in the house with Will when he set the bomb, or dynamite, or whatever it was."

Of course Charlotte had suspected Randy; everyone had. But the whole scenario was so awful, it was hard to imagine someone actually crossing that line. What kind of sick person would do such a thing? Randy knew Mike. Everyone in town knew Mike. He was the outgoing, fun-loving brother of Mayor Sonny Compton. He was one of the best craftsmen around. He had a wife and kids. But Mike wasn't the intended victim. Randy had intended to kill Will.

"They've got his whole confession on tape," Jack continued. "We're looking at murder charges here. I don't think Randy's gonna be bothering anyone for a long, long time."

The news came as a relief—but poor Krista and her family would be devastated. And Charlotte was the last person to offer advice on how to fix her life.

Chapter Twenty-Nine

ALLISON HUGGED CHARLOTTE like she was about to leave for war. "Listen, honey. Will is filled up with grief over Mike right now. Dang that boy, he's just like his daddy, only wants people to see his strong side." She touched a cold hand to Charlotte's cheek. Such a motherly gesture. "He's a mess. He feels like it's all his fault."

"He shouldn't, though. He didn't do anything," Charlotte said.

"I know it. And he'll get through it. I promise he will. But right now, we just need to give him a little space to think it all through." Allison's eyes were bloodshot but full of determination. "But don't you give up on him, hear? He may not be acting like it, but that boy needs you."

Charlotte nodded, and Allison rubbed her gently on the shoulder. "Alright, honey. Now that we've found our son, we've got to get on over to Mike's family. You get yourself some rest."

Birdie tapped her foot as she waited her turn with Charlotte. "Good Lord, child, you like to have scared the devil out of all of us with that face of yours. I declare. How many times am I going to have to remind you—"

"Birdie. Will doesn't want to see me."

"Oh." Birdie's hand went to her mouth. "Well, then." She looked around the almost-empty store. "You may be needing that tequila after all."

It took one hour and two tequila shots, but Birdie finally agreed to leave Charlotte alone. She waved vigorously from her boat-like Cadillac as she sped away with Pastor Crane at the wheel, his head practically touching the red fabric roof.

Each step up to Charlotte's loft felt steeper than the one before. Once inside, she went straight to the bookshelf and tenderly lifted the firefly jar from its spot. She studied the chipping gold paint on the tails of the insects, then touched its coldness to her cheek, imagining it was her mother's hand touching her face, like Will's mother so recently did. She closed her eyes, loneliness consuming her.

Birdie's unwanted voice popped up, stern in her memory. "Put your big girl panties on." *Gosh darn it, Birdie.* She opened her eyes and put the jar back on the shelf. A hot bath and a bite of chocolate might help her feel better. She took a step toward the kitchen.

An ominous feeling made her glance back.

Her precious jar teetered and rolled. She snapped her arm out to catch it, barely touching the lid as the jar slipped through her fingers. It landed, shattering into a thousand tiny pieces on the floor. She shrieked and fell to her knees, cutting them on the shards, brushing the pieces together as if by magic they would adhere and form the shape of a jar. The air was too still to breathe, the only sound the scraping of her hands and glass against the wood floor.

"*Noooooo!*" she cried. She could see the yellow room, her childhood home, her mother's face as she painted the bugs onto the jar. *They're not bees, Charlotte, they're lightning bugs. Someday, I'll show you how to catch 'em.* She heard the tinkling sound of her mother's laugh. *Swoop and scoop, that's the trick.*

The largest surviving piece of glass lay in her bleeding hand. It had the golden tail of a firefly, the body of which was somewhere in fragments, unrecognizable. Charlotte's heart hurt more than her cut knees and hands as she saw herself as a child, entranced by her mother's beauty and the shimmering little bugs on the jar. *We'll plant some honeysuckle in the backyard, some gardenias and azaleas, maybe even a little dogwood, and we'll have our jar. It'll be good enough for us.* Anna Grace kissed Charlotte on the head. *We'll have our jar all through the winter when the lightning bugs in South Carolina disappear. We'll have ours forever.*

For Charlotte, forever ended that moment.

She placed the largest piece on the bookshelf where the jar so recently sat and forced herself to sweep up the rest and dump it in the trash can with a sound that reminded her of rain. Alternately wiping tears and blood, she did her best to rinse out her cuts and, sitting on the closed toilet, cursed at herself while she used tweezers to extract the remaining microscopic shards of glass. Throwing the tweezers into the sink, she walked with purpose to the kitchen where her cell phone lay on the table and dialed Jack's number.

"Hey sis, what's up?" Jack answered.

"I shouldn't have called you."

"Of course you should have."

"It sounds ridiculous saying it out loud. I'm fine. Really. I'll just talk to you later."

"Is it Will?"

"No. It's my mother."

Silence. "Did you find out something about her?"

"No. And I don't mean to be so dramatic about it, but," Charlotte choked, barely squeaking out the words, "I feel like I just lost her all over again." It took her a couple seconds to calm down enough to explain to him about the jar, how it comforted her as a sort of stand-in for her mother. She needed that jar. She couldn't imagine going on without it.

"I'm so sorry, Charlotte. Until this moment, I never realized how much losing your mother impacted you," he said.

"Really? I feel like I wear it everywhere I go. Like my grief is tattooed on my forehead."

"No. No, you're just like the rest of us, still walking around while we're filled up with pain. We all have this in common."

She'd never stopped to think that Jack might be grieving, too. Surely, he loved his father as much as she loved her mother.

"On the day I left for the Citadel, my dad pulled me aside. I thought he was going to give me some big speech about becoming a man or making the family proud. But he didn't say a word." Jack sighed into the phone. "He just unbuckled his watch from his wrist and handed it to me. Charlotte, I wish you could have known him. I can't remember a day in my life when he wasn't wearing that watch. It was our grandfather's, a rare 1920 silver officer's Rolex. Dad's eyes were all glassy. He didn't have to say anything. That gesture said more than words ever could."

Charlotte waited, sensing he needed a little time, bracing herself for the sound of his voice. She wasn't sure how she'd handle it if he cried, too.

It was a few seconds before he began again. He sounded thoughtful but strong. "That watch stressed me out more than heading off to army training. I worried every day that I'd break it or I'd lose it, and my link to him and my grandfather would be destroyed. Even though I knew it was just a piece of metal, I felt the pressure of the responsibility of that keepsake." Charlotte envisioned him touching his forehead like she'd seen him do so often at the tea shop as he worked from his laptop. "The first time I came home on break, I opened a safe deposit box just for that watch. Sounds silly, but for my own peace of mind, I needed to know it was safe." He cleared his throat. "I'm not sure that made my dad very happy. I think he expected me to wear it. Would have been more courageous of me to do that, I suppose." He paused again. "The watch is still there. At the bank."

Charlotte said nothing. She'd called the right person. He really did understand.

"Listen," he said. "Ruth Marie has some jars in the cupboard. I'll bring one over. You can paint on it, make a new one. Hell, I'll paint on it for you if you want. I can probably manage a lightning bug or two."

Ruth Marie yelled, "What on earth are you talking about? You're gonna paint bugs on my jars?" She laughed.

"That's not right, is it? I'm sorry, Charlotte. That jar can't be replaced. Just like your mother can't be replaced. I know better, I do."

"Don't be sorry. I like that you want to make things better. That was very brotherly. Plus, the thought of you painting on a jar is kind of funny." She was feeling better. Just having someone understand made her feel less lonely.

"How about you just tell me how I can help."

"You did it already. Thanks for listening."

"You sure?"

"Yes. Tell Ruth Marie I said hi." Charlotte hung up and took the remaining piece of jar from the shelf before flopping onto the couch. She held it tightly in her hand, a little less devastated, a little less sad and overwhelmed and alone and miserable. She still wanted a pity party, or at the very least, a good woe-is-me cry. But now that she'd talked to Jack, the tears wouldn't come.

She put the shard of glass to her nose, hoping for one last

smell of honeysuckle. There was nothing. *Accept it. It's gone.* It was only glass and paint anyway, just like Jack's watch was only silver and steel. She leaned the piece upright against the base of her lamp on a small table next to the couch. The light made the remaining gold shimmer, like it was alive. *That is not a sign,* she told herself. *My mother's soul is no more in that jar than mine is in a cup of tea. She is in my heart.*

What a coincidence. Her heart was broken, too.

Chapter Thirty

S OMEWHERE IN THE middle of the sleepless nights following Mike's death, Charlotte came up with a plan. She had to get out of Crickley, far away from Will, Virginia, and Randy. If she could get away from herself, she would. Plus, she still had a storage unit full of her mother's stuff back in California that she needed to go through. There was a chance she'd find something like the firefly jar in there, maybe something handmade by her mother, or something special from her childhood. She had no idea what, but the thought made her hopeful.

She picked up the phone to call Birdie, then decided against it. Birdie would ask too many questions, and Charlotte wasn't clear enough on exactly how she was going to withstand the Birdie fifth degree. She simply needed to leave, and there was no way Birdie would accept an explanation like that.

Charlotte looked over at Krista intent on the cash register, pale and drawn, the corners of her mouth pulled down, clearly avoiding Charlotte's eyes. She put an arm around Krista's shoulder. "Are you okay?"

Krista nodded. "I'd rather be here than with my family right now. Half of 'em are mad as hornets at Randy, and the other half are cleaning their shotguns, only they don't know who to shoot."

"If you want to stay in my loft, I have some business to tend to back in California."

"Naw," she said. "I'm good. My family may be poor and crazy, but we stick together." She moved past Charlotte and started checking the coffee machines, then looked back. "Hey, Charlotte?"

Charlotte turned to her.

"Thanks."

By noon, Charlotte had every shift covered and an airline ticket. By six P.M., she was on a plane out of Charleston, heading to the West Coast.

To her surprise, she slept better on the red-eye flight than she had in weeks. When she arrived at LAX to tall palm trees, the landmark spaceship-shaped restaurant, and neon signs along the exit, she felt almost giddy. She drove her rental car to Santa Monica where she'd booked a room at a nice hotel on the beach. It was too early to check in, so she used their restroom to wash her face and change into her running clothes. She left her luggage with the concierge and could hardly wait to jog her old familiar route from the pier down to Venice Beach and back. It'd been ages since she'd exercised.

She passed rows of beach homes, pressed together, barely

two feet between them, several of which she'd been inside with one friend or another. Nothing had changed. It was like she never left, like her life in South Carolina never existed.

When she returned to the hotel, her room was ready. She took a quick shower and marveled at how even the water smelled different in California. Between that and the flood of memories, she was nostalgic for her old life, the one with her mom and stepdad.

She pulled into the lot of the mini storage, punched in the code to enter, and drove to unit 119. There wasn't much of value left, mainly boxes of her mother's books and clothing—things Charlotte didn't need when she moved to Crickley Creek and wasn't ready to face the pain of sorting through. It smelled like her mother's attic, and she nearly closed the door and left. Instead, she pushed up her sleeves, dusted off the top of the first box, and tried to muster the strength to open it.

To her right was a stack of books, the one on top featured a large pink bird with the title *Fancy Feathers*, by Virginia Rose Buchanan. It was like Virginia had followed her to California. Curiosity won out, and she picked it up. Sure enough, on the inside flap of the picture book about birds was a photo of Katu featuring Buchanan Manor. She probably should be impressed; Virginia's photos were fantastic. But she was here to find a replacement for her beloved jar. She would not let Virginia get in the way. She threw the book at the aluminum wall and was rewarded with a resounding thud.

Then a thought struck her like Carolina lightning. She had a blood tie to Katu Island. No one could claim that she didn't belong in South Carolina. Not that it even mattered, but Virginia had nothing on her. Plus, Charlotte had happily lived in California. She was resilient, able to adjust to all kinds of circumstances. She was strong. She had something to offer, too—a new way of thinking. A broader perspective. With renewed vigor, Charlotte opened the first box. She would find something poignant. She would find something perfect.

Chapter Thirty-One

CHARLOTTE BEGAN THE next day like the one before, with a jog along the beach. There was a certain feeling of safety for her here, the kind that came from knowing where the best parking spaces were, the shortcuts, the lane you need to be in five streets ahead of time. She knew the minute a man opened his mouth if he was a player or a liar. She understood what people meant without having to worry about what sinister meaning lay beneath.

Most of her friends from elementary school, high school, and many from college lived within a ten-mile radius. A big part of her wanted to call them, but she had work to do.

With each box, Charlotte's desperation grew. There was nothing that brought her mom back to her. Not one thing that sparked the same closeness as the firefly jar. What began as peaceful unpacking became a frantic search. Her "giveaway" pile was now much larger than her "keep" pile, and she fantasized about leaving it all in storage and trying again later—just in case she had missed something.

By that afternoon, Charlotte's rental car was full of photo albums, quilts, her mother's old notebooks, and assorted treasures. But despite many things she couldn't part with, like her stepfather's reading glasses and her mother's worn silk robe, her grandparents' Asian-inspired lamp and iron dog-shaped doorstop, there was nothing. She felt as empty as the dusty square storage space.

Still, she'd taken many walks down memory lane and survived them, and for the first time since her mother's death, she remembered her as the vibrant, loving person she was, not the brain-damaged woman who was too busy dying to be a mother. The pictures helped her remember, the feel of the silk robe on her fingers, the familiar objects from her childhood. She could see her mother's smile, and it felt safe and sweet and good. Now she needed to box it all up and have it shipped to South Carolina.

She finished earlier than she expected, so she decided to call some friends for a quick night out before she left. The quiet had been so nice, she hadn't made it a priority to buy a new cell phone charger for the one she forgot. She used the phone in her hotel room to call her friend Megan, whose number she would probably never forget. Megan called Sue, and after changing into a fresh pair of jeans, a white halter top, and her brown leather flip-flops, Charlotte was walking along the beach toward Gladstone's.

Sue and Megan were waiting outside the restaurant with huge smiles and open arms. They were even more beautiful than Charlotte remembered. Sue, the quintessential West Coast athlete, beach volleyball fanatic, and breaker of hearts.

Megan, the self-deprecating Korean-American who wore red lipstick, laughed at her own jokes, and could cure any ailment with something from her garden. The three of them pranced into the bar arm in arm. "Three Cadillac margaritas, please," Megan said to the bartender, stationing herself in the corner by the television tuned to ESPN. As time passed, the bar filled, and music blared across the beach and highway flanking the restaurant. With all the talking, not one of the girls thought to order dinner.

Over their first round of drinks, Charlotte told the girls about Tea and Tennyson, Scruggs, Krista, and of course, Birdie. "She's like a character from a comic book," she said. "Over-the-top funny and she doesn't even know it." Over the second round of margaritas, Charlotte told them about Virginia.

"What a nightmare," Sue said, pulling up the calendar on her phone. "That's it. I'm booking a ticket. Megan, you're coming with me. We have got to meet these people."

By then, several men converged on their corner. Some joined in the conversation. One took over much of Sue's personal space and another was angling for Charlotte. Megan, on the other hand, was masterful at brushing them off.

Over the third round of margaritas, Charlotte told the crowd about Jack. "I totally love him. But like a brother." Over the fourth round of margaritas, Charlotte was crying about Will. "I never thought a cowboy could be so...hot. Oh my God, you should see him!" Charlotte looked around to find a comparable example. "Kind of like that guy, there." She pointed at a man entering the restaurant. "But taller, with longer hair, maybe not so many muscles." She squinted at the man. He turned his head in her direction and, as soon as he saw her, he walked faster.

"Holy shit."

It was slow motion, like a beer commercial, his thighs bulging through his jeans, chest muscles flexing through his shirt, cowboy boots making a thud with each step. Megan and Sue must have been in the slow-motion trap, too. They appraised him, perfectly still, their lips parted, a sure sign they approved. "Hello, cowboy," Megan said, extricating herself from her spot. Sue giggled and Charlotte half fell off the chair, trying to stand. The guy who'd been flirting with her for the past hour left in a huff.

Megan reached out a hand to the man. "I'm Megan."

"Will," he said, taking her hand. Megan wrinkled her eyebrows at Charlotte. "*The* Will?" she asked. Charlotte nodded.

"From South Carolina?" Sue asked.

"Yup," he said.

Charlotte could barely focus to see him clearly. "How'd you get here?" she asked.

"I drove."

"In your truck?"

"Yup."

"That's, like, more than two thousand miles!"

"Took me thirty-six hours. I couldn't let you do this, Charlotte."

"Do what?" Get drunk? Did he know she was drunk? Of course he knew she was drunk. She could barely stand, and her tongue was getting in the way of her words, softening the consonants. She couldn't help it.

"You belong in Crickley," he said simply.

"Tomorrow?"

"What's tomorrow?" he asked.

"When I go back."

"Back where?"

"To Crickley. Where you live."

Will laughed, and it was like the laughter freed Megan and Sue from their trance. "You drove out here to bring Charlotte back to South Carolina with you?" Sue asked.

"Well, yeah. Scruggs didn't tell me she was comin' back. He kind of let me think she may be gone for good. If I'd known she was just spending a few days out here, I might have saved myself the trip."

"Oh my God! That's so romantic!" Sue spilled her margarita as her hands flew to her chest.

"Your accent is divine," Megan said.

"Can I get y'all something? Coffee? Bread?" Will offered. "Something to soak up whatever y'all been drinking?" Megan and Sue giggled. Charlotte just stared at him. "At least I can drive y'all home."

After safely delivering Megan and Sue, Will took Charlotte to her hotel. She managed to ask a few questions despite her thick tongue and her eyes spinning in her head. "How'd you find me?"

He had his arm around her waist, helping her down the hall to her room. "Luck, mostly, but I had some help, too. I've got a buddy from the Citadel who works for the CIA. He found you on the registry at this hotel."

"You were following me?"

"Not to the restaurant. That was the luck part."

He held her in one arm and opened the door to her room with the other. "How about we order some room service? You'll feel better after you get something in your stomach."

"I don't normally drink this much."

"I figured."

"You drove a long way."

"I had to do something big to make up for acting like a two-year-old."

Charlotte shook her head, trying to wake herself up. "Mike died. It's okay. You needed time."

Will spoke while on hold with room service. "I owe you an apology."

By the time Will had his first bite of french fries, she'd already eaten most of her chicken sandwich. He barely touched his food, clearly too focused and intent on convincing her how truly sorry he was. How Mike was dead because he didn't protect him, and it was now his responsibility to make sure Mike's family was taken care of. How he should have stopped Randy a long time ago. How he'd been living in a hell of guilt and remorse and felt the best way to protect Charlotte from Randy was to sever all contact with her.

Charlotte understood. She didn't need an explanation from Will. An apology, yes. "I think this makes us even," she said. "The way I see it, we canceled each other out, so neither of us has to be sorry anymore."

Will found her hand and held it tightly. "You're a good woman, Miss Sinclair."

A million tingles sparkled their way through her body at his words. "I don't miss this place," she said, looking out the window to the wide yellow sand beach. "Malibu is familiar and comfortable, but I guess there's too much of my mother in me. I had to get out."

Will chewed slowly and listened.

"But what if South Carolina doesn't fit me either? Where would I go? I kinda wish I was a loggerhead—just pick a beach and go back to it over and over again."

Will's eyes crinkled at the sides. "Charlotte." He squeezed her hand. "Crickley is your home. No matter the reason why, you chose it."

Home. The word squeezed her heart like a fist. "Yeah," she whispered.

"We should get an early start tomorrow," he said, "I'll find myself a place to stay."

"Stay here." She could barely hear her own voice. She dug deep and said it louder. "Stay. With me."

CHARLOTTE SLEPT LIKE a warm cat. Daylight streamed onto her. She stretched and burrowed into the bed before opening her eyes. It took a second to focus and another for her brain to register where she was. *California. Margaritas. Will.* With eyes as big as two suns, she turned her head toward the other side of the bed. It was empty. Had she dreamed it? She couldn't have. She sat up and looked toward the bathroom door. It was open, the bathroom empty.

"Mornin'," came a deep voice from a chair in the corner.

Simultaneous excitement and embarrassment made her jump. *It was true.* "Hi."

Will smiled at her, looking somewhat amused. He was fully dressed, his hair damp as he pulled on his boots. How long had he been watching her—and why didn't that seem creepy? Maybe it was the way he was looking at her. Nothing about him felt judgmental or lecherous or unsafe.

"You sleep okay?"

Yes, she slept wonderfully. *Only slept.* Nothing else happened. *Right?* She looked down to see what she was wearing. It was a cool rush of relief to see she was still in her clothes from the night before. "Mm-hmm."

They canceled her flight, checked out of the hotel, placed

everything from the rental car into the back of Will's truck, covered it with a tarp, and tied it down. He also had a car charger, which Charlotte used to power up her phone.

There were sixteen voice messages and about a thousand texts. Most of them from Birdie. She was shocked at how Southern Birdie sounded. "Miss Charlotte. It is very rude of you to ignore me like this. Ugly Scruggly says you've gone out of town, but that is no excuse for you not returning my call. This is an important time in my life, and you are ruining it by not calling me back." Charlotte didn't bother listening to the rest. It would be easier just to call her.

Birdie answered the phone without a hello. "Charlotte Sinclair. What in the hell is your problem?"

"I'm in California, Birdie."

"I don't care if you're in Swaziland, I need you here by day after tomorrow. When I truly needed you was yesterday, but since you skipped out on all of us, I had to take Virginia dress shopping with me. Good Lawd Almighty, don't make me think about it. Now, can you get here? 'Cause I need you to be my maid of honor."

"No way! Birdie! You're getting married?"

Will smiled knowingly and chuckled.

"Is it Ashby?"

"Of course it's Ashby," Birdie squawked.

"I knew it! I knew there was something weird about you two."

"I'm going to pretend like I didn't hear that." Birdie

cleared her throat. "Here I am, finally getting my big moment, and not only is my maid of honor not answering her phone, she is insulting me, too."

"Why didn't you tell me earlier?"

"It was nobody's business."

"How long have you been dating? Isn't this kind of fast?"

"Look, honey, neither one of us is a spring chicken. And that man has been saving himself a long time. I mean, a looooong time. After I gave him a small taste of how things were done, it was like I'd opened Pandora's box." She chuckled wickedly. "That man didn't know what hit him. I finally told him, 'Ashby,' I said, 'if you want to enjoy the complete pleasures of Birdalee Mudge, you are going to have to buy the cow. Plain and simple.' When he said okay, I figured we're too damned old to wait, so I booked the chapel for Thursday afternoon. I know a Thursday is not traditional for a wedding and you'd think the church would make an exception for their very own pastor, but they're booked and I don't care. I'm not waiting a minute longer. And you, dear girl, are going to be here in time for the ceremony. And you will be wearing a purple dress. I already bought it."

"That day at the store when you bought all those romance books. Is that when you got together?"

"We figured things out on the cruise."

"The cruise? You went alone on that cruise."

Birdie sighed deeply. "I purposefully did not tell y'all that the good pastor was accompanying me because it was none of y'all's damn business. Some of the church folks figured it out, considering we were gone at the same time, but I'm not gonna get in to that. Fact is, I brought him along as a friend and man of the cloth to help me choose. You never can be too careful when it comes to choosing a man."

"You can say that again," Charlotte laughed.

"Nothing happened with Ashby on that boat, mind you. Should have, but his whole remain pure for God thing was gettin' in the way. The man bought his own damn room." Birdie dropped her voice. "That's why I got myself all those books. I needed a little help remembering how to butter a biscuit, if you know what I mean. It'd been a while."

"Looks like it worked."

"Like the sun works on an ice cream bar. He can't live without me now."

"I'm happy for you, Birdie. We'll have to drive straight through to get there, but I guess we can switch off driving."

Will nodded.

"Good. You will be at the church by two thirty. Bye now."

Charlotte turned to Will, who'd heard the whole exchange. "I suppose if I'm the maid of honor in Birdalee Mudge's wedding, I am as much a part of Crickley society as anybody else."

"You are one hundred percent correct," Will said, patting her knee.

"I think I'm going to be my own brand of Southern. Whoever said we all have to be the same?"

"That's about the truest thing I ever heard," he said. "And I'm good for gettin' you to the church on time."

He was good for a lot more than that.

Chapter Thirty-Two

C HARLOTTE MADE IT to the church on time, dressed in the required bright purple taffeta dress with shoulder bows. Birdie was positively calm. Strangely composed. Serene, even. She hugged Charlotte as if she were a beloved grandmother. She smiled graciously at her guests, and even used big words like *exquisite* and *magnificent*. When the time came, Scruggs, in a coordinating purple bow tie, led her down the aisle to an awaiting Ashby Asa Crane IV, who was a bit sweaty but appeared pleased to be there. Ashby's brother, Samuel, stood on the groom's side and Charlotte stood by the bride. Birdie swore she'd rather have a new true friend than an old rotten one stand up for her.

Virginia manned the guest book, which, according to Birdie, "pissed her off something awful." Charlotte did her best to avoid her, and Virginia seemed to do the same.

In a short and sweet ceremony, Ms. Birdalee Middleton Mudge became Mrs. Birdalee Mudge-Crane. Birdie pulled Ashby's head down by the neck and kissed him with vigor before turning toward the crowd. They walked up the aisle arm in arm, Birdie proclaiming loudly, "Don't y'all even think about dropping in for any unannounced visits, 'cause I can tell you right now, my husband and I will not be answering the door."

WILL'S DANCE MOVES were sluggish, and Charlotte was too exhausted to stay in her role as cheery copilot. They teetered their way around Birdie's reception, the weariness from racing to make it across the country on time taking hold. She slumped into his warm chest in a near dream-state, his heart beating comfortingly in her ear. Dancing with Will was like being privy to the secret of a happy existence: togetherness, understanding, love. For the first time in a long time, she felt like she mattered. Like someone would miss her if she were gone.

Through her barely open eyes, Charlotte could see Krista sashaying her way toward them. If a person didn't know Krista was a Hassell, they sure couldn't tell by looking. She might be struggling on the inside, but she was a Hollywood starlet on the outside. Clearly, Birdie's wedding invitation was a big deal to her. The dress alone probably cost three days' pay.

"Charlotte." Krista's voice was drowned out by the music, but the twinkle in her eye was clear. "I need to talk to you about Mike's family."

Will immediately snapped to, leading both women off

the dance floor and out the back door.

"Okay, hear me out now," Krista said. Will and Charlotte both leaned in. "I want to do something good for Mike's wife and his boys since it was my stupid-ass cousin who got them where they are. So I was thinking, you know how Virginia is so proud of those paintings of hers? I've known about them my whole life. Everybody knows about Virginia's paintings."

Whatever Krista was getting at, if Virginia was involved, there was no way it would work.

"Let's put her paintings up in the store and sell them." Krista lifted her perfectly plucked eyebrows.

Oh hell no.

"She could give some of the proceeds to that fund Will set up for Mike's family. I'll be in charge. You won't have to do anything." Krista smiled wider than Charlotte ever saw her smile before. "Wouldn't it be great? People around here would love to have an original painting by Virginia Buchanan, and we could make some good money for the Comptons." She seemed so genuinely pleased with her idea, Charlotte hated to shoot it down.

"It's really not a bad idea," Will said.

Charlotte looked at him like he'd just grown a second head. "What if Virginia doesn't want to sell her paintings?"

"She'd get to show off and pretend like it's all for a good cause. It might just fit perfectly with her special kind of crazy." He turned to Krista. "Just be aware that you'll get absolutely no credit for helping." Krista's smile didn't fade. "Even if you deliver all the paintings, collect all the money and whatever else kind of work you're going to have to do for that woman, she will take every last bit of the credit."

"I know," Krista said. "And it's okay. I'll know in my heart I had something to do with it."

The fact that Krista tried so hard to rise above her family melted Charlotte's resolve. She threw up her arms in defeat. "I just can't get away from that woman." Shaking her head, she hugged Krista. "I'm proud of you. And I can't believe I'm gonna do this, but I'll call Jack. Don't get your hopes up, though."

A little charitable behavior might be good for all of them.

Chapter Thirty-Three

J ACK CARRIED A large painting in each hand, trailing behind Virginia like a servant. She held her head high, her eyes never landing on Charlotte, despite the fact that she was surveying every inch of the premises. "I suppose we can make this work," she announced.

Krista ran to greet her. "I was thinking that if we put one in the front window, we could attract some attention—"

"Only if we wish to destroy them with the sun." Virginia turned her back to Krista and gestured to the expanse of bookshelves lined against the walls. "We will put them in front of the books."

"Mother, there is wall space," Jack said. "This is a bookstore. Charlotte needs to sell those books."

Charlotte stepped forward from her carefully unobtrusive spot next to the front window display. "How about one or two on the bookshelves and the rest on the walls? I have some ideas for where we—"

"I am happy to take my paintings elsewhere." Virginia turned her head in Charlotte's direction but avoided eye contact, as if one look at Charlotte would turn her to stone.

It took all the self-control Charlotte had to keep from making a face at the woman.

"You agreed to this, Mother," Jack reminded. "Let's work together to get it done."

"I'm sure *you* wouldn't want *your* paintings bleached out from the sun," she snapped.

"The walls, Mother. You can hang them on the walls, you don't have to put them in the window."

"Put them wherever you want," Charlotte said. *I'll remove them soon, anyway.*

"I have some ideas for the layout," Krista said, eager to be of service. "If you want some help."

"I'm fine with Jackson and Mr. Scruggs helping me, thank you."

Krista slunk away.

I knew it. Anything involving Virginia would be a disaster.

Scruggs perked up at his name, nearly slamming a pitcher of sweet tea onto the counter. "I didn't think you'd remember me," he said, earning a scowl from Virginia.

"Jackson, why don't you get some more of my paintings from the car, honey?" She could actually sound nice when she wanted to. "Mr. Scruggs, you may fix me a glass of iced tea." He visibly cringed. "Two sprigs of mint."

"Yes, ma'am." Under his breath, Charlotte heard, "Freakin' old witch." Moments later, the sound system broadcasted the voice of Freddie Mercury, singing "Tie Your Mother Down." Jack walked back in with another painting and shot Charlotte a knowing, amused look. Virginia either ignored the song or was completely oblivious to the words. Charlotte couldn't help but love Scruggs more.

Two hours later, Virginia went home, Jack was back at work, and all twelve of Charlotte's tall bookshelves had a large painting, mostly of seabirds or coastal scenes, blocking a significant portion of her merchandise.

Ruth Marie ran in, a framed painting bouncing off her barely protruding belly. "Hey, y'all! I brought something to add to the sale." She turned the painting around, exhibiting the avocado-green, mustard-yellow, and orange hues of Virginia's oil painting of mums in a vase. "As much as it pains me, since this is such a good cause, I would like to take this opportunity to follow in my mother-in-law's generous footsteps and donate this item that means so very much to me." After a pause, she whispered to Charlotte, "Is she here?"

"Not anymore."

"Damn."

"I have a feeling that if you know what's good for you, you will run straight home as fast as you can and hang that thing in the foyer," Charlotte said. "With a floodlight shining down on it."

Birdie, who had matched her red hat to her red handbag, her red shoes, and her red fingernail polish to her red lipstick, and donned a red, white, and blue shirt, pulled her wide-brimmed hat from her head as she walked in, throwing it on a table near the front door while she took in all the paintings. "Who'd have ever thunk it? I believe I'm speech-less."

"Hallelujah!" Scruggs shouted from across the store. "Let's hope it lasts."

"Oh, pshh," Birdie said, waving him off and turning back to Charlotte. "Guess I've been too close to her all these years. Lost all my objectivity." She clicked her tongue twice. "They look good. Real good."

"I know," Charlotte said, touching Ruth Marie on the arm. "They're beautiful."

"Unlike the mums," Ruth Marie said.

Birdie squinted at the tastefully typed notecard in the corner of Virginia's nearest painting: PIPERS ON THE SHORE ORIGINAL WATERCOLOR BY VIRGINIA BUCHANAN. PRICE $450. TWENTY-FIVE PERCENT OF ALL PROFITS TO BENEFIT THE FAMILY OF MIKE COMPTON.

"Well, I'll be," said Birdie.

"We'll all be," Charlotte said. "We've already sold one and they've only been for sale since this morning."

Birdie's eyes opened wide. "Who bought it?"

"I'm not sure I should tell you. It's proprietary infor-mation."

"Don't mess with me, *Miss* Charlotte."

"Okay, okay." Charlotte planned to tell her anyway. "It was Maureen Smith."

"Oooooh. The Daughters are buyin' 'em. That makes sense, you know, with the whole Revolutionary War tie-in and all."

Charlotte understood about Virginia's ancestors and their connection to the Revolutionary War, and she knew about the Daughters of the American Revolution, but she had trouble understanding how that would entice anyone to buy a watercolor of seabirds.

"I might just have to get me one of those," Birdie said just before her cell phone rang to the tune of "You're a Grand Old Flag" at increasing volume, attracting Scruggs's attention as well as that of every customer in the store.

"You did not," he shouted from behind the counter. "That is too much, Ms. Birdalee. I mean, Ms. Libertee. Last I checked we still have a month to go before July."

"Oh hush, you." Birdie pulled out her phone and checked the number on the screen. "Lawd have mercy, can't a girl feel patriotic without getting hazed for it?" She turned her back on Charlotte and answered the call with a whispered, "What?" Then, "Is that right?" Charlotte heard what she thought was Ashby's voice on the other end. "Mm-hmm." The corners of her mouth tilted up. "Mm-hmm." Her voice dropped to a whisper. "You are a dirty boy, Pastor." The color rose in her cheeks. "Be right there."

Charlotte stood with her hip jutting out, her hand propped against it, head tilted to the side and eyebrows raised as Birdie turned to face her.

"Don't give me that face," Birdie said, evidently trying, and failing, to look innocent. "I am a happily married woman." She dropped her phone into her purse and stuck her chin in the air. "Now, I'm in a hurry, so if y'all will stop staring at me, I'll take my drink to go."

DESPITE THE FACT that they'd sold three paintings that first day, Krista decided that they weren't selling fast enough. An event was in order—an auction that would bring people into the store and their attention to a worthy cause. Krista would handle designing and distributing flyers, she'd make an announcement at church and surely, through word of mouth, plenty of people would come. Charlotte figured that during the auction, she would add to the sales by giving a portion of the profits from her own merchandise to the trust. Krista's idea might work, and it'd be great advertising for Tea and Tennyson.

A week later, the ARTIST AUCTION TO BENEFIT THE FAMILY OF MIKE COMPTON was exactly what they had. Who'd have guessed it? The normally reticent husband of Birdalee Mudge-Crane turned out to be a proficient auctioneer. "Hum a da hum a dah hum a dah, sold!" he sang. It worked. All of Virginia's paintings sold, many for well more than five hundred dollars.

Buchanan Manor was the location for the mayor's presentation of the check for $9,524.33 to Mike's family. Virginia stood beside Mayor Sonny Compton in her dining room like the guest of honor during the entirety of his speech. Mike's family embraced Krista with such a display of forgiveness and grace for her help that Virginia didn't outshine her, despite her best efforts. Krista publicly thanked her for allowing her paintings to be sold.

Virginia complained to Jack later. "She said thank you for *allowing* it, as if I had plans to keep them all to myself. I'll have you know I am in high demand. The Ice House has made me an offer." Charlotte was aware of the Ice House, a local art gallery housed in what once was a building for storing ice.

"Mother, that's fantastic," Jack said.

"Yes, but I'm not sure I have the time nor the inclination to sell any more of my paintings," she said in a tone that clearly implied how very fortunate Charlotte had been to have had the honor of displaying and selling the highly coveted art in her store.

"Well, Mother, I think you ought to consider it. Lord knows, you've got at least fifty of them stored in the attic."

Several minutes later, Virginia excused herself to oversee the catering staff's kitchen cleanup.

"Is she ever happy?" Charlotte whispered to Jack, loud enough for Will and Ruth Marie to hear.

"No," he said. "Not for a few years now. She was never smiley and optimistic like you and Ruth Marie. But when I was a kid, she did have some moments when she seemed truly happy."

"Really? I find that hard to believe." It sounded meaner than she intended.

He chuckled. "Try to imagine her in galoshes running through a swamp."

"You're kidding."

"Nope. She and our daddy used to love to go birding. They'd set out before the sun rose, Mother with her camera and Dad with his waders, stalking those birds like a couple of foxes. When they got home, Mother would go straight to her dark room and develop what she shot, and if something turned out good, the whole rest of the day she'd be in a good mood." Charlotte felt Jack's mood turn melancholy. "I loved it when they went birding."

Virginia appeared in the doorway. Perfect timing, of course. How much had she heard? "Jackson, before you leave, I'll be needing you to do me a little favor." The mock sweetness in her voice made it clear the favor was not negotiable.

"Can I do it now? I think we're just about ready to head out."

"That'd be fine." Jack followed her to the base of the stairs, where they could hear her tell him to pull her old paintings out of the attic. They heard his footsteps going up the stairs, and Virginia's voice back in the kitchen. It sounded lighthearted, her mood changing to pleasant as quickly and without warning as it did to angry. Charlotte, Will, and Ruth Marie smiled at each other knowingly.

Fifteen minutes later, Jack stormed into the sunroom. "We're leaving." Ruth Marie stood up immediately. "You too," he said to Charlotte and Will. "Let's go."

"What on earth?" Charlotte said under her breath as they hopped up to follow Jack.

"Meet me at my office," Jack said to them on the driveway as he helped Ruth Marie into the Jeep. Without question, she and Will did as they were told, barely speaking on the way to the law firm. Neither had a clue as to what could possibly have set Jack off. They parked in front of Tea and Tennyson and walked to Jack's office. He sat behind his large mahogany desk with Ruth Marie in a chair next to him.

"Charlotte," he began, motioning toward two empty chairs in front of the desk. "I found this in Mother's attic." He handed her several pieces of legal-sized papers stapled together. "I don't know what made me look. I saw something pushed off to the side between some boxes that looked like my dad's old briefcase. I guess I was feeling nostalgic, I don't know. I just felt like I should open it. This is what I found."

The bold print at the top read GRANT DEED. She scanned the document. *I hereby deed... all properties pertaining to... by the name of Katu Island... jointly to my son, Jackson Parker Buchanan, and my daughter, Charlotte Grace Sinclair... signed, William Jenkins Buchanan.*

"Oh my God." She inhaled sharply. She covered her mouth with her shaking hand. "Oh my God," she said again, high-pitched as the emotion reached her voice. She handed the document to Will.

He rose and paced the room as he read it. Jack typed furiously on the computer. "I'm pulling up the county record of who owns Katu Island." The room fell silent as Jack worked. He stared at the screen intently, barely breathing, until finally he looked up at Charlotte. "It's ours," he said, shaking his head as if still piecing together the information. "Mother owns the house and the buildings, but we own the land."

"He knew," Ruth Marie whispered, stating the obvious. Charlotte was beyond words. Things were both so clear, yet so confused. *He knew my name. He left me his land. Why didn't he contact me?*

Jack studied the computer. "The land is not in arrears for taxes." He thought for a moment. "Mother must have been paying them. She must know that we own the land. She has to." He didn't look convinced. "I'll call the county on Monday and find out for sure."

Ruth Marie placed her delicate hand on his shoulder. The shock on Jack's face softened as he looked at Charlotte directly. "He knew." With a swift movement, Jack rose from behind his desk and pulled her up into a hug. "Our father may not be here to speak for himself, but I can tell you that he loved you, Charlotte. Over Mother's dead body, he loved you."

Chapter Thirty-Four

"THERE IS NO way on God's green earth I'm gonna leave you to yourself after you just got news like that." Will took hold of her hand and walked with her along the sidewalk to Tea and Tennyson. "You talk, I'll listen."

"I'm tired, Will. I don't feel like talking. I think I just need to…process."

"Okay then, you process and I'll sit. I won't talk, I promise."

"There's no reason for you to sit there while I think. Go on home and I'll call you tomorrow."

"Charlotte, I'm gonna save us both some trouble by telling you that I'm not leaving you at a time like this. You can pretend like I'm not here if you want, but I'm not leavin' until I'm sure you're okay." She couldn't help but smile as they climbed the stairs to her loft. She was so used to having to handle everything on her own, it was nice to have someone willing to bear the news with her.

Neither of them were terribly hungry, so Charlotte put out a wedge of Brie with some crackers and grapes. Will opened a bottle of pinot grigio, laughing about how she didn't have beer, and they sat together at the table. Charlotte knew she was being uncommonly quiet, but where to begin? Will, true to his word, remained silent. For the most part.

"I have an idea," he said finally, excusing himself from the table and heading toward the bathroom.

Seconds later, she heard the unmistakable sound of water hitting her claw-footed bathtub.

Will reappeared. "How about you soak in the bath, and I'll see if there's a game on out here."

For a manly man, he was incredibly perceptive. She stood and hugged him. "Thank you. That'd be perfect."

Minutes later, as she soaked in the tub, the muted sounds of a football game made her smile.

How did Bill know he had a daughter? Did you tell him, Mom? Why didn't he find me? The urge to get up and find her firefly jar was overwhelming. *It's gone. She's gone. He's gone.* She gritted her teeth and sunk her entire head down into the water. What in the hell was she supposed to do with that land? It came with a crazy lady living on it.

She came up for air. *He knew.* He knew about her and he gave her his land. He accepted her as his daughter. Only he never met her. Had he planned to? Was he making plans to find her, but then died?

Charlotte got out of the tub and dried herself off, pulling on the robe she kept on a hook behind the door. After towel-drying her hair, she brushed it out, slightly embarrassed by its dampness but not enough to take the time to dry it. Will's eyes never left her as she walked in front of the TV and plopped onto her stepdad's leather recliner. He put the television on mute but said nothing. She tucked her feet up onto the chair, underneath her bathrobe, and stared out the window.

The brick courthouse buildings across the street dated back to the early 1900s. They looked invincible with their sharp corners and freshly painted white trim, like they'd be there forever. "My dad once lived in this town, probably walked along that very sidewalk," she said, still fighting for clarity through the emotion. "Technically, I might own part of his island. But I don't think I want it. It doesn't make things right, and I sure don't want to be tied to Virginia any more than I already am."

"You could make it yours. The piece that was your dad's. The part that never belonged to Jack or Virginia. He specifically left it to you."

"If I took it, it would only be to get back at Virginia, and I just can't get myself to be happy about that. She deserves for me to take it. I should throw it in her face. But I can't."

"Give it some time. You don't have to decide today."

"Plus, Bill Buchanan didn't even know me. And I certainly don't need something left to me out of guilt."

"How do you know his motivation?"

"It's pretty obvious. I was a mistake. Mom tried to make it right by never telling me anything, and Bill tried to make himself feel better about it by leaving me his island. I wish he would have just called me and said, *Hey, I know your mother's dying and you're gonna be all alone, so here I am. Your dad.*

You have a family. You're loved. Something. Anything would have been nice."

Charlotte breathed heavily. The place where sea turtles laid their eggs, the estuaries where birds flew low to catch fish, and thick old oaks dripping with Spanish moss. Maybe if she knew something about how to take care of a wild island, she could embrace it. But no, only Jack and Virginia lived on its land, only they knew its secret hideaways and hidden treasures. They even named an alligator Bert or Ernie—she couldn't remember which. It was Jack who showed her the turtles and Virginia who called it home. She was an outsider. She'd be lying to herself if she thought she wasn't.

It was better to just let it go. Anything Charlotte owned would be earned, created with her own hardworking mind and hands.

Will supported her through all of it, listening, asking questions, withholding judgment.

Around midnight, he stood to leave, but Charlotte couldn't bear it. Having him here showed her just how much she didn't want to be alone. They climbed into bed, exhausted. Cuddled against his chest, she knew how right he was. And despite the electricity between them, he never pushed for more than a snuggle. Somehow, he knew that the timing wasn't right for anything else.

Not even an island could fix the mistake Bill and her mother made.

Chapter Thirty-Five

J ACK DRAGGED INTO Tea and Tennyson, looking like he'd had a bottle of whiskey and an hour's sleep. Charlotte rushed to him. "Are you okay? Is Ruth Marie okay?"

"Yep. Yep," he said heavily. "We're fine." He lumbered to a chair and sat. Charlotte followed and sat beside him. "I'd love a cup of coffee before we get to talking."

"You got it." She hopped up to prepare a large black coffee for her brother.

A few minutes later, she returned, holding the coffee, her heart pounding. "Don't worry," Jack said. "Everything's okay." Charlotte wasn't buying it. He was too defeated, too concerned. She hated bad news, and she hated the anticipation of bad news even more.

"I went over to Mother's last night," he began. "It took a bit of liquid courage to bring up the subject of the land, but I just couldn't wait on it." His eyes were puffy and dark. "I don't know which hurts more, my head or my heart."

"What'd she say?"

"I assumed, you know, I assumed she knew about the grant deed, because the taxes were all paid up. So I laid into her for keeping me in the dark all these years. I accused her of keeping your daddy from you and the secret from me. I was mad, I was drunk, and I'd just had it up to here with her." He put his hand flat over the top of his head.

"Don't feel bad, Jack. She's had that coming a long time now." Charlotte felt a guilty surge of joy. Jack told her off!

"I thought so too, but as it turns out, Mother didn't have a clue about him giving us Katu."

"That can't be true."

"Oh, I believe it is. You should have seen her." His hand shook as he sipped his coffee. "She started out still as stone, so I figured she was thinking about how she was going to explain herself. Then, like a freaking exorcism, she let out this unbelievable yell." His lips turned white as he bit them together. "It was this feral sort of animal sound, like she was being strangled; a god-awful noise from the pit of her soul."

Charlotte, taken aback by the story and Jack's obvious alarm, reached for his hand, but he didn't notice, using it to pantomime Virginia. "She started half walking and half running around the room, shaking her arms like she couldn't stand to be in her own skin. I tried to get a hold of her, but, oh my God, if you could have seen the way she looked at me."

"We can fix this," Charlotte said. "She can have my portion. I don't want it."

"Don't talk crazy, Charlotte. I don't think it'd do any good, anyway. She's mad at our dad, and there's nothing we can do to change it. It's done."

"Where is she now?"

"Home. I stayed with her last night. Gave her a hot toddy and put her to bed after she finally calmed down. She refused to speak a word to me, but at least she had herself under control. She was sleeping when I left this morning." Jack ran a hand through his unkempt hair. "Look, much as I love my mother, my dad knew what he was dealing with. It's always been about the land, the house, and the name for her. It was never about family or love or decency." He shook his head. "I hate saying all that like she's the devil or something. She does love people, she truly does, it just wasn't what was most important to her."

"I actually feel sorry for her."

"Well, don't. I have a feeling she's gonna put all that anger she has for our dad on us. Or, maybe just on you. Brace yourself, Charlotte. Something's gonna happen, and it ain't gonna be pretty."

"There's nothing she can do. She has no power over me."

"I hope you're right." His hand was steadier as he sipped his coffee this time. "I wish I'd checked on those taxes before I went over there. I was just so sure, you know. I was sure she was in on it."

Scruggs brought over a warm, gooey pecan strudel and two forks. "Y'all look like you need some food."

"Thanks," they said together.

"Turns out those property taxes have been paid by a

trust," Jack said. "I called the county this morning and they led me to a law firm right down the street. They've been handling the trust as a third party with the stipulation of not telling us until either Mother died or we asked. I'm guessing Dad knew he wasn't in good health, even though I don't remember him ever talking about it. Not only did he leave us the island, he left us enough money to keep it and take care of it."

Charlotte put down her fork.

"I'm sorry, Charlotte. The law firm has no personal letters for us. But they did have strict orders to keep the information from Mother. If all had gone well, our dad wouldn't have died so soon and Mother could have lived her whole life never knowing she wasn't living on her own land."

"And I wouldn't know about my father for all those years? Until she was out of the way?"

"I'm sure he had a plan. I just don't know what it was."

She looked at the strudel and couldn't imagine taking another bite. Jack wasn't eating either.

Charlotte spent the rest of the day greeting customers, preparing drinks, serving pastries, helping locate books, cleaning and going about her normal routine. But beneath her cheery façade, she couldn't stop thinking about Virginia and what she might do next.

At the end of the long day, she was happy to finally be sitting on the couch with a cup of peppermint tea, on the phone with Will.

"If you'd asked me a year ago how I thought Mr. Buchanan would react in a situation like this, I'd have said, without a doubt, that he'd hop on the first plane out and find his baby girl," Will said. "I have a hard time understanding why he didn't track you down right away. Makes no sense to me."

"Do you think he was afraid of Virginia?"

"Afraid of his own wife? He'd be a sorry excuse for a man if that were the case." He paused. "Hold for a second, Charlotte." When he came back, he was in a hurry. "There's smoke coming from Katu. A lot of it. I'll call you back."

Charlotte hung up the phone. *I don't believe it.*

She was putting on her shoes when Will called back a minute later. She could hear that he was in his truck. "I called 911. The fire department is already on their way. I'm going, too. Call you soon. Sit tight, okay?"

"Okay." But she had no intention of sitting tight. She ran to her car, tires squealing as she reversed out of her parking space and headed in the direction of Katu. Sirens cut through the air from the fire trucks ahead of her. Driving with one hand, she called Birdie to find out if Virginia was with her.

Birdie flew into hysterics, repeating, "What, what, what?" Charlotte heard her slam down the phone. Presumably, Birdie was on her way, too.

When Charlotte arrived at the bridge, several firefighters appeared to be in the initial stages of blocking off the entrance. She zoomed past them without slowing down, following the smoke down the long, muddy, gravel road to Virginia's home. When she got to the circular driveway, she could hardly believe the scene. Good God in heaven. The broad white columns of Virginia's grand Greek Revival mansion stood like Atlas trying to hold up the world while flames grew toward the roof from the windows on the top floor. Ash covered Charlotte's windshield. She parked a good distance away and ran toward the house.

As she approached, her hair swirled around her head, propelled by the heat. She saw Will checking each of the lower windows, trying to look in, while Jack spoke intently with a firefighter and Ruth Marie sat in the Jeep several yards away. Ruth Marie shouldn't inhale any part of the massive clouds of billowing smoke. Maybe she was safe in the car. The whole scene was surreal, like they stepped out of reality and into *Gone with the Wind*. Surely, Charlotte wasn't really standing here, witnessing the violent demise of her family's ancestral home.

Will ran over to her.

"They haven't found Virginia yet. Can you call Birdie? Maybe she's with her."

"I called on the way here. Virginia's not there." They both turned toward the house, looking for Virginia, Middie, or any number of staff members who might be seen leaning out a window, waving madly for help. Flames, smoke, and water were the only things moving. *No one could survive that much heat and smoke.* The sound of panicked barking and whining came at her like an alarm.

"Oh my God, the dogs!" She moved forward and Will grabbed her arm.

"They're fine. The kennel is far enough away from the house in the back that they're not in danger. The firefighters know about them."

A sharp movement to their right caught their attention. They turned to look in time to see Jack break from the firefighter and run around the side of the house. Without hesitation, Will took off after him. Charlotte watched, horrified.

Ruth Marie came running up behind her, her slightly growing belly making her appear fragile. Charlotte grabbed her, trying to steady her from the turbulence taking place before their eyes. "What's he doing?" Ruth Marie cried.

"I don't know," Charlotte said. "I don't know." Thick smoke stung her eyes and lungs. She put her arm around Ruth Marie's waist, helping to hold her up, blinking away the haze and straining to catch a glimpse of Will or Jack. It was like their men were soldiers running into battle, brave and strong, intent on their mission, no matter what the consequence. She prayed for a happy ending and pulled Ruth Marie closer.

A firefighter forced them to move back, handing them each a face mask to help protect them from the smoke. From behind her head, Charlotte heard, "Give me one of them breathin' thingies." Birdie had arrived. She wiggled her way between the two girls and held them both tightly against her comfortingly soft body.

They were squished together only a few minutes, but to Charlotte, it felt like an hour before she finally caught sight of Will and Jack emerging from the side of the house. Between them, they carried Virginia, a life-sized rag doll dressed in a gray pantsuit. One arm flopped to the cadence of the boys' footsteps, her head thrown back abnormally far, mouth gaping open. Birdie yelped, pulling off her oxygen mask for a better look, and when she let go, Ruth Marie collapsed to the ground. Charlotte tried to catch her. Sitting on the ground, she placed Ruth Marie's head on her lap, trying to hold the oxygen in place with a vigorously shaking hand.

Firefighters descended upon Will and Jack, taking Virginia's unconscious body and placing her on a stretcher, where they pushed an oxygen mask onto her face and rushed her inside the waiting ambulance. Jack noticed Ruth Marie on the ground and for a moment looked torn before running full-out toward his wife. Birdie flapped her way to the ambulance yelling, "Hold up! I'm going with her! Don't you go to that hospital without me! You hear me?!" She climbed into the back of the truck just before they closed the doors. It took off screaming into the darkness.

Will jogged to Charlotte, who was still on the ground tending to Ruth Marie while Jack asked questions to ascertain her level of coherence. "I'm okay," said Ruth Marie. "Don't worry about me. Just got light-headed. How's Virginia?"

"She's alive," Jack said. "Barely, but she's alive." He stood Ruth Marie up carefully and walked her toward his Jeep. "Meet y'all at the hospital."

Charlotte plopped onto the ground. Virginia might die. The hatred she held for her disappeared like melted snow. So many of the things she hated about Virginia, Charlotte had been doing herself. She told her she would take the island. She told her she would be a better Buchanan. She'd been unable to look past her own desire to avenge her mother to see that Virginia was a human being, a widow, a mother, and a former impressionable young girl.

"You okay?" Will asked, kneeling beside her.

Charlotte nodded. She needed to get away.

He walked her to her car and opened the door for her. "See you at the hospital."

She gave him a thumbs-up, then drove with the windows down, hoping for fresh air. She smelled the mossy remnants of the recent rain. The trees, scrub, and undergrowth in the forest, all were damp. That was lucky. Very lucky. The stately home of her ancestors that, until that moment, had caused her to feel an intimidated pit in her stomach was no longer, but the island would most likely survive. She prayed Virginia would, too.

Birdie was pacing the waiting room when they all

showed up. She started talking before anyone could ask for an update. "So, she took in a bunch of smoke. I guess that can kill a person, but the good news is that she's not dead yet. I'm worried, though. Real worried. That woman never said so much as hello to me in the ambulance, even though she was looking right at me. I'm guessing that means it's bad, y'all. To not even acknowledge your best friend? It's got to be real bad."

Will put his arm around Charlotte and she pressed into him, looking over at her brother, who was helping Ruth Marie to sit down. Everyone was silent, listening to Birdie.

"Listen y'all," Birdie said. "Virginia Buchanan will not die in this manner. Nope. She just won't do it, especially when it is not yet her time. Right? We know her. This is not her grand exit. Anyway, the doctor said he'd be out again in about an hour, and there's nothing we can do until then anyway." She looked at each of them, and when she got little response, acted exasperated. "I'm gonna find me something to drink. Y'all want anything?" The group shook their heads and pulled up seats alongside Ruth Marie.

"How'd you know to go in that window?" Charlotte asked Jack.

"I guess I just know my mother," he said. "I was talking to the firefighter about where they might look for her, when it hit me: if she were going to try to kill herself, she would think about every detail, right down to where she wanted to be found." He made the statement as if this were a perfectly normal thought process.

"You think she set the fire on purpose?" Charlotte might have had that passing thought too, but dismissed it as ludicrous. Had she pushed Virginia to suicide?

"It's a possibility." He looked sad and exhausted. "I couldn't think for a while where she might be, but then it just popped into my head. The china room."

"Which one is the china room?" Charlotte asked.

"It's the sitting room at the bottom of the front stairs. She calls it the china room because it's where she has the family's Limoge china and Repoussé sterling. It's also where she hung the oil paintings of our more famous Buchanan ancestors. I knew she'd be in there. Even knew which chair she'd be in."

"It was just like Jack said," Will interjected. "When we busted in the side window, we found her slumped over in that chair."

"She meant to do this." Charlotte could barely stand.

"I don't know for sure," Jack said. "But I wouldn't put it past her."

"Was she trying to get revenge on us by burning down her house, or was she trying to kill herself?" Ruth Marie asked.

"The Mrs. Buchanan I know would never take her own life," Will said, his jaw clenched.

"I don't believe it." Ruth Marie nodded in agreement.

"She's too feisty for that," Jack said, his eyes betraying his deep worry and sorrow. "I think this was her revenge—position herself as a victim, get sympathy on her side, and make Charlotte feel like it was her fault for moving here to begin with. All because she no longer owns the land."

After stewing for more than an hour, sipping on diet sodas and listening to Birdie give every conceivable reason as to why Virginia would never set fire to her own home, the group was given the news that Virginia was awake and lucid. She was going to survive. Furthermore, by an odd stroke of luck, her staff had been given the day off. And it was an incredibly fortunate thing that she'd been on the bottom floor—the smoke and heat on the top floor would have killed her quickly.

The doctor might as well have said, "Obviously, the woman planned the whole thing." When he finished talking, he nodded with sympathy and walked back through the swinging doors he'd emerged from earlier, leaving the group looking at one another wide-eyed and shaking their heads.

Charlotte's guilt may have been misplaced. After all, Virginia's behavior was nowhere near normal. But, a thought kept nagging at her: if she'd never come to Crickley Creek, the Buchanan ancestral home would still be standing.

Chapter Thirty-Six

THE NEXT MORNING, while Virginia remained hospitalized, Ruth Marie stayed home to rest and recover while Jack, Will and Charlotte met at the island to assess the damage. Birdie was on hospital duty.

Charlotte felt numb as she crossed the caution tape and walked among the ashes and occasional smoldering ember. The island had been spared, but the house was a complete loss, the first floor barely recognizable and the second floor gone altogether. Nothing could be salvaged, the contents now charred wood or ash. The house would have to be razed.

Jack's waxy, pale face and red-rimmed eyes made him look twenty years older. He kicked over debris, looking desperately for something spared: a picture, a spoon, a paperweight, anything. Every memento of his childhood, every ancestral heirloom, valuables that survived the Civil War and the Great Depression, family artifacts passed down for generations, were lost forever. All the family photos—gone. She would never know what her grandparents looked like, or their parents before them. She would never see what her brother looked like at the age of two, or her father as a young man. She'd never eat from the family china again, never have a cuff link, or a watch, or even a tie as a token of her father. No family Bible, nothing to pass down to her children from the Buchanan side of the family. If she ever had children.

They are just things. We can do without the things. But inside, she grieved the loss of something she never even had.

A few professionals were still cleaning up, and two men in blue walked around, making notes on a clipboard as they spoke with Jack. Charlotte guessed they were from the insurance company. "We're still in the initial stages," said the uniformed man. "But it appears as though the fire began in the upstairs master bedroom." Charlotte pictured Virginia's bedroom, the grand mahogany bed, dainty sitting area, fireplace, the family portrait she stood below when she realized the man in the painting was her father. *Of course.* Charlotte had no doubt that the piece of wood that first caught fire was the frame of that family painting.

Jack joined her and Will. "Something just occurred to me," he said. "Now that I look back, when we rescued Mom, something was wrong with that room."

"What?" Charlotte asked, stuffing her guilt, pretending she was completely innocent.

"The shelves were empty," Jack said. "There was no china on display in the china room." He squinted as if to see the room better in his mind. "Her box of silver was gone, too. All my life, that box sat on its little table, holding her precious dinnerware. It wasn't there."

Will pointed to a portion of wall still standing. It was once a hallway on the main floor. "There are no pictures on the wall. Wouldn't there be *something*?"

"Where do you think it is?" Charlotte asked.

Jack walked to what used to be the entryway. "When we got here, the roof above the front door had already caved in." He looked around, adding it all up. "She stayed too long. Her escape route was destroyed." His face dropped as he looked at Charlotte. "Damn woman."

Will added, "And when we found her, the window was stuck. We had to bust through it. She couldn't get out that way either."

"Follow me," Jack said. They moved as quickly as they could over the remains of the house toward the woods. Once they could step safely, all three sprinted the short distance to the clearing where the old church where Jack and Ruth Marie were married stood. The double front doors were locked, but Jack had a key. When he swung the doors open, there was a collective gasp. The room was filled with Virginia's belongings. Like the holy grail, the box holding four generations of Buchanan family silver sat in front of the door in its high polish mahogany box atop its special table.

Charlotte delicately opened the lid. Everything was there, right down to the pickle fork. Jack walked down each pew, lifting the lids on carefully packed boxes of antique Limoges china and items ranging from photo albums to Lladro figurines.

"Whoa," Will said, taking it all in. "I think we just found Blackbeard's treasure." Oil paintings of ancient ancestors leaned against the walls, and watercolors of seabirds lay stacked next to them. A large jewelry box filled with rings, bracelets, and several pearl necklaces sat tucked beneath a pew, articles of clothing still on hangers swayed from light fixtures, and at least five boxes filled with loose photos were lined up near the door. Furniture of all sorts lay haphazardly around the room. It was nearly all there. Only one thing was conspicuously absent: the oil painting from the master bedroom.

Not only had Virginia set the fire on purpose, she'd spent a lot of energy planning it. How did a person ever get to the point of doing something like that? The nagging feeling kept growing in Charlotte's chest.

Jack walked among the items like it was a yard sale. He mumbled as he touched each of his family treasures. "She's crazy. She's certifiably insane." He found a pillow from his mother's bed and threw it on the floor. "Stupid woman. What in the hell are we supposed to do now?"

Charlotte was relieved that Jack hadn't lost his mother, that his treasures were still intact. She was relieved that she might now see those pictures of her ancestors, of her brother as a child, her father as a young man. But it didn't have to come to this. Jack and Virginia almost lost everything.

Jack finally sat. He looked like he'd been kicked in the

gut. How was a son supposed to react to a mother whose plot to gain revenge, or attention, resulted in such a loss? Virginia had taken the old "you'll be sorry when I'm gone" line to an extreme.

Moving slower than his usual hurried pace, Jack locked the church, patted Will on the back, kissed Charlotte on the cheek, and left to visit his errant mother.

Charlotte needed to get back to work. She had customers in the store, and Will had investigators to talk to and subcontractors to oversee. She kissed Will extra hard before getting into the car. What she needed to do was work, throw herself into appreciating her customers, finish her baking, organize her books. Maybe she'd design a new display. The distraction would help her escape the endless thoughts centering on her stepmother. Even Cinderella's stepmother never dared to burn down the castle.

Charlotte took in the passing scenery, quaint homes and kudzu-covered signs, every living thing a shade of green she couldn't find in California. Her mother, pregnant and alone, had been forced to leave everything familiar: the town she loved, her family, her friends, and the man she lost to a woman so caught up in *name* and *heritage* that she'd just rendered herself homeless. Virginia would now have to live with what she'd done.

And so would she.

Charlotte's head throbbed, probably because she inhaled too much smoke from smoldering embers. The smell of burnt wood coated the inside of her nose like creosote. She craved the comfort found in the smell of bread and coffee, cozy bookshelves holding promises of fictional or biographical escape, artful displays that pleased the eye and unique trinkets so cute or original as to warrant a special spot in someone's home. Oh, how she loved her store. She wanted nothing more than to see Waffles's fuzzy little face and listen to Scruggs's overly dramatic stories.

What she walked into was a store filled with concerned customers. Word traveled fast, especially when it had been on the local news. Birdie waited by the door, jingle bells hanging on a green ribbon around her neck. According to Krista, Birdie'd been there most of the day, eating and drinking and talking and eating and talking and talking some more. If a person didn't know about the Buchanans' tragedy before they stepped foot in the door, they were fully apprised of it by the time they stepped out.

Birdie ran to Charlotte's side, firing questions at her along the way, clearly desperate for the latest details.

"Why are you asking all these questions?" Charlotte asked. "Weren't you with Virginia today?"

"I tried, dammit," she said. "First, the pea-brained doctors wouldn't let me in to see her; said I'd been banned from her room for bringing her the teensy-tiniest nickel nip of whiskey or some such nonsense. Then, when they finally weren't looking long enough for me to squeeze in, she wouldn't so much as mumble hello. Nope, not a word came out of her fool mouth. She just stared me in the face, all pissed off, shooting them daggers at me with her eyes. Like *I* did something wrong. The gall of that woman."

"No kidding," Charlotte said. "Wait until you hear this." She told a slack-jawed Birdie all about what they found in the church.

"Well, I'll be." She shook her head sympathetically. "No wonder she wouldn't talk to me."

"Yeah. You don't think she was trying to kill herself, do you? Not if she kept all of her stuff, right?" For some reason, she needed Birdie's verification.

"I can't imagine anyone so full of sass would go that far."

"I hope you're right."

"Oh, she won't tell us why she did it, probably won't ever admit that she did, but I'm quite certain she had a plan—something that will make people think she hasn't completely lost her ever-lovin' mind."

"I don't know, Birdie. This whole suicide/arson thing is crossing a line."

"Mark my words, honey, she'll pull through. She'll pick herself up, dust herself off, and get on with life. Mostly because she has to."

"That's so Scarlett O'Hara." Charlotte picked up two coffee mugs from a nearby table and walked them to a bin while Birdie trailed behind.

"More like that mule our Nobel Laureate Mr. Faulkner wrote about, the one who'd *labor ten years willingly and patiently for the privilege of kicking you once.* Virginia waited and waited, and when the time came, she made her kick count. And I bet you that somewhere inside that crazy head of hers, she's happy she did it."

"Birdie?"

"Mmm-hmm."

"Do you think it's my fault?"

"Honey, now you're sounding like the crazy one."

Charlotte placed the mugs in the bin with a clink. "If you say so, Birdie."

Chapter Thirty-Seven

THE WEATHER WARMED, the sun bright but not too hot, with cool breezes blowing inland off the Atlantic. Plum trees bloomed pink, and a woodpecker worked hard in the oak on the back patio of Tea and Tennyson. Charlotte was happy to see the woodpecker. She knew they represented strength and wisdom by finding value in the most hopeless of things—like dead trees.

Charlotte was busy finishing the day-before preparations for Jack's birthday party. It would be the first time she would see Virginia since the fire, but daily updates from Jack gave her an idea of what to expect. Virginia's plan had backfired. No one was waiting on her hand and foot, no one was devastated that she almost died. No, the only people who suffered at the hands of Virginia now were Birdie and Ashby, who had given in and let her stay in their guest room. There was no end to Virginia's complaints: their house was too cold, too hot, too messy, the food was too rich, and Birdie watched those awful reality shows full of low-class talentless trailer trash. It was unbearable.

Ruth Marie had begged Charlotte to cater Jack's birthday

party at the store. In her second trimester, she tired easily and, despite her best intentions, just wasn't up to cooking for twenty. The lunch didn't have to be fancy, and Charlotte had been considering branching out into catering anyway.

Charlotte wore a safe, navy-blue wrap dress and strappy brown sandals, certain she was neither under nor over-dressed. She carefully set the finger sandwiches on top of the arranged cake plates: cucumber and cream cheese at Ruth Marie's request, a cold version of hot ham buns for Jack. She'd made more than enough, opting to have too much food rather than too little. Plucking apart stems of grapes, she artfully draped them next to the fresh fruit covering one of the larger cake plates, compulsively glancing every few seconds at the doorway. Next, she made a pyramid of miniature quiches on top of a porcelain cake plate made to look like lace. The other plates were topped with prosciutto rolls, a variety of meats and cheeses, and fifty spicy rice and Gruyere balls. Twenty-five cappuccino cups holding chilled gazpacho filled every empty space on the table. Ruth Marie had provided the handsomely decorated dark chocolate birthday cake, and Birdie was supposed to bring the punch.

There was still no sign of Virginia. Thank God.

Birdie barely walked into the store before her booming voice announced, "Where's my diamond tiara? This is like a feast for royalty."

"Hello to you, too, Birdie," Charlotte said. Thank good-ness someone else was in the room in case Virginia walked in.

After admiring the food, Birdie walked her giant bottles of ginger ale to the punch table. "You done good, honey. It looks like Martha Stewart herself was here."

Ashby strolled in a few minutes later, wearing a blue-and-white seersucker suit and holding a bag that appeared to be filled with several cartons of orange sherbet in one hand, and a sagging bag filled with champagne bottles in the other. "The punch fixin's have arrived," he announced, placing the items on the table. "Those are some excellent-looking hors d'oeuvres you got there."

"Thank you." Even though Charlotte was confident in the taste of her food, it was nice to hear the compliments on her presentation. She smiled, and was still smiling when she realized Virginia was standing in the doorway like an apparition. Will walked up behind her, his presence somehow making her less ghost-like.

"Oh, my dear friends," Virginia cooed in her syrupy voice, the smile on her face dazzling in its brilliance. She turned to Will and reached for his hand. "How lovely." Pulling him into the store as if he were her boyfriend, she never so much as glanced Charlotte's way. Will allowed her to pull him a few feet, then he dropped Virginia's hand and made a beeline for Charlotte. Virginia ignored the whole exchange.

The party roared to life as soon as Jack and Ruth Marie arrived. All eyes were on the beautiful couple on the precipice of parenthood, both of them happily glowing. Charlotte could honestly say she was glad for them.

Virginia worked the crowd like a seasoned politician, laughing heartily and making witty remarks. She was utterly charming.

"Charlotte!" Birdie nearly fell into her. "I will kill him for you, I promise I will!"

Charlotte nearly spilled her punch. "Kill who?"

"My stupid husband, that's who." Birdie smacked him on the chest. "He just casually slipped up ten minutes ago. *Bill would've been so pleased to see his son and daughter together*, he said."

"What are you talking about?"

"This man right here"—she jabbed Ashby in the chest with her pointer finger—"told Bill he had a daughter!" She glared at Charlotte, becoming aware that others were starting to listen. "Follow me."

Birdie let them to the outside patio. "I said, *Ashby Asa Crane, what in Dante's burning hell are you talking about?* Then he got all sorry like a little puppy dog and said he couldn't go on letting you wonder how your father knew about you. He thought he was doing what was best, blah, blah, blah."

"Well, that's great!" Charlotte said, sitting. "At least that mystery is solved."

If Ashby told Bill, her mother hadn't. Secretly, she'd hoped that when Anna Grace was diagnosed with cancer, she'd reached out to him, tried to make things right.

"Great? Number one: he is not supposed to share secrets under any circumstances. And B: he should have told you way back when we first talked about it." She rolled her eyes at him. "Your *I'm a pastor and I am sworn to keep secrets* crap makes me want to slap you upside the head sometimes."

With his long, skinny legs and bulging eyes, he looked like a guilty giraffe. He turned to Charlotte, his voice a whisper. "Truly, I apologize. Back when we were talking at the wedding, I didn't know if it'd cause more harm or good by telling you. I thought it might hurt your feelings, since you'd never heard from the man. I mean, how much can we expect a person to take in one day?"

Charlotte felt nothing but love for Ashby. Birdie, on the other hand, continued to glare at him.

"Withhold your judgment, woman. You did the same thing," he reminded her.

"Please don't feel bad," Charlotte said, patting his hand. He looked grateful.

"Hurry up and tell her about it, for God's sake," Birdie said.

"Well," he began. "I didn't know your mama was pregnant until Birdie shared the news with me just a few years back."

"He's the only one I told, I swear," said Birdie, crossing her heart. "The man is honor-bound to keep a secret. And it's important that he knows just how much his parishioners are sinning. You know, so he can pray for them."

Ashby waited for her to shut up. "I was at old Hinckley Youngblood's funeral," he said. "Bill didn't look right. I mean, he had dark circles under his eyes and he was all puffy and gray. When we walked up the hill to the burial plot, he was huffin' and puffin' like he'd just run a mile full-out. God told me in that moment that Bill wasn't going to live much longer. He impressed it upon my heart with such strength, that I knew exactly what I had to do. I had to tell him about you. I had no choice."

Birdie rolled her eyes.

"I saw that, Mrs. Crane," he said. "I am a man of faith, and I'd appreciate your cooperation as my wife."

"Okay, okay," she said. "Keep talking."

"So, we were standing there, next to the coffin, and I just blurted it out. That Anna Grace had his child, and that's why she moved to California. The poor man nearly fell into Hinkley's hole. Teetered like a weeble-wobble. Scared me half out of my wits."

"Do you have any idea how he found out my name?"

"Well, yes. I told him. See, Birdalee has had some contact with your mother through the years. That's why she took you under her wing back when we first heard you arrived in Crickley."

For some reason, that news didn't make Charlotte angry. In her own way, Birdie had done what she could to protect her friend's daughter. Looking up through guilty downcast eyes, Birdie must have sensed Charlotte's softening, as she lifted her head proudly.

"I never knew much," Birdie said. "Getting anything out of your mother was like trying to pull duct tape off silk."

"How long ago did Mr. Youngblood die?" Charlotte asked Ashby.

"Well, I guess it's coming up on two years."

She mentally calculated the timeframe. "It's been almost two years now since my mother died. If he contacted her after you told him, she was already really sick." He had deeded her his land soon after he found out he had a daughter. But in that year, he never contacted her.

Birdie seemed appeased by his story. "Well, I think we're done here."

Ashby patted her hand, then leaned over to Birdie and whispered in her ear, "Now, it's time for us to go home and make up."

"Well, then." Birdie flushed red as a beet. "Alrighty." Grabbing her purse, she stood, turned on her heels and walked briskly toward the front door. Ashby waved solemnly at Charlotte, then followed, grinning.

Charlotte found her way to Jack and touched him on the arm. "Hey, sis, what's up?"

"I have news."

She took a deep breath and told him what she'd just learned.

"It's just so odd," Jack said. "Our dad wasn't the kind of

man who didn't face up to things. Why didn't he find you?"

"Good question."

"Do you think your mother wouldn't let him?"

"I don't know."

Ruth Marie joined them, and Jack quickly filled her in.

"My guess is," Ruth Marie said, "if Bill had known about you before he knew about Jack, he probably would've married your mama instead."

Charlotte's stomach hurt at the thought.

Jack clinked his dessert fork against his glass. "If I could have y'all's attention, please." The room quieted immediately. "I just want to thank y'all for coming. It means so much to me to have you here to help celebrate my birthday. As y'all know, there have been some big changes since this time last year.

"First, I'd like to thank my sister, Charlotte, for the delicious food."

The crowd clapped and Charlotte's eyes went immediately to Virginia in time to see an annoyed look on her face before she quickly replaced it with a look of innocence.

"And I can't forget my beautiful wife, who arranged everything. Thank you, Ruth Marie."

Jack said nothing about his mother, who gave him a flared-nose smirk.

Thank God. The tide seemed to have turned.

Chapter Thirty-Eight

"WHATCHA WEARING THE frown lines for?" Will kissed her forehead, helping to relax the lines in between her eyebrows. Charlotte put down a dirty party dish and leaned into him. "Seeing Virginia today just got to me, I guess."

"I kept waiting for her to sprout wings and a stinger," he chuckled. "Never happened."

"Now I feel even more guilty about everything that has happened. It's like the whole town has conspired to punish Virginia for going too far. She lost everyone's respect. She has no home. And now she has no power. I mean, she might be a horrible person, but she's still a person."

"I know a thing or two about misplaced responsibility," he said. "We can't control other people, can we? I couldn't read Randy's mind any more than you could have known that Virginia would do something so reckless. It's on them, not us."

"Then why do we feel so guilty?" Charlotte lifted her head to look at his face.

His eyes held infinite understanding. "I reckon it's because we're good people."

"Is it really that simple?"

He kissed her gently. "I like to think so."

It took an hour to get Charlotte's dishes clean, the leftover food packaged for Jack and Ruth Marie, and the store back in pristine condition. By that time, Ruth Marie was seated on Charlotte's couch in the loft, her swollen ankles propped onto the coffee table.

"Well, at least that's over," Ruth Marie said when they all walked in.

Jack sat on the couch next to her and Charlotte and Will took the love seat. "That it is, sweetheart," said Jack. "Time for you to get some rest."

"It was a lovely party," Charlotte said.

"Did the birthday boy have a good time?" Ruth Marie asked.

Jack nodded and used his left hand to scratch his chin. He was wearing a watch. A nice one.

"Is that your dad's watch?" Charlotte asked.

"Yes." He looked pleased that she noticed. "Pardon the pun," he chuckled, "but I figured it was time. I took it out of the safe deposit box yesterday."

Charlotte was thrilled for him and his personal triumph. "So, you're wearing the watch." She smiled. How happy Bill would have been that his son was finally wearing it. How much courage it took for Jack to put it on.

"I've been thinking," Charlotte began. "If my mother

hadn't died, I might never have known all this. I wouldn't know you." She turned and smiled at Will, then to Jack and Ruth Marie. "I won't ever know Bill. But I think I'm beginning to understand what was important to him."

"What are you getting at?" Jack asked with a hopeful edge to his voice.

"Well, look what I found here—loggerheads, beach music, crabbing, old friends, new friends, Tea and Tennyson, family, and...love." She squeezed Will's hand. "I guess what I'm trying to say is...I've decided that I'm going to wear my watch." She sat silent while the meaning sank in.

"Really?" A slow smile spread across Jack's face.

"Just like our father didn't need to say anything to you when he gave you the watch, he doesn't need to say anything to me now." She looked to Will and he winked at her. "And the thing is, I'm not trying to get back at your mother. Through all of this, I finally found peace with her. My motivation feels pure." Charlotte shrugged. "The fact is, I love that island. I've known it since the day we went to see the turtles."

Barely able to control the building emotion, she pursed her lips and breathed deeply. "It scares me to have something so important. There are turtles and birds and alligators and deer and hundreds of species living on that island. It's a big responsibility to accept all that." Jack nodded, and she continued. "But our dad gave me part of his island. He knew what he was doing. He wanted me to have it. I will accept it and I will do my best to make my family—both families—proud."

"I'll start," said Jack. "I'm already proud of you."

Will stood and put his hand on her shoulder. She reached up and covered his hand with hers. "It's not just the island that I love. I love all of you, too. It was the fire that made me realize that belonging has nothing to do with where you came from. It's not about a place. It's not about fitting in either. They are two separate things. Belonging is about being your authentic self and finding people who appreciate you. It's about who you choose to love."

Jack's eyes were bright and locked on hers. She wiped at the tears moistening her face. "I've always wanted a big family, more than anything in my whole life. Craved it, actually. It's the one thing my mother couldn't give me. Now, I think I might have it."

Ruth Marie stood and hugged her. "We love you, too."

"I guess it's official." Jack looked pleased. "Welcome to the family."

The tears turned into laughter. She was just so *happy*. "I may never know how to be a Buchanan, but I understand now that I don't have to."

THAT COOL, SUNNY Sunday, Charlotte took a tour of the island with Jack. On the south side of the island, in a remote area near the sea turtle beach, something man-made in the middle of the natural setting caught Charlotte's eye. Long grasses nearly covered it over, but a glint of silver-gray peeked out of the ground from within what appeared to be a clearing in the woods.

Jack drove his Jeep toward the spot, and gasped when he saw a cement foundation and weather-beaten framing for a small home. "I never knew this was here," he said, jumping from the car. Charlotte hopped out, too, intrigued by the find. Judging from the size of the weeds and condition of the wood, it had been there awhile.

They walked along the foundation, guessing where the bedroom would have been, the bathroom, family room and kitchen. It was built to face the sea, and Jack pointed out stumps of several large trees, most likely felled to reveal the view. On the second step leading to what would have been a front porch was a metal lockbox, the lock missing. Jack opened it easily, and pulled out plans for the home, along with a pad of graph paper where it appeared Bill Buchanan had been working on perfecting a letter.

Jack stood still for a moment, reading, and when he finally looked up, his eyes were moist. He handed the paper to her.

My dear Charlotte,

I have only known of your existence for a short while, and I've never seen your face, but you've taken up a great portion of my heart. I would have contacted you

*sooner, but my wife is struggling to accept the news. I
wish I had contacted you sooner, and now I fear I am
horribly late. I have no desire to cause any problems in
your life. I don't want to upset you, but I want to be
your father. I would like to know you. We have a lovely
island here in South Carolina that has been a part of
the Buchanan family for well over two hundred years. I
am building you a home so you can visit whenever you
wish. I heard of your mother's passing and I am so sorry
for your loss. I loved her once very much. If you find in
the future that you would like to stay here permanently,
you have your own place, close enough to be part of the
family, but far enough away to have some privacy. My
wife will come to understand. I welcome you as my
daughter or not, if you wish. You should also know that
you have a brother, Jackson. I am certain you will like
him very much.*

Charlotte was too shocked to cry.

"Building you this house is just about the same as building you a fortress. One he could defend. Bringing you here
would start a war with Mother, and he knew it." Jack
grabbed her into a hug and held tightly.

"He wanted me." She smiled into his shirt.

Charlotte kept the letter in her pocket, reading it often
and grieving for the father she never knew; the man who
loved that island, loved her mother, and from the looks of
things, loved her. The house was his attempt to make things

right. Like his gift of the island, the house spoke to her better than words, because words were difficult and could be misconstrued. One thing became clear: the south side of the island was meant to be hers—miles of marsh, wetlands, forest and beach, including the sea turtle beach and the house her father began. Finally, her mind was at rest.

Down the way, closer to the shore, Jack was making plans to build a home in the style he and Ruth Marie loved. They would keep the church, the property around it, and most of the north side of the island.

Like the loggerhead sea turtle who dragged herself onto a beach and chose to build her family there, Charlotte had dragged herself to South Carolina and made it her home. With all her heart, Charlotte wanted to protect her island. She would keep it clean and safe for the turtles, alligators, birds, bobcats, cypress, old oaks, and every other living thing that made its home there. She would allow professionals to come over and study native plant and animal life, she would work to conserve the endangered species, like the brown pelican and the loggerheads. She would open it to tourists, but keep the numbers low so that the island could be appreciated without risking vandalism. It would never be sold or commercialized. Its history would be open for study, its secrets–good and bad–out in the open. It would forever be maintained, preserved, and used as a tool for learning. In her heart she knew she had much to understand, and that the island would make her a better person. She loved it like her store. More than her store—like family. It was a gift, a responsibility, a part of her heritage, and a reminder that she belonged right where she was.

Chapter Thirty-Nine

NOW THAT SUMMER was here, Will was busier than ever. The home-building business was booming, and he was able to employ almost everyone who lost their job when Randy went to prison. Tanned and happy, he was more handsome than Charlotte had ever seen him.

Charlotte's business was stable, and for the first time in years, so was her life. She spent every spare moment with Will. He never failed to walk her to the door after a date, or call her on his way home to make sure she made it safely into bed. He listened to her talk for hours, smiling his dimpled smile and teasing her about her California ways. Every now and then, he brought her flowers, or her favorite candy bar. Once, he bought her a green silk dress from the window of a boutique in Charleston. He said it made him think of her. A day never passed without a phone call or a hug.

It was July 21, Charlotte's twenty-seventh birthday. She wished she could share it with Anna Grace, eating her namesake dessert and opening gifts that only a mother could buy. Instead, she wore her mother's favorite shirt, the billowy white one with the colorful embroidery. At least that way, something of Anna Grace's was with Charlotte on the day she left the safety of her mother's body and entered into the world.

Early in the morning, as she set out the cream and prepared to open for business, Will stood at the door with an armful of roses, eager to start her day off right. The original plan was for Will to take her to Chaucer's restaurant for her birthday dinner, but Allison wouldn't hear of it. They'd be having a birthday dinner at the "big" house that evening.

The day dragged on, as days often did when she was anticipating something wonderful. Finally, Charlotte drove past the white picket fence of the Rushtons' home. She parked beside the stately red brick mansion and felt a shiver of delight when she noticed Will sitting on the front steps. As she exited the car, he stood.

"I have something for you." He looked like a three-year-old with a hand-drawn picture for his mother, hiding the treasure behind his back.

"What is it?"

"Pay the toll and I'll give it to you."

"The toll?"

He leaned over and puckered his lips for a kiss.

"Oooh, the toll." Standing on her tiptoes, she kissed him. When she stood back down, Will pulled a jar from behind his back and handed it to her. It was a regular Mason jar with a gold metal lid, one Allison probably used for canning. Holes had been punched through the top and on the bottom were flower blossoms. What made Charlotte cry, though, were the small, beetle-like flying bugs whose tails blinked light.

He'd given her a firefly jar.

Did he know that she saw this as a sign? He had to know this gift wasn't coming from him alone, that it was also a gift from her mother. A gift from the spirit of Anna Grace. It was proof. Tears streamed down her cheeks. They were her first real lightning bugs. Proof that it was okay that life was beginning again, fresh and new and better than ever.

Will chuckled at her tears, wiping them from her cheeks with his thumb. "All that for a jar of bugs?"

Charlotte held on tightly to the blinking jar as Will led her inside with his hand on the small of her back. The whole family was there, crowding around, hugging her and wishing her a happy birthday. Charlotte followed them into the kitchen where, sitting on the marble-topped kitchen island on top of a tall white cake stand, was a uniquely beautiful cake.

She looked closer. It was slightly slanted in at the top, encased by long, oval ladyfingers. Unlike the ladyfingers her mother would make, these had been dipped in chocolate. The inside was filled with Bavarian cream, artfully drizzled chocolate dripped over the top and mint sprigs had been set around the edges. Obviously, it was Allison's version of a Charlotte. Not only had Will remembered that detail, his mother went to the trouble of putting it all together. Charlotte hugged them both, saying "thank you" over and over.

The evening meal came straight from a recently purchased California cookbook. "For our California girl," Allison said. She served a salad of mixed field greens with candied walnuts, bleu cheese, cranberries and balsamic vinaigrette dressing. The entrée was a glazed pork loin with roasted olives and artichoke bruschetta. Then, as if worried there wouldn't be enough food, she also prepared her traditional cream of mushroom green bean casserole topped with French's fried onions.

At the family's insistence, after the meal, Charlotte and Will moved into the screened-in back porch. They were not, under any circumstance, allowed to help with the cleanup. Natalie and Brooke didn't even protest. Will sat Charlotte on a wicker chair in a windowed corner with her jar of fireflies on the table next to her. He handed her a glass of iced tea and told her he'd be back in a second. She put the icy glass against her lips and took a sweet and minty sip. Placing the glass next to the jar, she leaned back and closed her eyes, giving herself permission to indulge for just the tiniest of seconds. Each ray of the setting sun warmed her face, gentle beams of light enchanting her with their heat, beginning with her nose and spreading to her forehead and cheeks. Soon, her body was flooded with warmth. She felt the brilliant otherworldly presence of her mother.

"Hi, Mom," she said, barely audible. "I miss you." It was the first time she was able to speak those words without a wave of sadness attached to them. Instead, she felt peaceful and content. As a matter of fact, now that the grief wasn't getting in the way, she felt closer to her mother. Closer to heaven. Closer to happiness.

In the fuzzy center of her twilight mind, a whisper came through. *It doesn't matter where you are, my love. It only matters who you're with.* Charlotte soaked in the heavenly thought, the voice warm and familiar. But it was the next five words that freed her, that threw open the padlock she'd snapped into place over her heart.

I'm so proud of you.

A soft kiss on her forehead awakened her. "Wake up, Sleeping Beauty," Will whispered. Slowly, she opened her eyes and smiled up at him. She hadn't been asleep long, only a couple of minutes. Her grin grew wider. She was happy. Wonderfully, divinely, extraordinarily happy.

Will's eyes twinkled and she sat up with a start. He was up to something. Looking very serious, he bent over and knelt on one knee. His hand shook as he reached his right hand for her left, holding a small white box in the other. "Charlotte." His voice cracked. "Because of you, I am a better version of myself." His face looked so earnest, tears sprang to her eyes. "I can't imagine life without you. I want to build a family with you. I want to finish building your house on the beach, teach you how to fish, take you on vacations, I want to make you happy, and I…I want to make you proud. Charlotte, I love you. You are the one. You've been the one since the day I met you on Katu." He clumsily opened the box. "Please be my wife."

Inside her head, a symphony of yeses repeated, bouncing off the inside of her skull and floating behind her eyes. Yes, yes, yes, yes, yes. She hadn't said it out loud yet. He looked at her strangely. "Yes," she finally whispered. "Absolutely, yes."

He slid the antique platinum ring on her finger, the diamond in the center taking the fading sunlight and turning it into a million prisms of light. "It was my great-grandmother's," he said. "They were married nearly sixty years."

Whoops and hollers came from inside the house.

Finally, the couple made their excuses and left the family to finish the evening on Will's back porch. Holding hands as they walked to his truck, Charlotte inhaled the night air and cupped her jar of fireflies into her side. The yard was in its first spring bloom, showy and splendid, with gardenias perfuming the night air.

"Will? Could you wait a minute?" She dropped his hand and walked to the middle of the yard. Slowly, she unscrewed the lid of her firefly jar, releasing them into the night. One by one, the bugs escaped, blinking their excitement to be free at last. Her heart nearly burst with joy as they hovered around her for several seconds before taking off in all directions, a celebratory dance of light, a twinkling fireworks show in miniature.

Will stood leaning on his old white truck, smiling at her.

She looked at him, then down at the ring on her left hand before screwing the lid onto the empty jar and walking toward her future husband.

"If you don't mind, I'd like to keep the jar."

The End

Don't miss the next book in the Crickley Creek series, *Blink Twice If You Love Me*!

Join Tule Publishing's newsletter for more great reads and weekly deals!

Acknowledgements

Many thanks to Jane Porter at Tule Publishing for giving this book a chance, and to my editor, Julie Sturgeon, for making it even better. This book has been in the works for over thirteen years, so there are many people to acknowledge. Sue Backer knows Virginia better than I do, and took my dream to write a book seriously. My sisters, Susie Herring, Holly Wenzl, Noelle Reese-Noggle, Millie Steber, Alice Perrins, and Meggan Lokken have been my cheerleaders. Members of the Lowcountry Book Club are my expert panel and brilliant with their advice: Dawn Lee Schaeperkoeter, Pat Werths, Edi McNinch, Margaret Arnett, Becky Brown, Karen Newell, Susan Tyner, Meredith Knoche, and Patricia Brandon. Friends over the years who read the manuscript and gave encouragement: Krista Roodzant, Suzanne Johnson, Becky Wilson, Sherri Whiteford, Kim Mackey, Pamela and Kiki LeBaron, Sharon Allen, Clare Herring, Nina Amouris, Caroline Bridges, Summer Hanford, Zan Economopoulos, Lin Sexton, Kris and Morgan Battisfore, the Van de Pol family, Sarah Cusumano, Michelle Myers, Lynn Fiorindo, Suzie McCormac, Ellery Kane, and Diana Kallarias. I apologize to anyone I overlooked. Heartfelt thanks to my Facebook and Instagram friends who have been on this publication journey with me. Big thanks to Kathie Giorgio of All Writers Workplace and Workshop who worked with me as a coach for years. Love and gratitude to all of my parents—Bari Lokken, Bill Lokken, Maureen Lokken, Sharon Reese, and Barrett Reese. Endless appreciation to my wonderful children: Andrew Bixler, Emily Beers, Allison Reese, Natalie Reese and Brooke Reese. And finally, this book would not exist if it wasn't for my beloved husband, Bryan Reese. When our twins began kindergarten, he said to me, "You are being given the gift of time, do with it something you've always wanted to do." And *The Firefly Jar* was born.

Some of the names used in this book are of people I know and love. The characters, however, are completely fictional and are not representative of the actual person in any way.

If you enjoyed *The Firefly Jar*,
you'll love the next books in the...

Crickley Creek series

Book 1: *The Firefly Jar*

Book 2: *Blink Twice If You Love Me*
Coming in July 2023

Book 3: *Christmas in Crickley Creek*
Coming in October 2023

Available now at your favorite online retailer!

About the Author

Photographer: Stephanie Lynn Co

Laurie Beach is a hopeless romantic who refuses to subject anyone to unhappy endings. She is a former news reporter, advertising producer, and political press secretary who, after raising four children, is parlaying her love of writing into a career as an author. Having grown up in Alabama, she especially loves novels set in the South. Laurie now lives in California with her dogs and patient husband of 26 years.

Thank you for reading

The Firefly Jar

If you enjoyed this book, you can find more from all our great authors at TulePublishing.com, or from your favorite online retailer.

TULE
PUBLISHING